THE GUEST
OF HONOR

By Irving Wallace

Fiction
The Guest of Honor
The Golden Room
The Celestial Bed
The Seventh Secret
The Miracle
The Almighty
The Second Lady
The Pigeon Project
The R Document
The Fan Club
The Word
The Seven Minutes
The Plot
The Man
The Three Sirens
The Prize
The Chapman Report
The Sins of Philip Fleming

Nonfiction
Significa (Coauthor)
The Intimate Sex Lives of Famous People (Coauthor)
The Book of Lists 1, 2, and 3 (Coauthor)
The Two (Coauthor)
The People's Almanac 1, 2, and 3 (Coauthor)
The Nympho and Other Maniacs
The Writing of One Novel
The Sunday Gentleman
The Twenty-seventh Wife
The Fabulous Showman
The Square Pegs
The Fabulous Originals

IRVING WALLACE

THE GUEST OF HONOR

Delacorte
Press

Published by
Delacorte Press
Bantam Doubleday Dell Publishing Group, Inc.
666 Fifth Avenue
New York, New York 10103

Designed by Rhea Braunstein

Library of Congress Cataloging in Publication Data
Wallace, Irving, 1916–
The guest of honor : a novel / by Irving Wallace.
    p.   cm.
ISBN 0-385-29742-4
I. Title.
PS3573.A426G84   1989   88-27247
813'.54—dc19   CIP

Manufactured in the United States of America
Published simultaneously in Canada

July 1989
10   9   8   7   6   5   4   3   2   1
BG

FOR SYLVIA,
WITH DEEPEST LOVE

Love begins with love; friendship, however warm, cannot change to love, however mild.

—JEAN DE LA BRUYÈRE

THE GUEST
OF HONOR

ONE

WEARING their light raincoats against the evening drizzle, the two of them, the colonel and the major, left their car and driver between the Temple of the Emerald Buddha and the Church of Immaculate Conception, and proceeded on foot along the concrete path toward Chamadin Palace. When they reached the wrought-iron gate set in the ten-foot-high spiked wall surrounding the Spanish Colonial palace and the presidential compound, the taller of the two, the colonel, pushed the bell without a moment's hesitation.

They had rehearsed the operation so many times that no detail escaped them. They knew what to expect and were certain they would not fail.

In response to the bell, a captain of the presidential security command and three enlisted men, each fully armed, emerged from the protective guardhouse and came forward to meet the pair.

The colonel passed their identification papers through the gate.

The captain of the security command glanced at the papers and looked up.

From his side of the gate, the colonel spoke.

"The major and I are messengers from General Nakorn, and we have instructions to deliver a confidential document by hand to President Prem Sang. You need not announce us. As our papers indicate, the president is expecting us."

The captain of the guards shook his head. "Sorry, sir. We must announce your arrival." He unlocked the gate and opened it. "Step inside while I inform the president's secretary."

The colonel showed no concern; he had been prepared for this. He went into the courtyard, closely followed by the major, and they stood beside the sleepy enlisted men while the captain of the guards ducked into the guardhouse to use the telephone.

The pair could overhear him on the telephone.

"Miss Kraisri, the colonel and the major have arrived with a confidential message for the president from General Nakorn. Are you expecting them?"

There was a silence as the captain of the guards listened.

"You say the general's office called?"

He listened again and nodded in assent.

"Very well, Miss Kraisri, I will so inform them and admit them."

He hung up the receiver and emerged into the drizzle.

"Yes, Colonel, the president's appointments secretary has been told to expect you. She regrets to tell you the president has no time to see you, but requests that you bring the documents to her."

"Thank you," the colonel replied.

"Proceed across the court to the palace entrance. Show your papers to one of the guards inside the entrance. He will direct you to Miss Kraisri's office."

Both the colonel and the major bobbed their heads in acknowledgment, accepted the return of their papers, and headed for the palace entrance.

One of the palace doors opened as they reached it and they went inside. A guard studied their papers and, once satisfied, pointed to the two flights of marble staircase ahead of them that were interrupted by a broad landing.

"Up those stairs, sirs. Then to your right you will see guards in front of the door to the president's office. His secretary will be expecting you."

"Thank you, Sergeant."

The colonel preceded the major along the marble entry to the glistening staircase, paused to let his companion catch up, and then in step they began to ascend the staircase.

Both men found the going awkward, aware of what they were carrying beneath their raincoats.

Reaching the gilt console atop the landing, they turned and ascended the second flight more rapidly.

At the head of the flight they saw a lieutenant in full uniform, a rifle slung over one shoulder, awaiting them outside the reception room.

They went directly to him.

"We've been instructed to hand Mademoiselle Kraisri a personal document from General Nakorn for President Sang," the colonel said.

"Yes," the lieutenant replied. "Let me take you in to her."

He opened the door and led the colonel and the major into Miss Kraisri's reception room. A green metal desk and word processor dominated the room, but there was no one at the desk.

"Miss Kraisri must be inside working with the president," the lieutenant said. "If you will turn the document over to me, I will see that President Sang or his secretary gets it."

"Let me give it to you," the colonel said, beginning to unbutton his raincoat. He moved to the guard's left, and dug inside for the document.

The lieutenant turned fully left to face the colonel and receive the document. As he did so, one hand outstretched to receive the document, the major moved behind him.

As the guard waited for the document, the major at his back reached inside his own coat, tugged the long dagger from its sheath, pulled it free, lifted it high, and aimed it at the guard's back.

In an instant, with great power, the dagger flashed downward while the major's free palm clamped over the guard's mouth to muffle his outcry.

Inside the vast presidential office, Prem Sang, president of the nation of Lampang, having sent his secretary upstairs to read the latest draft of his agrarian reform bill to his wife, once more hunched over the pile of papers on his oversized desk.

He was a small man in his forties, with brown hair, sunken brown eyes, a prematurely lined face, altogether worn with fatigue by his three difficult years as chief executive. His smallness was accentuated by his cramped position on the breadth of the large desk.

His spine ached, and he decided that it was time to stand up and stretch. In doing so, he was able to survey the elegant office, from its parquet floor covered by Iranian carpets, to the mahogany wall paneling punctuated by gilt-framed mirrors and a mural of farmers at work in a field, to the gold wall sconces and crystal chandeliers. Through the windows to one side, near the presidential seal hanging on one wall, he could see the bulletproof enclosed balcony that encircled the building. There were three doors: one to his reception room, another to his downstairs dining room, and the third door that led to the staircase to the private apartment above that he and his wife shared. There was a fourth door, not visible, concealed by an extension of the mahogany paneling over its solid-steel entrance. This door opened onto a passageway that led to the garden where the presidential security command had its barracks.

Lowering himself into his leather swivel chair, Prem Sang focused upon the only object on his desk beside the pile of documents. This was a silver-framed photograph of his wife, Noy, and their son, Den. Then his eyes fell on his papers, and once more his mind was occupied by his work.

As he had been for months, President Prem Sang was absorbed by his dilemma. His domain consisted of three islands in the South China Sea off Thailand, Cambodia, and the southern tip of Vietnam. The main island, and by far the largest, was Lampang proper, where Sang resided in the capital city of Visaka. The two adjacent islands, Lampang Lop and Lampang Thon, were much smaller, with almost impenetrable jungles and hills, and there the Communist insurgents resided in troublesome number.

President Sang's immediate problem was how to satisfy both opposing sides of his population. On the main island of Lampang where the ordinary people—who were democratic, Catholic, English-speaking—had elected him on a platform of just distribution of land and wealth, he clung to his slim margin of popularity. On the nearby islands of Lampang Lop and Lampang Thon, the Communist guerrillas ruled under the leadership of Opas Lunakul, a pawn of the Vietnamese Communists who infiltrated daily.

The Communists had been propagandizing effectively that President Sang and Lampang were puppets of the United States, from whom they received considerable economic assistance. Lampang's independence was being eroded by this foreign dependency, they claimed. Only under communism could Lampang be truly free and economically sound.

But the Communists weren't President Sang's only problem. He had an internal one as well. The head of his army, his close friend General Samak Nakorn, was in total disagreement with him about the Communists.

The general wanted any money that might come from the United States to be spent on troops to wipe out the Communists. President Sang wanted the money to prop up his domestic economy, which he felt was the best way to defeat any Communist threat.

President Sang sat reviewing the columns of notes on his desk once more. Unemployment in Lampang was eighteen percent. For the employed, life was hardly better, the average family of five with an income of $110 a month. Dismal. If that could be improved, and land distributed, the Communists could be beaten peacefully.

There was a knocking on his entrance door.

He half remembered. General Nakorn had sent over a message to be turned over to his secretary or the guard.

With his secretary upstairs, President Sang called out, "Come in, Lieutenant."

The door opened. The president had anticipated seeing his

lieutenant. But there was no one. And then there was. The lieutenant lay sprawled in the hallway, a knife in his back.

That instant, two uniformed men, unknown to Prem Sang, stepped over the body of the lieutenant, each carrying a rifle.

As they raised the rifles, Sang was able to identify the weapons.

They were automatic Kalashnikov rifles, standard Soviet assault rifles, and they were being aimed at him.

Bewildered, President Sang jumped up from his desk, shouting, "What is this? Who in the devil—?"

In response, both rifles chattered hideously.

The muzzle velocity of each, the impact of the bullets, tore away part of Sang's face; ripped through his heart; penetrated his stomach.

The firepower momentarily lifted him off his feet and flung him backward against his chair, where he stumbled and slipped to the floor and collapsed to the carpet in death. As a pool of blood began to form, the two assassins gently closed the door and disappeared.

Upstairs, in the dressing room, the president's wife had been applying cream to her face as she listened to Prem's secretary, when suddenly she was startled by the sounds below.

She paused and listened.

Firecrackers, she told herself. Or maybe more. She snatched her silk robe off a hook, pulled it on, and made her way to the stairs. Hurrying down the stairs, puzzled, apprehensive, she burst into her husband's office.

She saw no one, and then, moving closer to the desk, peering behind it, she saw her husband's crumpled body. Then she saw its condition, riddled with bullets, and the dark pool that must be blood.

She gasped, and then she screamed. She screamed and screamed.

What followed was a kaleidoscope of people.

Miss Kraisri and the servants came on the run. Then the palace guards, led by the captain of the guards. Soon the police, and doctors, and ambulance attendants.

Someone had guided her to a straight-backed chair nearby, and there Noy Sang sat paralyzed by shock.

She had been seated there a long while before General Samak Nakorn and his officers arrived.

Even here the stocky Nakorn was in uniform, replete with ribbons and medals.

Nakorn was questioning the doctors as Sang's body was being carried out on a stretcher. Next, Nakorn was questioning the captain of the guards. "Two of them, you say? The president's secretary had told you I had informed her to let them in and expect a message. It's a lie! I never spoke to the president about such a thing. I never had a message for him. It's a Communist plot. When the coroner removes the bullets, you will see they are of Russian origin. This is terrible, unbelievable, horrible."

Only later did Noy Sang realize that General Nakorn was standing over her, addressing her.

Normally a gruff, hoarse man, his voice was oddly subdued.

He was trying to tender his condolences.

"I am sorry, very sorry, Madame President," he was saying.

Only then did Noy Sang realize that not only was she a widow, but as her husband's vice-president, she was now president of Lampang.

In the glass-enclosed control room in TNTN—The National Television Network—bureau on M Street, Hy Hasken settled his lanky frame in an armchair beside the one occupied by his editor, Sam Whitlaw.

The visit of Whitlaw from New York to Washington, D.C., was to be of short duration. One of the initial matters on his brief agenda was a talk with Hy Hasken, the network's White House correspondent.

After Hasken's broadcast stint had ended, Whitlaw had telephoned him in the White House pressroom. "Hy, I want you to come over and join me in watching the seven o'clock news."

Hasken had arrived just in time for the evening news and prepared to observe himself on the television screen in front of them.

Waiting for his own segment, Hasken tried to make small talk with his superior. But Whitlaw's concentration was on the news, his life's blood. So Hasken waited in silence.

At last he saw himself on the television screen, microphone in hand, planted in Lafayette Square with the front facade of the White House in the background.

Hasken tried to see himself as the millions of viewers out there saw him doing his stand-upper. Actually, he saw himself as his audience—longtime acquaintances—in a living room might see him. He was slender with sandy hair brushed to one side, a high forehead dulled by studio makeup, alert blue eyes, a long nose and small mouth, and a staccato, resonant, faintly prosecutorial voice and tone.

Watching himself, Hy Hasken listened.

"The most significant news to come out of the White House today is that President Matt Underwood is preparing to meet with Madame Noy Sang, president of the island of Lampang, a nation crucial to the immediate interests of the United States.

"Just one year ago this week, President Prem Sang of Lampang was assassinated by persons unknown, thought to be hit men representing the Communist insurgents who have been growing in power on two neighboring islands that fall under the jurisdiction of Lampang. The assassination of Prem Sang brought his vice-president to the presidency. His vice-president happened to be his youthful wife, Noy Sang. If this seems odd to Americans, it must be understood that the politics of Lampang carry over a social structure known as the extended family. A president always has, as his running mate and heir, his wife or son or another close relative. In a way this makes sense, for no stranger ever ascends to the presidency, but instead the replacement is always someone close to the president, one whose thinking is presumably compatible with the president's own.

"This has worked well in Lampang. Upon Prem Sang's death a year ago, his widow Noy Sang was able to slip effortlessly into his office fully conversant with her husband's ideas and goals. For a year, Noy Sang has served as president, and in this mourning period she has not traveled at all but has remained in Lampang to acquaint herself with her country's internal affairs.

"In the past year, Madame Noy Sang has become more acutely aware of Lampang's dependence on the United States. Now, with her mourning period behind her, Madame Sang is making her first trip abroad—a visit to the United States. She arrives this evening. After an overnight rest at Blair House she will come to the White House tomorrow for a business luncheon with President Underwood.

"This meeting tomorrow is crucial for both sides. On the Lampang side, there is no question that Madame Noy Sang is looking for a loan in the millions, one that will bolster her economy and be welcomed by her citizens, who are seeking social help and assistance in the land distribution program now under way. The United States, in turn, needs something more important and more costly. The United States needs a large and modern air base on the island of Lampang.

"To understand the importance of this air base, one must visualize where Lampang is located. Most viewers have heard of Lampang from time to time. Many may forget its strategic importance to America, which is second only in importance to the Philippines in the same general area.

"Lampang lies to the west of the Philippines, on the edge of the South China Sea and near the Gulf of Thailand. The main island, two thirds the size of Luzon in the Philippines, is south of Cambodia and Vietnam, yet still in the vicinity of the People's Republic of China. Lampang faces three Communist countries, two of whom openly receive weapons and aid from the Soviet Union. To complete our own anticommunist ring of islands in the Pacific Ocean, the United States needs a major air base on Lampang.

"Obtaining this critical air base will be President Underwood's principal goal when he meets with Madame Noy Sang tomorrow. Can he get it? There are obstacles. Madame Sang, like her husband before her, is under growing pressure to keep her nation free of dependence on the United States, and from American demands and influences. Much of this pressure comes from the local insurgent Communists who want to take over Lampang.

"At the same time, Madame Noy is a political moderate with a known affection for the United States and American ways, which began when she attended Wellesley College here in her twenties. But the key fact is that Madame Noy Sang needs something of immense value from the United States—a large cash loan to bolster her economy—and she is well aware that to get, she has to be ready to give.

"So the luncheon tomorrow between President Underwood and Madame Noy Sang appears to be more than a social meeting. It is a confrontation that involves a trade-off. Will the trade-off take place? We hope to report the outcome to you tomorrow. This is Hy Hasken of TNTN at the White House."

Sam Whitlaw jumped up and switched off the television set. Returning to his chair, he faced Hasken.

"Hy, I've seen your segment twice today. Earlier, I saw it live, and just now I saw it again on videotape. I wanted to speak to you about it. The question I have is—why?"

"Why what?" Hasken said, bewildered.

"Why a whole segment on prime time about Lampang? Who gives a damn about Lampang?"

"But you heard me," Hasken protested. "It's strategically important. It fills a big hole in our defense perimeter. You consider the Philippines important, don't you? Well, it's on our side. Lampang is just as important. Only it's not on our side."

Whitlaw shook his head. "I'll bet you ten to one that half your viewers haven't the faintest idea where it's located."

"Maybe not," Hasken conceded. "But it's a story."

"A poor one. And President Noy Sang coming here to discuss it with Underwood. Among world leaders, Noy Sang must be one of the least known."

"She's just been in office one year," Hasken said. "Give her a chance. She'll be better known after tomorrow."

"I doubt it, Hy."

"Besides, in herself, she's dramatic. I mean just a year ago her husband was assassinated. She was his vice-president—in itself unusual—and was sworn in immediately. Furthermore"—Hasken hesitated—"she's a looker. She could catch on."

"Maybe, but unlikely," Whitlaw said. "Another good-looking woman in the White House isn't going to mean much when we have a first lady who was once Miss America." Whitlaw sighed. "Certainly you could have found a better lead piece for prime time."

Throwing up his hands, Hasken said, "There is no better lead piece, at least none that I was able to find. My problem was and is President Underwood. As I've said many times on the air, he's a lazy president. He simply does not generate news."

Hasken thought about it. He had known Underwood from very early on, when Hasken himself was a beginner at TNTN and Underwood had reached his zenith on television as the most popular and beloved anchorman on the air. Underwood's partially gray mop of hair; finely chiseled features, somewhat seamy, certainly kind; and his warm voice had made him a household name. What made him even more colorful was that he had actually married a former Miss America, Alice Reynolds, who did women's features for the network. When Hasken had graduated from Columbia University in New York and obtained a lowly job at the network, Matt Underwood had reached his peak.

Early on, Hasken had stood in awe of the renowned anchorman. Then, gradually, as he learned more about television, Hasken's admiration for Underwood had diminished. Hasken had been a curious and aggressive reporter. His disrespect for Underwood had grown out of the fact that the anchorman lacked curiosity. Underwood was what Hasken secretly called a "reader." Dig up the goods on any story, foreign and domestic, and Underwood read it to his audience as if he had invented it. His strength was not his originality but his absolute sincerity.

Hasken thought his superior counterfeit. An actor. Not dumb at all. Quite smart, actually, and with a wide range of knowledge about many things. His real strength was in his ability to convince millions that what he spoke was his own and the truth. People believed in him as youngsters might believe in their fathers.

Then, abruptly, Underwood had left TNTN for politics. When a senator from New York died in office, there was the remainder of his term to be filled. The governor, a fan of Underwood's and aware of his incredible popularity, had made the daring choice of a television anchorman for senator to serve an uncompleted term.

From his experience as a reporter, Hasken knew that joining the pack in Congress often obliterated a man or woman. But Matt Underwood was different. Underwood simply transferred his popularity from television to the United States Senate. He continued to be more than ever the media darling. When the time came for seeking presidential nominees, Underwood was in effect drafted by his party. In the primaries he ran away with Iowa and New Hampshire, and in the election he swamped his opponent in a landslide.

And so the White House was occupied by a former television anchorman and a onetime Miss America.

Meanwhile, Hy Hasken, with all his initiative, had moved up swiftly in the network ranks, and two years ago he had become TNTN's White House correspondent.

Hasken didn't like President Underwood from the outset. He was a lazy president, as lazy as Calvin Coolidge had been, and presently Hasken began to say so on the air. This drew fire from the president and his chief of staff, Paul Blake, but Hasken persisted in his criticism of a president who held almost no press conferences and rarely received foreign leaders.

How his staffers had got him to sit still for a lunch with the female president of Lampang was beyond Hasken. Neverthe-less, Hasken thought it a story and had used it today.

And his editor, Sam Whitlaw, had objected. The story was too dull.

Hasken reached back for the thread of his conversation with Whitlaw, and after some difficulty found it.

"Let me repeat," Hasken resumed, "this president simply does not generate news. I've got to go with something, so I went with what I had."

"There was not another news lead you could find?" persisted Whitlaw.

"Nothing, Sam, believe me. The only scrap of real news I can imagine would be word that Matt Underwood has decided to run for reelection and grab a second term. That would be news. I happen to know the first lady wants him to run again. So does Chief of Staff Blake. It would give them both continu-ing power. But I suspect Underwood doesn't want to run again and doesn't intend to. I say again, he's too lazy for the job and bored by it."

"But Alice Underwood wants him to run?"

"Oh, yes, she adores the limelight and all those photo op-portunities."

"Well, why don't you say that on the air?"

Hasken looked helpless. "I'd like to, Sam. But I can't prove it. I'm a good investigative reporter, maybe the best, but what I investigate has to be provable. I believe the first lady wants him to run again. Yet I don't have a shred of proof."

Whitlaw seemed enthusiastic at last. "Then go out there and beat the bushes, and get the proof. The first lady wants him to run. The president doesn't want to. Conflict is the essence of any worthwhile story. I don't care if Underwood runs again or doesn't. The story is what will he do? Now, that's a good story, not some crap about Lampang."

"I'll do my best to get it," said Hasken earnestly.

"To be sure you get it," said Whitlaw, "I'm giving you a new job. No longer Hy Hasken, White House correspondent. From now on Hy Hasken, presidential correspondent. Think you can do it?"

"I can try."

"Starting tomorrow you are President Underwood's shadow. Follow him like a guilty conscience."

They slept in separate bedrooms on the second floor of the White House, and they had been doing this for some time, at least a year.

The reasons behind this separation were twofold. First, Alice Underwood was an insomniac and a poor sleeper. She took a low-dosage pill twenty minutes before going to bed, and when Matt Underwood came to bed shortly after, he inevitably awakened her. This made her cranky and harsh. Second, Matt Underwood always took two or three—usually three—snifters of cognac before going to bed. When he awakened his wife, she could smell the cognac on his breath, and this made her more irritable and angry. "Goddammit," she would say, "can't you come to sleep once without brandy on your breath?" Pulling up the blanket, he would say, "No, those snifters are my light sleeping-pill. I tolerate yours. You can tolerate mine."

This had set off a bitter exchange full of old recriminations, and after that both of them had trouble sleeping at all.

Alice made the initial move. She backed herself out of the First Family Bedroom and staked out her own place in the canopied bed of the Queens' Bedroom down the hall.

This morning at seven thirty the president's cheerful black

valet, Horace, knocked on the door several times and entered. He did not have to shake the president awake. Underwood lay there, still groggy, but gradually coming alert.

"I'll lay out your pin-striped light blue suit, Mr. President," Horace said, starting for the dressing room. "I believe you have a foreign visitor for lunch."

"Oh, shit," groaned the president. "All right. Whatever."

The president crawled out of the spacious bed and headed for the bathroom.

There he showered, brushed his teeth, towel-dried his hair and brushed it back, and sprayed some cologne on his chest.

When he returned to the bedroom in his bathrobe, his clothes were waiting, carefully arranged on the freshly made-up bed.

As he slowly dressed, the president's mood improved. He liked the airiness of this bedroom next to his second-floor study. The hand-painted Chinese wallpaper depicting birds in flight, gentle, placid, pleased him. Between the windows was the Willard Metcalf landscape that always soothed him. Even the 1818 marble mantel was comforting.

After knotting his necktie, Underwood slipped into his suit jacket and felt ready for the day.

Emerging into the hallway, Underwood determined to make another effort with his marriage. He had not breakfasted with Alice for several weeks. This morning he made up his mind to join her.

Walking down the hallway to the Queens' Bedroom, Underwood tried to recall—which he did often—how his estrangement from Alice had come about.

He had first set eyes on her after she had won the Miss America contest. Actually, earlier, but not in person. He had seen her on television, parading in the Miss America contest, watched as she became a finalist, and approved when she was crowned. He remembered her body in the tight white swimsuit. She had been flawless. A beautiful Grecian face, long neck, broad shoulders, magnificent protrusion of bosom, narrow waist, curved hips, and long, long shapely legs.

When she arrived at work for TNTN, Underwood was introduced to her and saw her for the first time in person.

In pink blouse and skirt, Alice was every bit as attractive as she had been in the Miss America contest. She was, at the time, a momentary celebrity. Underwood himself was a national star of the first magnitude. Naturally she gave him time and attention. He was glued to her by her breathtaking beauty.

Presently, they went to dinner and became better acquainted in a discreet corner of an Italian restaurant near Fifty-ninth Street and the Avenue of the Americas. After dinner they went to his apartment and made love.

Their lovemaking taught him more about her. She had not been warm and soft, but she had been experienced and aggressive. Above all, she was beautiful beyond belief.

For Underwood, Alice Reynolds was irresistible.

Realizing he would never find a woman more perfect, he wanted her for his own.

He was happy to marry her.

They had their only child, a daughter, Dianne, in the second year of their marriage. In the years that followed, Underwood continued to be satisfied being rated the most popular anchorman in the United States. He could detect, however, that Alice had become restless playing mother and having her work cut down at TNTN.

What gave her a lift, and briefly stabilized their marriage, was Underwood's appointment to the uncompleted term in the United States Senate. Underwood accepted it as something one doesn't turn down, especially when he had a wife who wanted him to take the new job and desired a change.

After that, it was politics and Washington, D.C. In his new role Underwood was more popular than ever, and Alice received greater attention.

Then the polls for the presidential nomination began to reveal a surprising thing.

While other candidates for the nomination were tried and true politicians, each well-equipped to serve as president of the United States, it was Matt Underwood who was the best known and the most popular among them.

He had gone into the primaries not seriously, not believing he had a ghost of a chance to be nominated. But his affable personality, his informal talks, his familiar face that seemed part of everyone's family, turned the trick. After resounding victories in Iowa, New Hampshire, and the South, Underwood became the party favorite for the nomination.

Once he gained the nomination and began to campaign, he found the steady public appearances tiresome. Still, he was good at reading speeches, very effective, and the public took him to their hearts. And so did Alice. She had come alive again at the thought of being the first lady of the United States.

The election came and went in less than a single day. The votes were not yet in from Illinois when Matt Underwood had become the next president of the United States. Alice Reynolds Underwood had become the first lady.

They were the most glamorous couple in the White House since John F. Kennedy and Jacqueline Kennedy.

Alice reveled in her position. She adored the chance to dress up, to meet diplomats, to be with her husband at the center of media attention.

The hang-up had been Matt Underwood. He disliked the

routine of seemingly endless hours, the details, the dull conferences with staffers. He disliked the socializing with people who did not interest him.

More than anything, he disliked the disagreements with his wife. They were at odds constantly. What she enjoyed, he found boring. There were moments when he considered the presidency illuminating, with all the firsthand information that poured across his desk, with all the newly acquired knowledge and power that came to him. But what he missed most was privacy, and the chance to devote himself to an absorbing book.

Their most severe difference came when he had made up his mind that four years was enough.

That had been a year ago. He remembered the confrontation as if it had been yesterday.

He had been absorbed in a news program on television when Alice appeared and snapped the set off.

"I want to have a serious talk with you," she had said.

Annoyed, he had waited silently.

"I've tried to bring it up several times, but each time you've been evasive. I want to have it out now, once and for all."

"Go ahead," he had said, suspecting what lay ahead.

"It's about your plans, and my own," she had said. "I want to know if you are going to run for reelection. Tell me."

"Well, actually, I haven't made up—"

"Of course you have," she had interrupted. "You know for certain. Now I deserve to know. Will you go for a second term?"

"No," he had blurted out. He had been surprised how easily it had come. "No," he had repeated, "I've had enough."

Alice had stood stunned. "I can't believe it. You really mean it? Matt, what are you going to do with yourself?"

"I have a world of things to keep me busy. You know most of them. Above all, I want to devote myself to my People's Nonnuclear Peace Plan. You've heard me speak of it often enough."

"Trying to convince nine leaders of nations that have nuclear weapons—or the capability to make them—to give them up. Matt, you can do that more effectively as president."

"I can't. Not as leader of the United States. My self-interests are suspect. But as an ex-president—"

Alice had not been mollified.

Underwood had tried to understand his wife. For Alice, four years were not enough. She wanted eight years. It was like being Miss America again, only bigger. She welcomed the spotlight. She would have loved it forever.

Also, Underwood knew, she was competitive toward the first ladies who had preceded her. Alice was aware that Jacqueline Kennedy and Lady Bird Johnson had each had forty persons on their secretarial staffs as press and social aides, and Alice hoped for more. During two terms, Pat Nixon had been hostess at sixty-four state dinners, and Alice wanted to equal that record or surpass it. She liked to have a major domo in charge of seventy-five servants for the 132 rooms of the White House, and she did not want to give up any of it.

So contention over a second term remained the strongest disagreement between them. He tried to retreat into himself, avoiding any further mention of the matter. Alice would not let go. She was as aggressive as ever, missing no opportunity to chastise him for his unwillingness to continue.

Arriving at the Queens' Bedroom, he was resolved to patch things up, get closer to Alice, heal their differences.

He opened the door without knocking.

Alice, in a flimsy white negligee, was comfortable in the American Sheraton canopied bed, a bed that had been used by five famous queens during their official visits to the White House.

"Top of the morning," Underwood called out. "I thought you'd like me to join you for breakfast."

Only then did he notice that there was a breakfast tray across her lap, from which she had been eating.

"Too late," she said cheerfully. "Next time let me know in advance. I've been busy with Monica—"

Shifting his gaze, he realized that Alice's social secretary, Monica Glass, was also in the bedroom, standing by the tall windows. Monica, who had been riffling through her briefcase, stared at him coldly.

Underwood ignored the social secretary. For Underwood, Monica was too ugly to look at. She was bright and efficient, but her thick features were a put-off.

"Too bad," Underwood grunted, annoyed.

"You busy today?" Alice asked, making a polite effort at public friendliness.

"Fairly," he said. "See you around."

Underwood closed the door, not softly.

Proceeding to the northwest corner of the hall, Underwood reached the President's Dining Room, a small room furnished with Federal pieces from the White House collection. Underwood liked the historical feel of the room, especially a sideboard that graced the west wall and still bore the inlaid initials D.W. for Daniel Webster.

At the mahogany table in the center of the room the president's appointments secretary, a clean-cut young man named John Zadrick, was already seated with his papers, waiting as the dining-room waiter, Babcock, poured his strong coffee, and then went to the serving cart to bring the president's breakfast to the table. As usual, the president's breakfast was austere—orange juice, a small bowl of cereal, and buttered toast.

After Babcock had departed with his cart, Underwood sipped his orange juice and raised his eyes to his appointments secretary. "How does it look?"

Zadrick said, "A light morning. You've got your usual meeting at nine o'clock with Chief of Staff Blake and Secretary of State Morrison."

Underwood showed his surprise. "Ezra Morrison? What's Ezra doing there?"

"As secretary of state, I suspect, he wants to brief you on your lunch."

"My lunch?" Then he half remembered. "Oh, yes, some diplomat—"

"Not exactly a diplomat," interrupted Zadrick. "Your guest —the guest of honor—is the president of a nation."

"What nation?"

"Lampang, Mr. President."

"Lamp—what?"

"The island nation not too far from the Philippines. You are to lunch at twelve thirty with Madame Noy Sang."

Underwood finished his orange juice and started spooning his cereal. "Noy Sang? What kind of name is that?"

"It's a native name, Mr. President. She's been president a year, since her husband's death. She's been allocated two hours with you. Mr. Blake and Secretary Morrison will be lunching with you. I gather it is important."

Underwood wolfed down his cereal and reached for his coffee and toast. "How important can anything be about Lampang?"

"Well, sir—"

"Never mind," said the president, stopping him. "I'm remembering now—Lampang and the woman who runs it." He snorted. "What's on the agenda before that?"

TWO

BECAUSE of the early-morning traffic, Secretary of State Ezra Morrison was running eight minutes late.

Normally this was a relatively short ride from the Department of State to the CIA headquarters in Langley, Virginia. Actually, it was less than a ten-mile ride from the center of Washington, D.C., to Langley.

Although his driver did his best, the traffic was intense every mile of the way.

At last his driver took the limousine through the Dolley Madison entrance to the CIA headquarters. A guard with a clipboard routinely entered Morrison's name.

Once deposited in front of the blocklike glass-and-concrete building, Morrison stood to straighten out his gray suit—although of considerable bulk, he was always dapper—and then patting down his peaked, bushy eyebrows and scratching the itch on his potatolike nose, he went inside the foyer. The walls and columns, all marble, were as formidable as ever, with the walls carrying fifty-two small stars carved into them, one star for every CIA man who had lost his life in the service. The CIA motto etched on a single wall made Morrison inexplicably uneasy: YE SHALL KNOW THE TRUTH AND THE TRUTH SHALL MAKE YOU FREE.

On the floor, as he crossed it, Morrison was once more conscious of the CIA emblem: a circle bearing a star on a shield and the bold lettering CENTRAL INTELLIGENCE AGENCY/ UNITED STATES OF AMERICA.

At the far end of the foyer two guards signaled Morrison up the flight of stairs that led to the badge room, where Morrison, to his annoyance, was still required to obtain his identification badge.

There were five elevators waiting—CIA Director Alan Ramage's private one, and four others—and Morrison took the one that led him nonstop to the CIA director's penthouse office on the seventh floor.

Once inside the vast office, with its signed Giacometti lithographs on the walls, along with a row of portraits autographed to Ramage from four presidents of the United States, and windows that gave a view of most of the 219 acres of wooded country on the Potomac, Morrison could make out that the others were already there. He nodded to the president's chief of staff, who was comfortably seated across the desk from Director Ramage and his CIA deputy director for operations. Morrison gave a brief smile to the deputy director. She was Mary Jane O'Neil, a pretty and petite young lady, and Secretary of State Morrison had been sleeping with her for over a year. True, he had a wife and three children, but they were no problem, since his family understood that in his job there were no formal quitting hours. The year before, when he had first dined with Mary Jane, he had not only been taken by her but had been delighted at how friendly she had been toward him. Two weeks later, Morrison was blissfully ensconced in her double bed.

"Sorry to be late," Morrison said to the CIA director, setting down his fedora hat and his briefcase. "There must be a gold rush the way the cars are lined up out there."

"You're on time," said Ramage, shifting some long strands of hair from one side of his scalp to the other in a futile attempt to cover his baldpate.

Ramage sat erect, as a former admiral might, and since he was a tall Texan, it enabled him to look down on his visitors and aide. He was an urbane man, given a sanguine look and dignity by his gold-rimmed spectacles.

Absently, Ramage shuffled the papers before him. "Lampang," he announced, and with that the meeting came to order. "I understand, Ezra, that you and Paul are briefing the president"—he checked his wristwatch—"in an hour. Does Underwood have any idea of what's at stake here?"

"I'm sure he knows," Blake said, "but I wouldn't say he's very interested."

"He has to be," said Director Ramage emphatically. "He must be made to understand."

Morrison waved off the director's concern. "Don't worry, Alan. There's a cabinet meeting scheduled before he has his lunch with Madame Noy Sang. We'll pound the facts, and our goal, into his head."

"The president will remember," Blake reassured the director. "Even though he's so laid-back, he'll remember. He was good at that on television, and he's just as good at it in the White House when he has to be."

"I hope so," said the director.

"Not to worry," Blake reassured him again.

"All right," said the director, "let's be sure we have it all exactly together before we try to brief him."

Director Ramage twisted toward his aide. "Mary Jane, you have copies of our memorandum on Lampang. Want to pass them out?"

Mary Jane O'Neil stood up. No more than five feet two, Morrison knew, with a tremendous pair of boobs for one so small. Morrison pictured her as he liked best to see her. Nude and acrobatic.

She was handing the memorandum to Director Ramage, and then she came around to pass one to Blake and saved Morrison for the last. As she gave him his memorandum, she allowed her hand to touch his.

Morrison peered up at her excitedly, and she offered him a promising smile.

As she returned to her chair, Morrison fixed on her undulating backside. Unforgettable cushions of love, Morrison thought, when you held each buttock in one hand.

Morrison was beginning to get an erection, which he didn't get often with his wife but always with Mary Jane, when the CIA director's voice brought him up sharp and into the reality of the morning.

"Lampang," announced Director Ramage. "Let's get right into it."

"All set," said Morrison.

Ramage sat back a moment. "Does the president know anything about it?"

Chief of Staff Blake leaned forward. "A little. He knows a little about everything."

Ramage nodded. "Then you've got to brief him thoroughly, simply but thoroughly."

"We've got two opportunities," said Blake. "I'm meeting with him shortly in the Oval Office. Then again after that at a full cabinet meeting."

"And he meets with Madame Noy Sang at noon."

"At twelve thirty," said Blake, more precisely, "for lunch and talk. I'll be in attendance and so will the secretary of state."

"Very well," said Ramage. "Right off you should prepare the stage. Locate Lampang for him."

"I think he knows where it is," said Blake.

"Make sure," said Ramage. "Be as precise as possible. He's got to know its relationship to Cambodia and southern Vietnam, and he must be made to understand how it will complete our defense perimeter."

"I'll take care of that," promised Secretary Morrison.

Ramage was uncertain. "What he achieves with Madame Sang is vital to our interests." Ramage began thumbing through the papers on his desk. "At the same time, he must be made aware of what kind of resistance he can expect from Madame Noy Sang."

"Do you expect much?" Blake wanted to know.

"I can't say." Ramage found the sheet of paper he had been hunting. "Percy Siebert, our CIA station head in Lampang, gave me a rundown on Madame Noy Sang. I'll give you the essence of his sketch." Ramage consulted the sheet in front of him. "She comes from a good family; they own rice plantations and are well-off. They sent her to the United States for her college education. So she has a real awareness of our country. She married a left-wing liberal named Prem Sang, a scholarly man of forty-two, and ten years her senior. They had one child, a son named Den, now six years old. When Prem became president of Lampang on a platform of agrarian reform, his vice-president was his wife. Odd to us, but that's the custom in that neck of the woods. I wouldn't say Prem was exactly a friend of the United States, but he wasn't an enemy either. He was really a nationalist. He wanted Lampang to be free and independent."

"Where does his wife stand politically?" Blake inquired.

"I really don't know," admitted Ramage. "From what Siebert has told me, she goes along pretty much with her husband's ideas. Now, after a year in office as president, and confronted with all the problems that exist, she may have relaxed her independent stand about the United States. Two things for sure. America's only powerful friend on the island is General Samak Nakorn, head of the army, and his deputy, Colonel Peere Chavalit. America's only powerful enemy on the island, or islands, is Captain Opas Lunakul, head of the Communist insurgents who dominate the two outer islands of Lampang Lop and Thon. Madame Noy Sang is walking a fine line in between."

"But she has to stand for something," Blake stated.

"She does," said Ramage, "based on the information we've assembled. She needs our help to get her agrarian reform policy going. At the same time, she doesn't want the Communists to propagandize that she's selling out to a capitalist country that will exploit Lampang. Madame Noy Sang has the people behind her—mostly peasants who take a dim view of communism. They want the land divided, the economy improved, and to get this they'd settle for U.S.-style democracy."

"Yes," said Blake. "That would satisfy most of us. The question is how to achieve it." He stared at the secretary of state. "That's your department, Ezra."

Morrison acknowledged his responsibility. He came to his feet, opened his briefcase, and pulled out a folder. Returning to his chair, he leafed through the folder.

At last he found what he wanted and extracted a page. Skimming it, he raised his head to take in the others.

"It's a trade-off," Morrison said. "What it comes down to baldly is a trade-off. We give Madame Noy Sang something she wants to get what we want."

"She wants a loan," said Blake. "Big dollars."

"Exactly," Morrison agreed. "In return we want a big air base on Lampang."

Ramage roused himself. "That's a tough decision for her to make," he commented. "Considering her political situation, allowing an air base for our jets and bombers and agreeing to thousands of our personnel parked on her island is going to draw heavy objections not only from the Communist insurgents but the Madame's own People's Party. If she does it at all, she'll want a lot of money in return."

"If she doesn't do it," said Morrison firmly, "she doesn't get a dime."

"I can't see that happening," said Blake. "She needs us."

"And we need her," said Morrison. "That's why I say it's got to be a trade-off."

"Well, let's start with our part," said Blake. "How much do we authorize the president to offer her?"

"We'll start low and work our way up slowly," said Morrison. "Much of it depends on the numbers she brings to us. Meanwhile, I'll confer with Secretary of Defense Cannon for his thoughts on what we can give for what we want. We'll agree on a top figure and pass it on to Underwood at the cabinet meeting." He turned to Blake. "Do you think you can handle the president on his pre-briefing—give him facts, no figures—before the cabinet meeting? I want to spend some time over at Defense first."

"I can manage," said Blake.

"Remember, save all figures for the cabinet meeting so that the president has them firmly in mind before his lunch. In any case, I'll make notes for him to use as reminders. If he forgets, I'll be there to back him up." Morrison glanced around at the others. "That should cover it," he said. "We're ready for Noy Sang."

"I hope so," said Blake, a little nervously.

"Well, let's just be sure the president is ready," Morrison added. "This lunch, it's an important one. Underwood has to come through. A little charm wouldn't hurt."

Blake shrugged. "The question is—who'll be more charming—Matt Underwood or Noy Sang?"

Leaving the CIA building for the White House in his chauffeur-driven black limousine, Paul Blake, the president's chief of staff, had entered the west basement. After nodding good morning to several National Security officers, Blake hastened up a narrow flight of stairs to his own office, two doors down from the president's Oval Office.

Inside, three of Blake's aides, informally attired, were lounging about discussing the contents of a speech the president would soon deliver on cuts in domestic spending. After returning their greetings, Blake dismissed them, postponing the conference on the speech for later in the day.

At the moment, he was expected in the president's Oval Office to give his chief a general picture of the lunch with Madame Noy Sang.

Seated across from the president, Blake felt at ease. He had known Underwood a long time. A graduate of Harvard Law

School, Blake had eventually become a partner in a prestigious New York law firm that had among its clients Matt Underwood. Blake had been assigned to handle Underwood's affairs from the start. Blake was a smallish round man with a cherub's face. Clean-shaven, pleasant, with a constantly benign expression, his affability suited Underwood. So did his intellect and his ability at organization.

Now Blake tried to fill the president in on the situation in Lampang. The president appeared to be only half listening. Gradually he managed to turn the subject matter to the heavyweight boxing championship fight in Las Vegas late in the afternoon. Who did Blake think would win?

Blake wasn't sure, and double-talked, knowing only who would lose if he didn't get the president back on the rails about Lampang.

The president was impatient. "Look, Paul, let's get to Lampang later. Do I have to hear it all twice? Let's go over it at the cabinet meeting, then it'll be fresh in my mind when I settle down to lunch with Madame Sang."

"As you wish, Mr. President."

"It's what I wish, Paul."

In ten minutes it was agreed the challenger would dethrone the champion in Las Vegas, and the president showed some enthusiasm for the first time that day.

When Paul Blake returned to his quarters, annoyed at his failure to get anywhere with the president, he considered phoning his aides to pick up on the speech about cuts in domestic spending. Surveying his office, it amused him that if cuts were to be explored, they might begin with those he had made in his own office. It was a modest white-paneled cubbyhole, and the desk he used was an oak one of routine government issue.

Blake moved to the desk, skimmed the overnight cables, decided that there were none that required the president's immediate attention. About to ring his aides, he realized that he had not completed his task of drawing up Underwood's remaining schedule for the day.

Bringing a white pad and pen before him, Blake began to outline the schedule. He jotted the following:

> 10:00—Full cabinet meeting.
>
> 11:30—Sign papers.
>
> 12:30 to 2:30—Lunch in President's Dining Room with President Noy Sang of Lampang, to be joined by Secretary of State Morrison and Chief of Staff Blake. After lunch, conversation to continue in the Yellow Oval Room.
>
> 3:15—Photo opportunity in the Rose Garden. Awards to the Boy Scouts of America.
>
> 5:00—Watch heavyweight title fight in the Red Room on the third floor.

Having completed his list of notations, and after reviewing them to be certain he had omitted nothing, Blake buzzed his secretary and requested that she type it and distribute it immediately.

No sooner had his secretary departed than the blue intercom White House telephone rang.

This usually proved to be the president.

Blake lifted the receiver at once.

The caller proved to be not the president but the first lady in person.

"Good morning, Paul, did I catch you at a busy time?"

In his courtliest manner, Blake replied, "It's never a busy time when I have a chance to speak to you, Alice."

"How nice of you. There's something I want to talk to you about. Do you have the president's final schedule for the day ready?"

"Almost. It's being typed this very minute."

"I'd like to see it, Paul."

"It'll be distributed to you automatically."

Blake could almost hear Alice Underwood pout on the phone. "I'd like to see it sooner if you please," she said.

Blake was immediately pleased. He welcomed any opportunity to be in the first lady's presence. "I'll get it to you sooner than soon. I'll bring it to you myself."

"I don't mean to interfere with your work."

"Not at all. Give me five minutes. Where will you be?"

"In the First Lady's Office."

"I'll be there in a jiffy."

There was a pause. "The president's schedule hasn't been distributed yet, has it?"

"Not yet. Do you want me to hold it off for any reason?"

"Possibly. We'll see. I want to look it over first."

It was ten minutes before Blake, hair freshly combed, necktie in place, schedule in hand, entered the First Lady's Office.

She was behind her polished desk in a quilted swivel chair, staring through the window at Lafayette Square.

When she heard him, she came to her feet. She started across the room to the chintz sofa beneath the wildflower prints on the wall.

As she signaled him to the down-filled armchair beside the sofa, he hesitated an instant to watch her walk.

She was perfection. He had never in his life seen a woman better put together. Alice was wearing a sheer white silk blouse, the lace brassiere visible underneath, and a short shan-tung skirt. Her long legs, in the flesh-colored stockings, were breathtaking.

Even his own wife, who had good legs and regular features, seemed somewhat less and even dowdy by comparison.

Alice Underwood was seated on the sofa, crossing her legs, and Blake found himself hard put to remember what he was expected to do next. Then, with effort, he remembered and walked stiff-legged across the room to settle in the armchair beside her.

"Paul," she said, "the president's schedule—did you bring it?"

He reached into his jacket pocket, pulled the schedule free, and unfolded it.

She reached out impatiently. "May I see it?"

He handed the schedule to her, and she quickly scanned it.

"What I'm interested in," she said slowly, "is what the president has lined up after lunch. I see he's having lunch with that woman from Lampang."

"Yes, Madame Noy Sang."

"What an odd name," said Alice absently. "Is this some kind of social lunch or what? I mean, is it a courtesy thing?"

Blake could not see where she was going, but he decided to be forthright. "It's somewhat more important than that. Which is the reason Ezra Morrison and I will be there, too."

"I see you've allocated two hours for it," said Alice. "Isn't that a long time for lunch?"

"The time isn't set aside only for the lunch," said Blake. "First there will be the amenities, the usual process of getting acquainted. The really serious business of the meeting will take place after lunch, when we all move into the Yellow Oval Room."

"Does all that have to take two hours?"

"Well, not necessarily," said Blake cautiously. "It could be compressed to an hour and a half."

Alice leaned toward him. It caused her breasts to jiggle, and Blake was momentarily disconcerted. Alice asked, "Can you compress it to an hour and a half?"

"I'm not sure, Alice. What do you have in mind?"

Alice spoke earnestly. "You remember when we came into the White House and you wanted me to have some do-good activity? We felt anti-drugs and anti-alcohol and help for re- tarded children had all been opted by previous first ladies. You were the one who suggested arts and education for me."

"I still regard it as a good choice," said Blake.

"Okay, you know that among other things, I became very involved in the new Contempo Museum. Well, we're having a high tea there as a fund-raiser, mostly for patrons. I'm expected to speak and I will. But I'm far less effective at that than Matt. I want him to join me at the Contempo and say a few words, too. Surely that's as important as Lampang. I mean, he can still have his talk with that woman from Lampang and find time to be effective at the Museum. Isn't that possible?"

Paul Blake hesitated. When he had gotten Alice into arts and education, he had specifically had in mind doing things for the poor and underprivileged. The patrons and backers of the Contempo Museum were hardly in that class. They could not be thought of as needy. The tea and the appearance of the president would merely be added icing on a cake that was already overly rich.

"I—I don't know, Alice—" Blake began.

Alice was immediately on her feet. She had made an inroad, and did not mean to lose it. "Come on, Paul, dear, you can do it, an itty-bitty favor. Please." She bent over him and kissed him on the cheek, and in doing so one of her breasts brushed his uplifted hand.

Shaken, Blake retreated. "Well—"

"Come on," Alice burst out. She hugged him, and he could feel both those magnificent breasts. "For me, for my cause."

For Blake, any further resistance was gone. He tried to adjust himself to her face over his. "Well, I suppose it could be done."

"You're a doll!" Alice exclaimed, pressing her lips against his. "Thank you."

"I—I'll rearrange the schedule."

"It's easy," said Alice briskly, straightening up. "Matt hasn't seen his final schedule yet. Mark in that Lampang woman from twelve thirty to two, and then have Matt drive over to the Contempo Museum with me by two thirty." She handed the schedule back to him. "Will you do it immediately?"

"Immediately," he said, staggering out of the deep chair.

Alice had him by the arm and was leading him to the door. "I'll expect Matt to pick me up at two thirty."

He was out the door and in the corridor. Alice had closed the door behind her.

Blake knew that he had been manipulated.

Those warm lips. Those soft breasts. They had been worth it.

Starting away, Blake asked himself, What did it matter? An hour and a half more or less with some woman from the South China Sea.

Blake told himself the president might even be grateful to escape a half hour sooner.

Forty minutes earlier, Chief of Staff Blake had made another change in the president's schedule and had sent out a special memorandum by hand to the interested parties.

He had postponed the full cabinet meeting.

He had been concerned with his failure to brief the president on Lampang earlier, and felt that the meeting in the Cabinet Room should concentrate on Lampang entirely, on what the president should be ready to give and expect to receive. With this concentration on the immediate subject of concern, there was no need to be burdened by the secretary of agriculture, the secretary of commerce, the secretary of transportation, the attorney general, and other members of the president's staff.

Entering the Cabinet Room, Blake could see at a glance that the necessary officers had been alerted and were on hand. Blake greeted the secretary of state, the CIA director, the secretary of defense, and the three officers of the National Security Council, and then he took the leather chair next to the president's vacant one.

"How did your pre-briefing go with the president?" Morrison wanted to know.

Blake grimaced. "Lousy."

"What does that mean?" Morrison asked.

"It means lousy," said Blake. "The president didn't give a damn about Lampang. He only wanted to speak of the heavyweight fight in Las Vegas later in the afternoon."

"Then our work's cut out for us," said CIA Director Ramage.

"Right you are," said Blake. "It's got to be Lampang and more Lampang. That's why I cancelled everyone else. I wanted to concentrate on what's waiting for the president at lunch."

They were beginning their briefing of the chief executive when a door opened and President Underwood came into the room.

Tall and erect, he appeared to be in good humor. He

brushed back his hair, grinned at the assemblage, and said to no one in particular, "What's been going on behind my back?"

Making his way to his leather chair, he greeted everyone in the Cabinet Room by name.

"We've been discussing your lunch with Madame Noy Sang," Blake told the president as he settled into place.

"Is it going to be a long lunch?" the president asked.

"It doesn't have to be," Morrison assured him. "After some get-acquainted talk with the Madame, you can wind up lunch and we'll move into the Yellow Oval Room. That can be strictly business."

"I just wanted to know because I didn't want to miss the big fight," the president explained.

"You'll have plenty of time for that," Blake promised. "This lunch and meeting with Madame Noy Sang is scheduled to last one and a half hours. Then the first lady expects you to accompany her to the opening of the Contempo Museum and say a few words, maybe five minutes' worth, about an important fund-raiser. That'll give you plenty of time to get back for the fight."

The president surveyed the room. "I see a lot of our friends are missing and you've brought in only the big brass."

"Deliberate," said Blake simply. "Since you're going to be bargaining with Madame Noy Sang, we wanted our full concentration to be devoted to a treaty with Lampang."

"Fair enough," said the president. "This lady I'm lunching with—can anyone tell me what she's like?"

Secretary of State Morrison leaned forward. "We don't know exactly. None of us has met her. You remember her husband was president of the island when he was assassinated. She was vice-president, as per custom in those parts. So she inherited his seat."

Underwood nodded. "Yes, I remember. I've seen her picture in the press. She doesn't look too formidable."

Ramage entered the conversation. "She isn't, Mr. President. Our station head in Lampang, Percy Siebert, says she's a small, gentle woman, and was in shock and retreat a long time after her husband's death. In effect, she gave it a year of mourning and the entire year to learn her job for herself."

"And now that a year has passed," said Morrison, "Noy Sang is coming out of seclusion. Her first trip abroad is this one to the United States. I suppose mainly because she needs us."

"Money, I'm sure," said the president.

"There might be a little more," said Blake, "and it could be sentimental. Noy Sang has been in America before. Some while ago. She spent four years doing undergraduate work at Wellesley."

The president seemed to perk up. "That's where Dianne is at school," he said proudly. "She's now in her senior year."

Everyone was supposed to know, and did know, that Dianne Underwood was his twenty-one-year-old daughter.

"That'll give you something in common to talk about," said Blake, "before you settle down to the nitty-gritty."

The president nodded. "All right, what's the nitty-gritty?"

Morrison had been busy drawing a map on the page of a long yellow pad. He tore it loose and came around the table to the president. Addressing Curtis Cannon, the secretary of defense, he said, "Curtis, take my seat and give me yours. This will make it easier for me to explain a map of the South Pacific and beyond, which I've been drawing."

The exchange was made, and Morrison squirmed into the chair beside the president and placed the yellow sheet before him.

"What's this?" the president wanted to know.

"A crude drawing of the Far East, highlighting our major air bases that help us contain any overenthusiasm that may occur in North Korea, China, Vietnam, and Cambodia." Using his pen as a pointer on the map, Morrison resumed. "As you can see, Mr. President, our Pacific Air Force has three major wings. Not counting Hawaii, which is Pacific Air Force headquarters for the 15th Air Force, we have three large air bases. Here's our air base in Japan for the 5th Air Force. Here's our air base in South Korea for the 7th Air Force. Here's our air base in the Philippines for the 13th Air Force. Do you see anything unusual about my map?"

The president shook his head. "Not especially."

"Well, look down here. What do you see?"

The president stared at the map. "An island, a large island and two small ones."

"Lampang," said Morrison. "We have no air base there."

"And you want one there?"

Morrison raised his head and met the president's eyes. "We not only want one there, we *must* have one there. That would give us a base a stone's throw from Cambodia, Vietnam, and China, all Communist."

"I see. How do we get it?"

"By depending on your own power of persuasion and undeniable charm to reduce Madame Noy Sang to a compliant puddle," said Morrison. "We'll outline what we want from her, and what we can give her in return."

"Go ahead," said the president.

Morrison looked down the table. "Curtis," said Morrison to the secretary of defense, "let's trade seats again."

They did so.

Firmly settled beside the president once more, Cannon said,

"Mr. President, I'm going to tell you exactly what we want from Madame Noy Sang. You don't have to commit it all to memory. I have our demands typed out on several cards for you. You can refer to these when you and Madame Sang get down to hard business."

He drew several cards from a pocket and passed them to the president, who placed them in his own pocket.

"Okay, go on," said the president.

"What we want is an air base on roughly a hundred and thirty thousand acres in Lampang. About ten thousand of those acres will be needed for various buildings and other facilities. There should be room for ten thousand Air Force personnel, and about fifteen thousand native civilians and contract employees."

"What about the airstrips?" inquired the president.

"There'll be plenty of room for two vital runways," said the secretary of defense. "One long one will take about fifty fighter planes—F-5s, F-4Es, F-4Gs, and maybe room for twelve F-5Es."

"Do we have to buy all this property?"

"I wouldn't dare to suggest that, even if it were possible," Secretary of Defense Cannon said. "The base itself, excepting planes and buildings, would be owned by Lampang. What I foresee, and what Madame Noy Sang will undoubtedly want, will be a mutual agreement between Lampang and ourselves. We get a long-term lease on the base—perhaps ninety years if you can swing it—in return for substantial aid to Lampang in American dollars."

"What's substantial aid?" the president asked.

Cannon looked across the cabinet table at Morrison. "Have you got a figure, Ezra?"

"I have two figures," said Morrison. "These are based on

inquiries I've made of my Far Eastern experts. Alan Ramage has also been helpful and given me a lot of input from the CIA. The first figure is the low figure. It may work, because Noy Sang is so desperate. Play around with that figure, Mr. President."

"How much is it?" Underwood asked.

"A hundred twenty-five million dollars."

"That sounds substantial enough to me," said the president.

"To you, sir, but it may not to the president of Lampang," said Morrison. "While she might not be too sophisticated, she's been in office a year and has an idea of what we need. She knows her ace in the hole is the air base. She knows its importance to our national defense. So she may be a little hard-nosed about all this and bargain for more." Morrison considered what he wanted to say next. "The fact is, Mr. President, you can go for more. Put on the appearance of being a good guy and go for the higher loan."

"Which is?"

"We could go for a loan of a hundred fifty million—that much, but not a dime more. Then it becomes too costly, considering our outstanding loans to other countries. Oh, Madame Sang may ask for more. They always do. Those little countries are impoverished and feel Uncle Sam has bottomless pockets. But we don't have that much to fling around, especially on a relatively obscure place like Lampang. You can be a hero and go up to a hundred fifty million, but I repeat, that's the limit."

"What if she says no?"

"Then you say good-bye to the lady. We'll hunt elsewhere for another base and a more reasonable trader."

The president frowned. "But I thought you were saying we really must have this Lampang base?"

"We want it, no question," said Morrison. "Yet there are

limits to what we can give. We can't allow ourselves to be blackmailed." He smiled at Underwood. "You can do it, Mr. President. Just turn on the old charm. We're lucky Lampang's head of state is a woman. A few words from you, a generous smile, and she'll melt. Diplomacy often comes down to that."

Underwood seemed uncertain. "I hope so."

"You'll pull it off," said Morrison. "I don't have a doubt in the world. You'll come up a winner."

"I'll do my best," said the president, and with that the meeting in the Cabinet Room was adjourned.

In the heart of the capital city of Visaka on the island of Lampang, Noy Sang sat in her husband's office in Chamadin Palace behind her husband's oversized desk, signing papers into law before her departure for the United States.

The office and desk were still, even after a year of her occupancy, her husband's office and his desk. He had been brutally killed here, and buried in the ground after great ceremony, but for Noy Sang her husband Prem was not entirely dead. It was as if he had simply gone away on a long trip, without saying good-bye. Some memories of him had faded, details mostly, and in recent months she had felt less alone because she had been busy with her work.

But the office and desk were Prem's. She could not be disloyal. Everything she had learned and knew—well, almost everything—had come from Prem, and she could not completely believe that she was her own person.

What brought all this to mind as she signed her papers was that the mourning period was over, and she was about to leave Lampang on her first official trip abroad.

Truly she now was—would be—President Noy Sang of Lampang.

Noy peeked at the dial of her gold watch. It was time for young Den to depart for school. She wondered where he was. Then she realized that her own departure from the airport and the flight to the United States with Chief of Foreign Affairs Marsop Panyawan would take place in a half hour, and that she had better finish signing her papers.

She resumed scribbling her signature by pen, and had just finished with the last document when she heard the clatter of footsteps on the staircase that led down from the family apartment.

Little Den bounced into the office, hastily followed by Noy's sister, Thida. Den was dark-haired and dark-eyed with a pug nose, and small (even for his age). Her sister Thida was three years her junior, taller and slimmer than she, with more angular features. She was single again after having had an early marriage annulled and was now vice-president of Lampang—a worthy one, because she was as politically knowledgeable as Noy and with as much empathy for the poor.

Noy put down her pen, came out of her chair, and knelt to kiss and embrace her little boy.

"Get right down to the car or you'll be late for school," Noy told him. "This won't be a long trip. Three or four days and I'll be back. Thida will go along to school with you today."

This had been a special arrangement, sending Thida with him, to keep Den's mind off her trip. Normally, there was only Chalie, a faithful driver always around to take Den to the public school—Noy would not permit a private school—and bring him back to the palace when school was over.

Noy stood up and hugged her sister. "You're in charge while I'm gone," Noy whispered to her sister. "Be strong. Don't let General Nakorn begin acting on any of his anticommunist ideas. I mean to keep Lunakul and the insurgents in a talking posture with us until we can work something out."

Thida smiled and patted her sister's hand. "Don't worry, Noy. You leave Lampang in safe hands. Maybe I can't manage Lampang the way you do, but still I can do a good job of imitating you. As for General Nakorn, I'll never take an eye off him."

"Thanks, Thida. . . . Good-bye, Den. I love you. See you in a wink of days."

She watched Thida take the boy by the hand and lead him out of the office.

About to return to her husband's desk, she saw Marsop Panyawan come briskly into the office. He was an intense skeletal man, with an air of gravity.

Not only was Marsop her chief of foreign affairs, but he had been her husband's best friend, and her own most dependable ally.

Marsop was slightly taller than the average Lampangian male, about five feet seven, with brown hair combed sideways, sunken eyes, and gaunt features. Greeting Noy, he crossed over to her desk and seated himself opposite her.

"Well, we're on our way to Washington, D.C.," said Noy.

"A visit vital to our interests," said Marsop. "I'm pleased you'll be lunching with President Underwood."

"Obviously not a social lunch," said Noy.

"I would not characterize it as that. We know we need money from them. I've learned clearly what they want from us, not in detail but in general."

"We get a loan," said Noy simply. "We give an air base."

"I'm quite certain that will be the arrangement."

Noy was thoughtful. "The loan. How much do we want from the United States?"

Marsop grunted. "As much as we can get, Noy."

"But in practical terms. You've already felt out the United States ambassador here. You know what they're thinking about."

Marsop shook his head. "I really don't know. I know what we need. I've met with the cabinet and I have a fair idea."

"What do we need?"

Marsop picked a package of cigarettes out of his jacket pocket and loosened one. He considered the cigarette before lighting it. "We need two hundred million dollars," he said at last.

"Can they give it to us?"

"They can, but they won't," said Marsop, puffing at his cigarette.

"Will they consider it excessive?"

"Only in the sense that they already have huge loans outstanding in Mexico, Brazil, Argentina, and a dozen other countries. Congress has been putting pressure on their president to tighten up and stop the handouts."

Noy showed her concern. "All right, I ask for two hundred million. What if they refuse it?"

"You're in trouble with our program at home."

Noy was considering something else. "Dare I hold the Soviet Union over their heads?"

"No, absolutely no. Not even as a bargaining chip, a threat. They'd be appalled to imagine you'd consider letting the Russians in here, especially with America's Pacific problem and their reason for meeting and negotiating with you. They want an air base for the very reason that it would be anticommunist."

"Well, what am I to do if they refuse the two hundred million?"

Marsop was quick to reply. "They mustn't be allowed to. You must demand the two hundred million and be steadfast in your demand."

Noy sighed. "You're making me very nervous, Marsop."

He smiled. "I mean to. Actually, you don't have to be. Don't forget, President Underwood wants something from you. He wants it very much."

"He can have it. We agreed to that."

"Not quite," said Marsop. "He'll want an extremely large air base. I don't think your followers would like that kind of giveaway. It would hurt you domestically. You've got to be very stingy about the air base. We'll talk in more detail on the flight to Washington. Actually, you have one more bargaining chip. It is the one I rely on most of all."

"What's that?"

"Your charm, Noy."

"Please, Marsop, that's impossible. I can't be a femme fatale for an American."

"You don't have to be." Marsop smiled broadly. "You can just be your regular everyday natural self. Believe me, you can't fail to impress him."

"I wish I could believe you. I wonder what he's like?"

"You mean President Underwood? I've got a complete run-down on him. I'll give it to you on the plane. Now we'd better get ready to go and meet him in person."

THREE

HIGH over the Pacific Ocean, Noy Sang and Minister Marsop Panyawan were seated on a velvet sofa aboard the Lampang presidential plane, finishing their late dinner. When they were done, and a dusky stewardess in jacket and pants had removed their trays, Noy leaned to her right to peer out of the small window.

"I think I can see the coastline of California," Noy said.

"Not yet," said Marsop. "The horizon is deceptive. We won't reach the United States for another hour."

"Then on to Washington, D.C."

"Yes, almost another five hours."

Noy gave a shudder and turned back from the window. "Too soon," she said. "Maybe I can sleep away some of the time."

"A rest would be helpful."

"Marsop, I need more than a rest. I need an anesthetic. I'm afraid I'm not quite ready for my first foreign affairs meeting."

"I'm sure you'll get on with President Underwood just fine."

"I wish I could be half as confident." She reached for her purse, then did not open it. "This is one hell of a time to give up smoking. Marsop, can you spare a cigarette?"

He fumbled for his pack, opened it, and held it out for her while she extracted a cigarette. Finding his lighter, he rolled his thumb across it and lighted her cigarette.

She inhaled deeply, exhaled, and then stared through the smoke at her minister of foreign affairs.

"I'm really not scared of dealing with President Underwood," she said slowly. "I'm just scared of being face-to-face with him for two hours. Who am I dealing with? Abraham Lincoln? Theodore Roosevelt? Richard Nixon?"

Marsop gave a short laugh. "Hardly. He's none of those, as you very well know. Last night, when I ran an hour of video-tapes of Underwood for you, you could see that he is not that formidable."

"What could I tell from those? Public speeches. Interviews. But no human being. I keep trying to think of him as a human being, and to imagine what he's truly like. Who will I be talking to?"

"A person no different from yourself, with his own ambitions, frustrations, aggravations, pleasures. Make believe Prem is beside you. Relax tomorrow. Feel secure."

She shook her head gravely. "Dear Prem is not beside me. I saw him dead. I can't play that game anymore. I'm on my own from now on. It's me alone." She reached out and gripped Marsop's hand tightly, then released it. "Of course, you'll be there standing behind me."

"I will be. But essentially you will be on your own. Just as the president of the United States will have his chief of staff and secretary of state with him, but finally both of you will be on your own together."

"What's he like, Marsop?" she said suddenly. "What's he really like?"

"I have a fair amount of intelligence on him," said Marsop. "You really want to know? Let me dig out my folder and read you what I have." He unlatched the leather briefcase beside him on the sofa and pulled out a blue folder. "Let me read to you a bit more about President Matthew—they all call him Matt—Underwood. I hope the knowledge will make you feel easier."

"Any light you shed will illuminate."

Marsop was parting his folder. "All right, let's find out what there is to find out, and pray that it is accurate."

"Tell me everything," said Noy.

"Everything, Noy."

He studied the contents of the first page in his folder. He raised his head.

"Matt Underwood is fifty-two years old."

"I thought he was older."

Marsop smiled. "It's his manner. A trick of solemnity when he was a television anchorman. To make him seem more fatherly."

"He was a television star, a real one?"

"A very real one, and an important one in his day."

"It's very hard to conceive, a television actor becoming president of the United States."

"Everyone has to be something, even a television star," Marsop said. "They had a Hollywood actor once before him. And a peanut farmer earlier. And a male model before that. It's very hard to be born a politician and stay one."

"Go on."

Marsop consulted his notes. He absorbed what he was reading and turned closer to Noy.

"According to our intelligence," Marsop said, "Matthew Underwood went to Columbia University—"

"I remember. That's in New York City."

"Yes. As a young man Underwood was blessed with a deep, resonant voice and a wonderful easy presence. He took speech and journalism courses and became captain of his debate team. Columbia finished first in everything in those years. One of Underwood's professors was so impressed with him that after his graduation the professor sent him to a close friend who was an executive of The National Television Network—that's the largest cable network in America. It broadcasts out of New York and Washington, D.C. The executive was equally impressed with Underwood and hired him to do reports around America from Pittsburgh, Chicago, New Orleans, and Los Angeles. This was one of those rare cases where an individual's charisma affected all the viewers. In two years Underwood was hired as anchorman for the national nightly news. It was his personality and weight that held a whole team of reporters in place. The anchorman starts off the news every night, and his person and style become so familiar to so many millions of Americans who welcome him into their homes that he becomes famous. Before Underwood there were such ones at the CBS network as Edward Murrow and Walter Cronkite. When Underwood became even better known than the others, he became a legend. His word was law. Everyone believed everything he reported. Anyway, his name began showing up on the popularity polls."

"That's how Americans choose their leaders?" Noy marveled.

"Underwood's name was pitted against the biggest political names, movie names, sports names, and he always came out ahead as the one whose name was most easily recognizable and whose person everyone trusted. That's what led him into politics. You recall that in America there are two senators from each state?"

"Yes, you forget, I have studied the American system. I know about senators to Washington."

"Very well," said Marsop. "One of the two from the State of New York died in the middle of his six-year term. The governor of New York had the right to pick a replacement for the deceased senator, to finish out his term."

Noy understood. "So he picked the anchorman Matthew Underwood, and Underwood accepted the appointment."

"Yes, he quit the network and marched off to Washington to be sworn in as Senator Matthew Underwood. He was an instant celebrity in a new profession. He was better known than any politician. He was an ongoing media event, someone to write about and report on, especially considering the similar celebrity of his wife."

"Alice Underwood," said Noy, nodding. "The woman he married after she became Miss America."

"You know about Miss America?" asked Marsop.

"I have read about it," said Noy. "I have seen many photographs of her. She is still very beautiful. Isn't it unusual for an American president to marry a woman only for her beauty?"

"You are misinformed, Noy. Underwood was not the American president when he met and married her. He was still an anchorman, and Alice had been hired by TNTN as a reporter. Of course Underwood was moved by her beauty. There is no denying that. But"—Marsop dipped into his sheaf of notes again—"Alice Underwood is known for more than her beauty.

She is intelligent as well. She is also well known for being aggressive—you know, pushy, wanting to get ahead or see to it that her husband remains ahead."

"Marsop, how can you know such a private and personal thing as that?"

"That's the purpose of having a first-rate intelligence service. Our country may be small, as small as Israel, but our intelligence is top-notch, just as Israeli intelligence is unbeatable."

"So," said Noy, "the American first lady is ambitious. But how much farther can she go? She *is* first lady already."

Marsop said flatly, "She wants to stay that way. She wants Matthew Underwood to remain president. In short, she wants him to run for reelection, for a second term."

"Is he interested?"

"No."

"How surprising," said Noy. "How can he not want it again? It's the single most important job in the world, much more powerful than that of the Soviet Union's general secretary."

"But it is not the most interesting job, at least that's what our intelligence source reports on Matthew Underwood's feeling about the presidency. Underwood is an intellectual man and a curious one, despite his facade of bluff geniality. The presidency of the United States is not a job you hold if you want to pursue matters of intellect. It is a job of taking advice, weighing advice, and of decision making. I'm led to believe that Underwood finds it tiresome."

"Why did he run for president in the first place?" Noy asked. "We know how I became a president. It was thrust on me. But Underwood had a choice."

"Not quite," said Marsop, "not quite. He was a wildly popular senator, and his party needed a presidential nominee. The offer was hard to resist. And then there was his wife, Alice."

"She wanted him to be president?"

Marsop offered a smile to correct Noy. "She wanted to be first lady."

"And she won."

"A landslide victory for both of them," said Marsop. "He'd have the same kind of victory if he ran again. He's immensely popular."

"Is he as hard on communism as I've heard?"

"Almost every American president is. It comes with the turf. To defend the homeland against Communists who are out to destroy capitalism and democracy. That's why you were invited to the White House. They want to fit you in—Lampang, actually—as part of their defensive ring in Asia against communism."

"I feel I'm going to be used."

"Not actually," said Marsop. "After all, homegrown communism is a problem for you, too."

"True. Yet I'm willing to negotiate a compromise."

"I'm afraid the United States is not as trusting."

"Will he trust us? Will he feel I'm being soft on communism?"

"He'll just want to know you wish to make the world safe for democracy."

"But I do," said Noy fervently.

"Then tell him so."

"How can I make him believe me?"

Marsop smiled. "By being yourself, Noy. Whatever Underwood and the others say, do not bend to them merely to please them." Marsop paused. "Be yourself, Noy, from the first to the last minute you are with President Matthew Underwood."

* * *

The president and Chief of Staff Blake were at the mahogany sideboard in the President's Dining Room on the second floor of the White House when the door opened and Secretary of State Morrison showed Noy Sang into the room.

Immediately Underwood looked up from his Scotch and soda, and set the glass down as he watched Noy Sang proceed across the carpet toward him.

Something about her surprised him. He tried to discern what it was. Probably her unexpected attractiveness and grace. He was familiar with beautiful women. After all, he had married a Miss America. But Alice's beauty was technical, more professional. This woman from Lampang was utterly different.

Underwood's eyes held her. He had been prepared for a diminutive native type of woman. She was indeed small, delicate really. Her light brown skin was flawless. She had long black hair (a barrette held it in place at the small of her neck), a high forehead devoid of makeup, penetrating green almond-shaped eyes, a broad tilted nose, and full red lips set in an unaffected smile. Her approach toward him was fluid and graceful.

She was wearing a gauzy soft yellow dress. He assumed she had worn the dress because of the heat outside. The dress disconcerted him briefly. It clung and highlighted every protrusion of her body—the full, gently bobbing breasts, and the wide hips above slender shapely legs.

One word fleetingly passed through Underwood's head, a word that had not been inside it for years: erotic. This woman exuded natural eroticism.

How, he did not know, but it was there.

Noy was before him, Secretary of State Morrison beside her.

"The Honorable Matthew Underwood, the president of the

United States of America," Morrison announced. "Her Excellency, Noy Sang, the president of the Republic of Lampang."

To his surprise, and her own, Underwood took Noy's hand, bowed, and kissed the back of it.

"This is a pleasure, Mr. President," Noy said.

"The pleasure is mine, Madame President," Underwood said. Then, releasing her hand, he laughed. "I'm afraid we're going to be presidenting each other to death. There must be a better way."

It was Noy's turn to laugh. "Everyone calls me Noy," she said.

"And everyone who knows me well calls me Matt," Underwood said. "I hope today we will know each other well."

Underwood's sidelong glance caught the secretary of state's expression. It was one of pain at the breach of protocol.

Underwood ignored his secretary of state and returned his gaze to Noy. "I know you arrived last night. Did you have a comfortable flight?"

"Smooth, but I was unable to sleep. When we reached Blair House, I made up for it." She added with enthusiasm, "What a wonderful guesthouse. I've never seen one as exquisite."

"It was originally two joined houses built before the Civil War. In 1942, President Franklin D. Roosevelt bought it for the United States government. Since then, two more houses have been joined to it."

"I slept in the guest bedroom on the second floor. The four-poster with the canopy was like being wrapped in a cloud. I know this was all prepared on purpose to weaken me for our meeting." She searched behind her, and beckoned Marsop to join her, and then she introduced him around as her minister of foreign affairs.

Turning on her heel, she took in every aspect of the President's Dining Room.

"How cozy and lovely this is," she said.

Underwood was quick to take her by the elbow and give her a closer view. The furniture, he pointed out, was Federal period, the hunt table was Hepplewhite, the wallpaper Scenic America. The pedestal dining table was Sheraton.

Chief of Staff Blake took this as a cue to intervene. "Perhaps we can all sit down to lunch now," he suggested, leading the way to the dining table.

"Not before I ask Madame Noy—"

"Noy," she said firmly.

". . . yes, Noy, if I may mix her a drink."

"No, thank you. I can speak for Marsop in saying we're both famished."

As the president stepped forward and drew out her chair for her, he indicated the inscription on the mantel at the east wall. "Can you read that? 'We have met the enemy and they are ours.' "

Noy squinted and nodded. "Yes, from your Commodore Oliver Perry after the Battle of Lake Erie."

Underwood was impressed. "You've been to the White House before?"

"Once on a tourist visit, when I was studying in the United States."

They were all being seated now: President Underwood at the head of the table; Noy to his right, with Blake beside her; and Marsop to his left, with Morrison beside him. Once the two waiters had made them comfortable, they joined the white-capped chef at a second sideboard to begin serving the chopped salads.

Underwood pursued Noy's last remark. "You studied in the United States?"

"At Wellesley College, near Boston in Massachusetts."

"Wellesley!" exclaimed Underwood. "I'll be darned. What a coincidence. My daughter, Dianne, is an undergraduate there. Her major is political science. What was yours?"

Noy was pleased. "I majored in political science also. I took everything from comparative politics to American politics and law to international relations."

"I'll be darned," Underwood repeated. "You must know more about politics than I do."

"I doubt that, Mr. Pres—Matt," she said awkwardly. "I have not had your experience. But in history and theory I was an avid scholar. I even audited a course on Karl Marx."

"Karl Marx," said Underwood, his eyes on Noy as he ate his salad. "Did you know that Marx once worked as a foreign correspondent from London for a New York newspaper?"

"Oh, yes."

"I'll tell you something that astonished me. I've been told that Lenin never liked Marx's work. Couldn't stand Marx the man, either."

"Is that true? I never heard that before."

"I think it's true. There was more to Marx's life than his books. Did you learn anything of his private life?"

"A little."

"In London, I believe, he had an affair with his housekeeper and she had a child by him."

"I knew that." Noy smiled mischievously. "Matt, you're testing me. Now it's my turn to test you. Did you know that after Marx and Engels had written the *Communist Manifesto*, Marx himself later wrote *Das Kapital*, he expected his ideas to be taken up in Germany? He never dreamt that Russia would become the first Communist country."

"News to me," admitted Underwood.

Finishing her salad, Noy said, "I suspect that would have astonished him just as he would be astonished to learn that his ideas took root in Nicaragua and to some extent in Lampang in the South China Sea."

Secretary of State Morrison interrupted the exchange. Addressing Noy, he said, "We have some idea of your conflict with communism in your homeland. Is it as grave as our intelligence reports indicate?"

Noy admitted that it was. "The Communists are guerrillas and they give us trouble from two outer islands, where they are entrenched with military aid and troops from Vietnam. I am seeking to undercut their appeal by vigorously pushing a land reform program, dividing the estates of the wealthy to give property and independence to the poor. Even the estate owned by my parents will not escape my reform."

"What does your father say to that?" Blake interjected.

Noy laughed sweetly. "He suspects I've been won over to Communist ways."

"Have you?" Underwood asked quickly.

Noy gave him a sharp look. "Of course not," she said emphatically. "I will deal with the Communists, possibly compromise with them, but I will never give in to them. I will never let communism supersede democracy in Lampang. I'm a devout believer in Jefferson and Lincoln."

There was a brief silence while the waiters served the medallions of veal and asparagus.

Matt Underwood's eyes remained on Noy. "Jefferson and Lincoln," he said. "Do you consider them our greatest Americans?"

"No," said Noy positively.

"No?" repeated Underwood, startled. "Who, then, do you consider the greatest American?"

"Thomas Paine," Noy said without equivocation.

"More than Jefferson and Lincoln?"

"They were great men. Jefferson was the most brilliant among all the presidents before you to inhabit this White House. Lincoln kept the Union together at a terrible time in American history. But Thomas Paine gave it independence—"

Underwood screwed his face in thought. "I always thought Thomas Paine unstable, a corsetmaker, a bankrupt who came over from England—"

"More, much, much more," insisted Noy. She turned to Marsop to enlighten him. "No American colonist was thinking of independence from England when Thomas Paine arrived on the scene. He wrote and himself published 'Common Sense.' One in every twenty Americans read it. Paine never saw a shilling for his effort. He gave half his profits to his printer and reserved the other half to buy mittens for the soldiers of the Continental Army. Six months after Paine propagandized for freedom, the Declaration of Independence was signed."

Those at the table were finishing their ice cream desserts by now when Morrison restlessly backed his chair away from the table. "Perhaps it's time to move to the Yellow Oval Room," he announced, rising. "We can have our coffee served there, and perhaps get down to business."

Matt Underwood pulled back Noy's chair and, touching her arm lightly, he led the way into the corridor and toward the Yellow Oval Room, followed by the others.

Entering the bright formal room, Noy held back a moment to take it in.

"Even lovelier than the dining room," she said.

Underwood had her arm again as he propelled her past the flat-topped leather-inlaid desk to the yellow sofa facing the marble table that stood beside the white fireplace mantel. He directed Noy to the sofa, indicated a place for her among the cushions, and lowered himself a few inches from her. He waited for Morrison, Blake, and Marsop to be seated, and then he waited longer as the waiters entered, rolling a table that bore the coffee.

Once the coffee was served, and the waiters had left them, Morrison came forward in his patterned maroon armchair.

"Maybe it's time," he said briskly, "to discuss Madame Noy Sang's business agenda for this meeting."

President Underwood had been sipping his coffee. He set his cup down. "Not so fast, Ezra," he said to his secretary of state. "We have time enough. I'm eager to hear more from Noy about what she knows of our history and our democracy."

"Your Constitution," Noy began. "I think it's the best document of its kind in the world. In fact, my husband and I worked to improve our own Constitution in Lampang by following yours. That is not to say yours is perfect. I've often thought there were several ways yours might be improved."

Underwood arched an eyebrow. "You do? Tell us."

Noy immediately and fearlessly launched into a discussion of the American Constitution. "When we modeled our Constitution after yours, we made changes that were long overdue. We dropped the electoral college provision, which we considered obsolete. We added an equal rights provision, which you had rejected as an amendment. At first our Assembly was fashioned after your House of Representatives. It allowed members to be elected every two years, as yours still does. We knew that was wrong and changed it. Two years gives a new member just enough time to find his or her office and start running again.

We changed that to four years. Most important, the great flaw in your Constitution is the presidency." Noy smiled. "It should be abolished in the United States as we intend to abolish and change it on Lampang."

Underwood laughed. "You want to get rid of me?"

"Not quite. We want to get rid of primaries and public elections. As I read somewhere, it would be wiser if the chief executive were to be elected by both houses of Congress and the leading party in each house. Each senator should have two votes, and each representative one. The chief executive elected would remain in office until his party loses a key vote in Congress. Key vote would be defined. Once defeated, the chief executive would resign and there would be a new national election for both houses. Once in place, they would vote for another chief executive all the more responsive to the people. There would be no vice-president. What do you think?"

Underwood smiled. "I'm beginning to feel uneasy. You're a radical, Noy."

"Just trying to improve democracy," she said.

Underwood pressed her for more ideas, and was intrigued by her originality and wit. He hung on to every word.

The dialogue went on and time was passing.

At the first interlude, Chief of Staff Blake pointedly held up his hand and considered his wristwatch. "Uh, Mr. President, if I may remind you of your schedule today. . . . In ten minutes you are due to pick up the first lady and take her to the Contempo Museum opening. You remember, you were written in to say a few words."

Secretary of State Morrison shifted in his seat. "Why don't you go on, Mr. President. I can stay behind with Madame Noy Sang a little longer and get into the political agenda we wanted to cover."

President Underwood frowned. "Not necessary, Ezra. I'd prefer to handle the foreign policy matter myself." He turned toward Blake. "You can take off now, pick up Alice, and accompany her to the Contempo Museum. Tell her I'm too tied up with our country's affairs to waste my time on art contributors."

Noy touched the president's arm. "Matt, if you are due somewhere else, please don't let me hold you. I can carry on our business with Secretary Morrison."

"No, I prefer to do it directly with you. Ezra Morrison can take Minister Marsop back to his office at the Department of State and outline our thoughts on Lampang. Meanwhile, we can talk it out ourselves. Please go ahead, Ezra, and give the minister some background on our own needs."

Morrison reluctantly rose. "If that is your wish, Mr. President—"

"It is my wish," said Underwood firmly.

As the secretary of state and Marsop prepared to leave, the president addressed Blake once more. "You just go ahead, Paul, scoop up Alice, and stand in for me at that museum affair. I'd like to carry on with Noy alone."

He watched Morrison depart with Marsop, and then waited for Blake to leave also.

Swinging toward Noy, he said, "At last we're alone. I prefer privacy in meetings."

Noy smiled. "I feel privileged," she said.

Underwood considered her silently for a few moments. He was taken by her naturalness with him, and her artless manner of saying whatever was on her mind. He was totally captivated by her broad knowledge and her fearless habit of contradicting routine opinion, his own included.

"There's something else I'd hoped to discuss with you about

America, Noy," he said gravely, "before we get down to heavier business."

"Whatever you wish," she said. "Please go ahead."

"Do you like American movies?"

"American movies?" This was so unexpected that she burst into laughter. "You ask seriously?"

"Of course. You can tell more about a stranger by learning of the movies they enjoy and the books they read than anything more serious. I want to know more about you."

She caught his mood and answered solemnly. "I adore American movies. In their way, they are a unique American art form. Recently I have been watching reruns of your old films on our television, and most are truly magnificent."

"For instance?"

"A few weeks ago," said Noy, "I sat through one of the best American films I had ever seen."

"What was it?"

"It was called *The Petrified Forest,* with Leslie Howard and Humphrey Bogart—"

"Ah, Duke Mantee."

"—and Bette Davis. It was a very meaningful film to me, an echo of how many in life are trapped."

Underwood agreed. "I remember seeing it three times."

"And you?" Noy asked. "What others have you liked?"

"I still remember one of my favorites," said Underwood. "A comedy starring Claudette Colbert and Clark Gable called *It Happened One Night.* I was so entranced by Gable smoking a pipe that I went out and bought one for myself." He fumbled at a top pocket of his jacket. "I still have it, or one like it." He withdrew a battered dark briar. "You see?"

"I enjoy the smell of a pipe."

"Then I'll smoke it." He found his leather pouch, filled his pipe, and applied a lighter. "There. How's that?"

"Sweet and mellow."

"Another movie I enjoyed," he said, puffing, "was *Citizen Kane,* with Orson Welles."

"I never understood it well because I did not know much about the American it was based on. *It Happened One Night* was easier for me because it was about a man and a woman and pure fun."

They went on about men and women, and Underwood grew more entranced by her sense of humor and vivacity.

Their exchange continued without pause, and when Underwood got up to pour them each a Scotch, he realized that two and a half hours had elapsed since lunch. He had been with Noy four and a half hours, and it seemed as though ten minutes had passed.

Handing her the drink, he knew that he owed her something. She had flown all the way from Lampang to discuss business with him, and business had not been addressed at all.

He wanted to talk more about her, but he also wanted to be constructive and make her happy about her job.

"Well, I'm glad you came here, Noy," he said. "Meeting you has been delightful."

"For me, too, Matt," she answered.

"Much as I'd like to continue socializing, I know I'm not supposed to," he said. "I know that you came here to discuss business."

She seemed mildly surprised. "I'd almost forgotten," she admitted.

"So had I." He stared at her. "Do you want to discuss what we were expected to discuss?"

She nodded, not too happily. "I suppose we must. The afternoon is almost gone. I'm scheduled to fly back to Lampang tomorrow. I have to justify this trip by discussing a serious matter."

He nodded. "Let's get it over with quickly and get back to more enjoyable conversation. I'm sure Marsop has told you as Morrison has told me, you and I are expected to make a trade that will satisfy each of our countries."

"A trade, yes."

"I give you something you want," said Underwood, "and in return you give me something I need."

"So I was advised."

Underwood's attention was devoted to her serious face. "What do you want, Noy?"

"A generous loan for a good cause. I need American money to bolster our economy."

"I planned all along to give you a loan. Do you want to name a ballpark figure?"

"A ballpark figure?" she said, puzzled.

"An American expression that means we are in the same baseball park, not too far apart, near enough to come to an agreement. How much do you need?"

"To survive, you understand," said Noy. "I will give you the sum I must have to fend off two pressures—from the Communist insurgents on the far left and my army on the far right."

"What is the sum?" Underwood persisted.

"I was told you could spare a higher sum, but to settle for two hundred million dollars."

Underwood could not contain his chuckle. "You are certainly frank, aren't you?"

"I am not a politician," she said. "I must be honest. Anything else is a waste of time. Does my sum meet with your approval?"

"It's a bit overwhelming," said Underwood. "Let me be honest, too. My advisors told me to offer you one hundred twenty-five million and then bargain and settle for one hundred and fifty million. Can you live with that sum, Noy?"

"I'm afraid not, Matt."

"All right," he said, setting aside his half-finished drink and putting his hands in his lap. "Why don't we talk it over? We'll both be honest."

Normally Underwood disliked the technicalities and bargaining involved in foreign affairs meetings. Whenever possible, he avoided them. But now, almost eagerly, he looked forward to an extended discussion with Noy. Speaking to her, listening to her, he was aware that he was dealing with a remarkable woman. He had never felt more comfortable.

Consideration of the loan went back and forth, and he heard her out on the situation on Lampang and her problems as successor to her husband.

At last Underwood came to a decision and he made it. Noy was plainly pleased, and even spontaneously reached out to touch his hand in a show of gratitude.

"But this is a trade," she said. "Now you must give me your demand."

"It's about the lease of an air base," he said.

"I know, Matt. But I must know the details."

He outlined the details carefully for her, consulting the cards he had been given to be certain that he had it right. He told her everything that Secretary of State Morrison and Secretary of Defense Cannon had given him.

Noy was attentive, understanding his demands, and when it was time she countered with her point of view.

She was so logical that he found it hard to resist her, but he continued to lay out America's needs.

After half an hour, they arrived at a compromise.

"Well, there we have it," Noy said. "Are you pleased?"

"If it satisfies you, I am pleased."

She gathered up her purse. "I've taken too much of your time. I'd better find Marsop and get back to Blair House to help the maid repack."

She started to rise, but he restrained her.

"Noy, must you return to Lampang tomorrow?"

"It was my plan. It is not urgent, but I am needed there."

Underwood hesitated. "In a different sense, I need you here, at least one more day."

She met his gaze. "But why, Matt? We have concluded our business."

"Only our foreign policy business," he said. "I have not concluded my personal business."

She wrinkled her smooth brow. "What does that mean?"

"I've had such a wonderful time with you that I hate to see it end. For one thing, I'd like to give you a closer look at Washington, take you on a guided tour. I know you've been here before. Did you see much?"

"Except for the tourist visit to the White House, very little."

"You must see more," Underwood said with conviction. "I'll personally take you on a drive around Washington. Then we can have lunch, one to one, and talk about personal business."

"What kind of personal business?"

"You," said the president. "I want to know more about you. And I want you to know more about me. We should know each other, not as heads of state but as human beings."

She cocked her head and bathed him with a smile. "That sounds appealing. I find you almost impossible to resist."

"Then, don't."

"Haven't you got a heavy schedule tomorrow?"

He grinned. "Yes, the day with you. I'll pick you up at Blair House at eleven twenty. Show you about. Then we can dine together at one o'clock. I'll get you back to your guesthouse by late afternoon, in time for your return to Lampang by early morning. What do you say? It would not be courteous to veto the president on a matter like this."

Noy laughed. "Who says I'm going to veto you?" She rose to her feet. "I like the bill of goods you offer. It stands passed. I'll be looking forward to seeing you in the morning."

After Noy Sang had gone, he saw that there was still time to go to his office and see if there was anything on his desk that required his immediate attention.

Starting for the elevator and his office, he felt in high spirits, higher than he had been in months. He hadn't enjoyed the company of a woman as much since he had become president. He tried to reason out her effect on him. It could not be her beauty alone. He had a wife who might be considered more beautiful. He thought of Noy again, her unaffected manner and style, her forthrightness, her knowledge and intelligence, her naturalness.

She was truly one of a kind.

And it made him buoyant that he could have almost the entire day with her tomorrow.

It was certain to be a memorable day.

Then, nearing his office, one cloud remained. He must summon his chief of staff and secretary of state and inform them of what had transpired between Noy and him. He must brace himself for that confrontation.

Entering the Oval Office, he saw that he would not have to summon his chief of staff and secretary of state. They were both already there, Blake and Morrison, each slouching on chairs on either side of the Rutherford B. Hayes desk, awaiting him. He walked around his desk, half saluting Blake and Morrison, and sat down in his leather chair, which was flanked behind the presidential flag and the Stars and Stripes.

He glanced at the presidential flag, as if to remind himself who was really in charge here.

He shuffled the papers on his desktop, and finally he spoke. "Well, it's done," he said.

Blake tried to keep the reproach out of his voice. "You took long enough, Matt. You were penciled in for two hours with her. You were with her over five hours. Fortunately you didn't have a heavy schedule today, except for the visit to the Contempo Museum. I can tell you the first lady was pretty upset you missed it. But still—"

"What counts is how you made out," said Morrison.

"Was it five hours?" Underwood said. "It felt like two. I guess there was a lot to talk about."

"How did you make out?" Morrison repeated. "Did you make the swap?"

"Oh, yes. We gave and we got."

"What did you give, Matt?" The secretary of state wanted to know.

"Lampang has a lot of problems," Underwood said evasively.

"The whole world has," said Morrison. "How much did you settle for? Did you have to go to one hundred fifty million?"

"No," said Underwood. "That wouldn't have helped her or us." He settled himself. "I agreed we would loan her two hundred fifty million, half of it immediately."

Morrison was incredulous. "You what?"

"They need money there, and we need them."

"But two hundred fifty million. That's the kind of money

we might consider giving some major nation, not a mere island."

"It'll be well spent, you'll see."

"I mean, if you gave it to General Nakorn, I might understand it," Morrison protested. "At least he's totally on our side."

"He's not interested in democracy. He doesn't give a damn about the people. If he were in power, he'd wipe out the Communists. There'd be a bloodbath."

"But he is on our side," Morrison implored. "He's our kind of dictator. Noy Sang is too weak. She's not dependable."

Underwood was adamant. "In my judgment she's entirely dependable. When she has the money, she'll turn Lampang into a real democracy. We'll have a democracy to work with."

Blake suddenly intervened. "Matt—"

Underwood faced him. "Yes, Paul?"

Blake hesitated. It was as if he had a question to which he didn't want to hear the answer. "All right, we know what you gave, but, Matt—what did you get?"

"An air base, just as we wanted."

"Just as we wanted," Blake said suspiciously. "You mean exactly the space we wanted?"

Absently, Underwood doodled with a pen. "Well, not exactly. Almost, but not exactly."

Morrison bent forward. "Exactly was to be one hundred thirty thousand acres. How much is not exactly?"

"Noy has obstacles to overcome. She couldn't give one hundred thirty thousand acres and pretend Lampang was still an independent nation. I had to be sensible."

"What's sensible?" Morrison demanded.

"We agreed on an air base of ninety thousand acres."

For seconds Morrison was speechless. At last he found his

voice. "That's for Piper Cubs," he said. "That's not for the jets in our Air Force."

"We can make do," said Underwood. He came to his feet. "I'd better get upstairs and have a few words with Alice. She must be furious about this afternoon."

As Underwood reached the door to start under the colonnade past the Rose Garden, Blake's voice caught him. "You missed the big fight in Las Vegas, Matt."

"I quite forgot."

"Your man won. The challenger won the title by a technical knockout."

"Good, good," said Underwood uninterestedly as he pushed the door open.

He did not leave. He addressed his chief of staff. "Paul, what's on the agenda tomorrow?"

"You know," said Blake. "You and Alice are entertaining the Senate wives for lunch. Then a press conference. In the evening the formal dinner for the governors together with their wives."

"Fine," said Underwood. "The evening is on. Cancel the afternoon, except for the press conference. I mean, you and Alice can handle those women."

"Cancel your appearance in the afternoon before the press conference?" said Blake. "What are you going to be doing?"

"I've convinced Noy Sang to stay over an extra day. I'm going to take her sightseeing and then off to a private lunch in some restaurant." He paused. "We'll discuss the air base further."

With that, he left the Oval Office.

Once he was gone and they were alone, Blake and Morrison sat in silence.

After a brief interval their eyes met. "What's going on?"

Morrison said, not quite to himself. "Five hours instead of two with the president of something called Lampang. A reckless loan far beyond what we agreed upon. A shrunken air base in return. Now, tomorrow, yet another day with that woman. What's happened to President Matt Underwood?"

"Easy," said Blake. "It even has a name."

"A name?"

"For ordinary men it's called middle-age syndrome. Why shouldn't that happen to a president, too?"

FOUR

THE following morning, Matt Underwood was determined to have this day for himself, or rather for Noy and himself.

The White House was a goldfish bowl, and escaping it had not been easy. He had begun the day with a series of lies. He called in Paul Blake and instructed him to inform the first lady that the president would be tied up for the afternoon—serious consultations with the National Space Agency—and unhappily would have to miss the Senate ladies' tea. He expected Alice and Blake to carry on in his stead. Yes, he would be available for a press conference at four thirty. He ordered Blake not to say a word to anyone about his absence from the White House. After that he lied to Jack Bartlett, his press secretary, about his afternoon's schedule, telling Bartlett that he had major policy decisions to make in seclusion. He expected Bartlett to invent a palatable lie for the press.

His earliest intention had been to lie to Frank Lucas, director of the Secret Service, also, but then he had second thoughts about that. He did not mind endangering his own life without the Secret Service, but he felt he could not take the risk with Noy.

He called Lucas in and told him the truth. He explained he had to have a confidential meeting with President Noy Sang about Lampang. Yet he wanted protection for Madame Noy more than for himself and therefore felt that it was his duty to inform Lucas.

"You're doing the right thing," said Lucas, a burly ex-police captain with a wide nose that looked as if it had been punched flat long ago.

"But I want only minimum protection," added Underwood. "Two or three Secret Service agents at most, so that I don't draw outside attention."

"Impossible," said Lucas. "I'll need a full shift of twelve, including several to sweep the restaurant you choose for surveillance devices and to supervise the preparation of the food in the kitchen. Understand this, Mr. President, we have a computer that lists all persons who've threatened you. There are at least forty thousand of those, and three hundred fifty we regard as serious threats. Disgruntled assailants have wounded or killed ten presidents and two nominees despite our protection, and we've lost eight agents in the line of duty."

"Still, I don't want a motorcade. Can't you cut my protection detail down to six?"

"It depends. Six isn't much." Lucas considered it, determined to do his duty, but eager to please the president. "What's your timetable and itinerary?"

"I'll have a car and driver at the South Portico just before eleven fifteen. I intend to go to Blair House to pick up Madame Noy. Then maybe an hour or two of sightseeing, the obvious sights around the city. Then I want you to find me an obscure restaurant in Georgetown—not a celebrity waterhole—someplace I'm least likely to be recognized—and reserve a booth for Madame Noy and myself."

Lucas shook his head. "There are no obscure restaurants in Georgetown. You'll be recognized anywhere you go. Unless—" He ruminated over a possibility.

"Unless what?"

"Unless I can find one that can be closed down for the afternoon, ostensibly for repairs, and have a notice posted to that effect. Then you and Madame Noy would have the place to yourselves."

"Is that possible?"

"Anything is possible with the right contacts," said Lucas. "In fact, I may have the ticket. There's a small restaurant, the 1776 Club, in Georgetown, that has a light luncheon crowd. It's usually almost empty at lunchtime and is quite easy to make secure. I know the owner and could talk to him. Of course, we'd have to bear the costs of the business he'd lose. I think I could talk him into that."

"Then do it. Book it for one o'clock. I'll need three hours. Maybe a little longer."

"Done," said Lucas. "You understand I'll have to place an agent in the limousine with you."

"Acceptable," agreed Underwood. "Our private conversation will take place during lunch."

"I'll have to have at least two cars with agents to precede you and follow you. There's no guarantee you won't be spotted by someone."

"I'm not worried about that. Those blacked-out windows in the limousine will conceal us."

"There are no blacked-out windows in the brownstones surrounding the restaurant."

"I'll take my chances, Frank. Just see that the CLOSED FOR REPAIRS sign is posted."

"Never mind, it will be."

"Know this, Frank. No one is aware of my meeting except you, my chief of staff, and the secretary of state. They won't talk. The press doesn't know. Even my wife doesn't know. The only leak could come from you or your men."

"You have my word, it won't," pledged Lucas. He rose and headed for the door. "See you at fifteen after eleven."

The limousine and driver and the Secret Service arrived on time.

The president left the White House by the back entrance, virtually unseen.

He had dressed his dapper best, a summer-weight gray suit, darker gray shirt, and a red tie with white polka dots.

At Blair House he stepped out of the limousine to escort Noy from the guesthouse. To his eyes, she was a dream of youth. She wore a blue Chanel sweater, and a pleated white chiffon skirt, and she took his hand with warmth.

Once seated in the rear, Underwood explained to Noy where they would be going, as he had earlier to the chauffeur.

At each sight they stopped briefly. Underwood's flashes of commentary were in his old television style and he was at his best.

"An odd American city," he said as they cruised along. "It was planned by a Frenchman. The majority of its inhabitants are black. Two thirds of its working population live in Virginia and Maryland. . . . That's the Capitol dome, which is a cast-iron copy of St. Paul's Cathedral in London. The interior of the dome is partially decorated with sculptured tobacco leaves, and no warning about smoking endangering your health. . . . There's the Washington Monument, an obelisk over five hundred fifty-five feet high and 90,854 tons in weight. At first it tilted like the Leaning Tower of Pisa but was straightened out in 1880. No one is allowed to walk up the eight hundred ninety-seven steps—an elevator takes you to the top in seventy seconds—but you can walk down and see a hundred and eighty-eight tribute slabs from various states, countries, the Cherokee nation, and Brigham Young's Deseret, where polygamy was allowed. The Monument celebrates our first president, who led us to freedom yet made millions of dollars on slave labor. . . . The Japanese cherry trees in blossom are a gorgeous sight, aren't they? The first shipment from Tokyo was infected with fungus and had to be burned down. The trees you see were planted in 1912. . . . They face a memorial to the revolutionary you referred to yesterday, Thomas Jefferson. There was a great fuss when a hundred and seventy-one healthy trees had to be destroyed or removed to make way for his memorial. . . . Over there is the memorial to Abraham Lincoln. Imagine, an Illinois rustic raised in a log cabin, now seated in a Greek marble temple that resembles the Parthenon. . . . That's the J. Edgar Hoover Building that houses the Federal Bureau of Investigation. It hoards two hundred fifty million fingerprints to identify murderers or people suffering from amnesia."

Near the end of the tour, Noy turned to him. "You are really irreverent, Mr. President."

"Mr. President is never irreverent. Only Matt Underwood is." He covered her hand. "You are spending the day with Matt Underwood."

The limousine had slowed down.

"The 1776 Club," the driver announced.

Underwood came forward, waving away the Secret Service. "Now to a long, leisurely lunch. Not irreverent, but certainly private."

"Why are you doing this, Matt?"

"Because I wanted to know you better without talking of loans and air bases."

"Know me better? But why?"

Helping her out of the car, he said, "Because I hope to be seeing more of you, much more. Any objections, Noy?"

She stepped down and smiled up at him. "I'm flattered and I'm pleased."

And they went down the steps that led them into this obscure and closed restaurant.

Frank Lucas, who had himself headed the Secret Service detail, was awaiting them at the entrance, standing next to the CLOSED FOR REPAIRS sign. He led them past the empty tables of the restaurant to a booth at the very rear.

As they sat down alongside each other, Underwood said to Noy, "I took the liberty of asking Marsop what you usually eat at home. He told me fish, you like fish."

"I'm accustomed to fish," said Noy. "We're an island country and fish is our staple."

"So that's the lunch, if you don't mind, bouillabaisse, baked salmon loaf, some French fries, a lettuce salad, and your own choice of dessert. Why don't we start with a drink?"

"Scotch and soda will be fine."

Underwood looked up at the waiter. "Make that two Scotch and sodas."

After the waiter had gone, Noy rested her eyes on Underwood. "I'm curious about something—"

"Yes?"

"Yesterday, Matt, after we parted, did you go back to your office?"

"I did."

"Were the others waiting for you?"

"My chief of staff and the secretary of state were there."

Noy licked her upper lip. "I supposed they would be. They wanted to know how you made out with me."

Underwood grinned. "Very much." He met Noy's gaze. "I told them of course."

"The larger loan and the smaller air base?"

"Of course."

"How did they react?"

Underwood chuckled. "As expected. They gave me hell."

Noy's face was suddenly serious. "I'm sorry." She hesitated. "If you want to renegotiate, we can do so."

Underwood shook his head. "You're kind, but I gave my word and I'm keeping it."

"Even with your staff against you? You've got a lot of—what is the American word?—guts, you have that."

"It's more than that. I'd never break my word with anyone, well, almost never, and especially not with you."

"I appreciate your kindness."

"Never mind," said Underwood. "Let's keep talk of affairs of state at a minimum. Let's talk about each other. After the death of your husband, you were left with a family, weren't you?"

"Not extensive," said Noy, "but enough to be comforting. I have a son, Den, six, and he is in school, as you know. I have a younger sister, Thida, unmarried, and smarter than I am. Den and Thida and I are close. I'm also close to my parents. They live in a village outside Visaka. In fact, my father owns the village and everything around it. I get on well with my mother, but less so with my father. I adore him, but often he's annoyed with me. There are in my country often arranged marriages, but I refused that and chose my own mate. My father didn't like that; and more than that, he felt Prem was too liberal. He's also annoyed that I want to keep my husband's promise to the people to parcel out the big estates to the poor. My father doesn't like that. He knows his estate will be among them. He thinks it is too communistic. He knows I'm not a Communist, but he thinks I've gone too far left. I tell him that by doing this, trying to share the land, we can take away the only appeal the Communists have. In a way preserve what he enjoys, capitalist democracy. But my father can't quite see that."

The drinks had been served, and Underwood held up his glass in a toast.

"To capitalist democracy," he said.

She raised her glass and touched his. "Yes. And to two democratic leaders—us—who believe in people."

"Well spoken," Underwood said, and he drank.

Noy sipped her drink. "I have two uncles and one aunt in the countryside. We feel close to each other, too, and always gather together during holidays, especially Christmas and New Year's Day. There is another I consider my family, although he isn't in the family. I refer to Marsop. He would have given his life for my husband, as I'm sure he would for me."

"Were there other men before your husband?" Underwood wanted to know.

"A few childhood affections in the lower grades and when I went to Wellesley."

"Did they amount to anything?"

Noy was puzzled. "What do you mean?"

"Were you intimate with any of them? Did you have sex?"

She was startled. "You are frank, aren't you?"

"Not really. I want to know all about you. I don't want to skip a beat."

Noy was quiet a moment. "Very well. I don't mind telling you."

Underwood was quick to interrupt. "You don't have to answer me."

"I want to," she said. "We don't do anything like that in my social class when we are unmarried. Never before I married Prem, and not since his death, have I had such a relationship."

"I didn't mean to intrude on your intimate—"

"No, Matt, it is good to air such things."

"There's more I want to know," said Underwood. "You've told me of those you care for on Lampang. Who do you care for least?"

"I'm not sure I understand you."

"Your opposition, your enemies," said Underwood. "Who do you dislike most?" Then he answered his own question. "I suppose it's Lunakul, the head of the Communist insurgents."

"You're wrong," she said. "Lunakul is not your stereotypical Communist. He's a mild, scholarly man, who does not believe in violence. He will use it, of course, if it's the only way to help our people achieve equality, as he uses what he can from Cambodia and Vietnam to achieve this end. But at the core he is decent, and I am convinced I can deal with him peacefully without turning our nation into a Communist state."

The drinks had been removed, and she did not want a second. Both waited for the bouillabaisse to be served.

They tasted the soup and Noy made delicious sounds of approval.

Underwood was pleased, and spooned his own soup. He was midway through when he spoke again. "You haven't answered my question."

"Whom I dislike most on Lampang? Actually, I dislike no one. However, there is someone I distrust. That is another matter. It is not personal. It is politics and one who I think is bad for Lampang."

"Who is that?"

"General Samak Nakorn," she said, "the head of our army. He is the one your Pentagon respects the most."

"They do? Why?"

"Because he's a Red-baiter. The only good Communist is a dead one, he says. Solve our problems by wiping out every living Communist. Make Lampang safe for an ally like the United States."

Underwood considered this. "But you're the president, Noy. Ultimately your defense department must go to you."

"They don't have to." She paused. "Does yours go to you on everything, Matt?"

"I think so, but I can't be sure."

They sat back and were quiet as a waiter removed the plates before them and served their next course.

When the waiter had discreetly disappeared, Noy was the first to resume their conversation. "Of whom can you be sure in your government, Matt?"

"Well, that's not an easy order."

"Let me give you an easier one," said Noy. "You wanted to know about those close to me, and I told you. Now I want to know who's close to you."

"That's obvious," said Underwood. He chewed on some salmon and tried the salad. "I have a wife, as you know, and a grown daughter."

"Tell me about your wife."

"There's not much to tell. She was judged the most beautiful young woman in the country, Miss America—"

"I'm familiar with all that," said Noy. "Tell me more."

"What's there to tell?" Underwood said lightly.

Noy bent her head to her food. "I heard she's ambitious."

"I'm not sure what you mean. Where can she go from being first lady?"

"She can go for being first lady again."

Underwood was briefly silent. "Yes, that's true. Alice would like me to run for reelection."

"Do you want to?"

"Not especially. I've done what I can. Advocated and pushed programs against poverty, unemployment, crime. There are so many other things that need doing, putting over a national health service, instigating a voucher program for education, curbing defense contractors, making our foreign policy less imperialistic. I know I won't achieve them in one term, not even in two. There's too much opposition." Then he added, "I've had enough of television and I suspect I've had enough of the White House. I don't like waking up every day to decisions. Often there's something to say for both sides of everything. I don't like trying to satisfy everyone, with the Congress, my staff, and the press on my neck all the time. Don't you find it difficult?"

"Impossible," said Noy. "When this term is ended, I'd like to retire from public life. Between us, I don't intend to run for election."

"Despite General Nakorn?"

Noy nodded. "Despite him or anyone or anything. I mean, I can't promote my policies forever. Someone else is going to take over sooner or later and do things I don't agree with."

Underwood was of the same mind. "That's the way I see it. I've given it my best shot. After this I'd like to stay young by reading books I never had time to read and playing some golf, spending more time outdoors, trekking, skiing, and then devoting myself to something I call the People's Nonnuclear Peace Plan."

"What's that, Matt?"

Eagerly he explained it to her.

"That's marvelous, Matt, if you can make it happen."

"I can try. So there's all that to keep me busy. And then I'd like to get to know my daughter better."

"You made no mention of your wife."

"I know my wife well enough. Once out of the White House she'll be dissatisfied. She'll want something to do that keeps her in the limelight. She'll probably go back to television. But she'd prefer to do that after an extra four years in the White House. I can't see myself doing that, even for her. I can't bear the thought of conferring with one more foreign leader while I'm president. After, it would be another thing, but not as president."

Noy smiled. "Yet here we are. You've given me two full days."

He did not look up. "You're different."

She stared at him. "How?" Then she teased him: "Or maybe you don't see me as a leader."

He met her eyes. "Oh, you're a leader all right. No doubt about that. The way you went after me on that loan and bargained on the air base. I gave our differences my full attention because it was the price of spending more time with you. I like time with you because I can talk to you in a way I couldn't possibly talk to Alice. She's too concerned with herself, her body. You're interested in other things, everything. Moreover, you're warm, a forthright person who is also warm."

"Maybe that's pretense," she said.

He shook his head. "You can't pretend about what you really are. I trust my instincts about you."

Noy pushed her plate aside. She changed the subject. "What are your instincts about those around you, your staff members?"

"Of course, they're all people I selected on advice of others, and appointed."

"But whom do you trust most and whom do you trust least?"

Underwood picked away at his salad. "I'm not sure. I depend on my chief of staff, Paul Blake. He's well organized and efficient, and a nice enough fellow. As to trusting him entirely —not quite. He's got a lech for my wife."

"A lech?"

"American slang. Lech, for lecherous. I watch him when he watches Alice. He can't take his eyes off her buttocks and legs. He's reasonably fond of his wife, but he's mad about Alice. One glance from her and he's putty in her pocket. So how can I trust him completely?"

"And the others?"

"Generally trustworthy, although I haven't given them much thought. Secretary of State Morrison is honest. We don't always agree, but he's competent and honest. Secretary of Defense Cannon, I don't know. He may be a Nakorn man, very anticommunist, but for the good of the United States. I can't fault him for that. CIA Director Alan Ramage—who in the devil ever knows what the CIA is up to? I'm supposed to be told, to know everything, and maybe I do, but I wouldn't bet on it. Anyway, that makes him good for his job."

They ordered fruit tarts for their dessert, ate them slowly, and then talked some more.

Momentarily, Underwood glanced at his watch. The tea

with the Senate wives was over, thank God. Presumably Alice and Blake had taken care of that. Alice would be annoyed by his absence, but would still enjoy the tea. She was good at that sort of thing.

Then he remembered the rest of his schedule. There was to be a long-postponed national press conference at four thirty, then, after a short rest, a dinner with the governors and their wives.

He'd better hurry to make the press conference, reluctant as he was to bring the adventure with Noy to an end.

It was nearly a quarter to four in the afternoon when Underwood returned Noy to Blair House.

Despite his haste now, the farewell to her was more important than anything else. He instructed his chauffeur to remain behind the wheel, even though the Secret Service detail, the agent in the front seat, and those in the other two cars were already on the sidewalk. Underwood insisted on opening the rear door of the limousine and assisting Noy out.

Holding her by the hand, Underwood walked her to the wrought-iron gate that led into the entrance to Blair House. Two Secret Service men opened it, and Underwood and Noy went through it, and hand in hand they ascended the steep white steps until they reached the portico between the columns that flanked the front door. Two more Secret Service agents had announced their arrival, and a Filipino houseboy had the door open.

Noy stopped and squeezed Underwood's hand lightly, and instinctively he bent down to kiss her good-bye on the cheek. Instead, she turned her head toward him and met his lips with her own.

"Thank you for everything, Matt," she said breathlessly. "You've been more than wonderful."

"You, too." He gulped. "I hope we can see each other again soon."

"I hope so," she said, turning away.

"We will, Noy," he promised.

He stood and watched her going toward the door to Blair House, and for the first time he was conscious that she had buttocks as fully rounded as Alice's and probably softer.

At the door she pirouetted to wave to him, and he observed her smooth, lustrous face one more time before waving back.

Not just an intelligent face, he thought.

It's a sensual face, he thought guiltily, and yet he was pleased.

Somewhat dazed, he reentered the rear of the limousine and ordered the driver to hurry to the White House.

He had twenty minutes in the Oval Office with Blake to prepare for his press conference and steel himself for the combat.

Sitting down to the question and answer cards that Blake had efficiently readied for him, he barely skimmed them before asking a question of his own.

"How was the Senate ladies' tea with Alice?"

"She was a bit upset you couldn't make it, but she understood the priority of an emergency meeting with the National Space Agency. Besides, I reminded her, you'd be personally greeting all those governors and their guests at the dinner tonight."

"Thanks, Paul. Now, what have we here?"

He started examining the cards.

"Not too demanding," said Blake. "I think what you want to be sure to get in are announcements of the new space shuttle, your speech at the United Nations, and your successful meeting on Lampang and acquiring a vital air base there."

"How long should the press conference last?"

"The lady from United Press promised to say 'Thank you, Mr. President' after one hour."

Watching the time, Underwood absorbed himself in the questions and answers on his prompter cards. Underwood had a good mind for retaining this sort of thing. He had done it for years on television, long before the White House, and he would carry it off again, even if there was something unexpected.

He slid his hand over the cards, making them into a pile like a poker deck, and then he slipped them into a jacket pocket as if to give himself reassurance. "All right, I'm ready, Paul. Let's go."

The rows and rows of reporters in the East Room stood up in one hostile wave, as if to encompass him.

Underwood signaled them to be seated.

He had arranged in advance to make no policy announcements. He would handle his announcements through planted questions. He had insisted on this because it would use up more of his hour, and because he wanted an air of informality and spontaneity.

Also, for a president who was perceived not to be on the ball by some columnists, his answers would prove that he knew what he was going on.

A dozen hands went up, and Underwood pointed to the White House correspondent from *The Miami Herald.*

"Mr. President, we understand the new, foolproof space shuttle will be ready for takeoff from Cape Kennedy shortly.

Do you want to tell us about its improved safety features, and the date set for the first shot?"

Deftly, and with all the technical facts he had managed to memorize, Underwood outlined the latest safety features in the new space shuttle. He spoke of the goals of the space shot, and he announced that it would take place four months from the following day.

Underwood selected a woman from CBS for the next question.

"Mr. President, there's been word out that you intend to address the United Nations in the near future," she stated. "Is this true, and if it is, can you speak of its purpose?"

"What you heard is true," said Underwood. "I intend to address the United Nations in the near future, probably in six weeks. The exact date of the speech is under preliminary discussion. It will depend on when the general secretary of the Soviet Union speaks to the UN.

"My speech will follow his by one hour, and what I say will depend upon his response to our charges of Soviet arms buildup in Third World countries. Any buildup in that area of the world could be characterized as a breach of our Summit Disarmament Agreement."

Underwood expected the next question to concern his agreement with Lampang.

That question did not come next, or immediately. The questions that followed involved the state of the economy, amendments to the revenue bill before Congress, the increase in unemployment, and a new program for civil defense.

Then, at last, came the question about Lampang. It was posed by the White House correspondent from *The New York Times*.

"Mr. President, yesterday you had lunch with President Noy

Sang of Lampang. We understand you discussed a defense alliance with Lampang. Are you prepared to announce the result of the agreement?"

Underwood was well prepared.

"Yes, I had a fruitful meeting with President Noy Sang. I am prepared to announce the results of that meeting."

Promise of results meant news, and Underwood saw most of the 400 correspondents in the room flourishing pencils and note pads.

He gave them all time to get set, and then he undertook his prepared announcement.

"As you all know," said Underwood, "the island of Lampang in the South China Sea is vital to American strategic interests. Until now, Lampang has maintained a withdrawn policy in regard to other nations. But President Noy Sang, who became chief executive of the nation upon her husband's assassination, has deemed it useful to Lampang to undertake a close alliance and friendship with the United States. Since the country is in dire economic straits, and under constant pressure from the mainland to yield to communism, we decided that as an ally we could strengthen Lampang's independence by agreeing to a loan. I informed Madame Sang that I would do my best to see that the United States loans Lampang two hundred fifty million dollars, and—"

There was a hum of reaction in the room at the enormity of the sum.

"—and, as a show of gratitude on their part, and a desire to cement our alliance, Lampang has agreed to turn over ninety thousand acres to the United States for us to build our second largest air base in the Pacific."

"Uh, Mr. President, if I may expand my question . . ."

"Please."

"What will be the length of the main airstrip?"

Briefly Underwood was stumped, but then a figure he had heard came to mind.

"I believe eight thousand feet."

"Isn't that a little cramped for our F-4s, F-5s, and T-33s?"

Once again Underwood was not sure.

"I'm not certain. All the figures are not in yet. In due time, in fact very soon, I'll consult the Air Force on that. If the airstrip is inadequate, I'm sure Secretary of State Morrison and I can renegotiate with President Noy Sang to our satisfaction."

There were many more hands up, and one of them came from Hy Hasken, of TNTN, in the front row. Underwood knew that it was a steadfast rule never to ignore an inquiry from a major network. He had already taken and answered questions from CBS, NBC, and ABC, and he did not dare to avoid TNTN.

He was tempted to avoid Hasken, because invariably Hasken was unkind to him—or at least difficult—and he did not want to deal with the man now. But he saw that there was no choice.

"Mr. Hasken," he said, pointing to the TNTN newscaster.

Hasken was on his feet. "Mr. President, today you cancelled a meeting with the Senate ladies because of an emergency meeting with the National Space Agency. I was curious about the emergency and I telephoned a contact at the agency. The contact was puzzled by my call. He said that the Space Agency was not meeting with you today. I decided you were occupied with something else."

Listening, Underwood's heart sank.

Trouble.

"Eager to know what it was, I kept my eye on Director Frank Lucas and the Secret Service the entire morning. I saw you leaving the White House in the late morning. I used my car to follow your limousine from Blair House, where you personally received President Noy Sang of Lampang and took her on a sightseeing tour of Washington. After that, you drove with her to a little-known restaurant in Georgetown, the 1776 Club, and disappeared inside with her for almost three hours. I know this to be a fact because I stationed myself across the street and timed you. My question is this: Why did you secretly take her on this sightseeing tour and the prolonged lunch? What were you up to and why did you have to see her at such length a second day, especially without letting anyone know about it?"

Hasken waited for Underwood's answer.

For short seconds, Underwood stood paralyzed. The dirty bastard had found him out and followed him. The bastard had him by the short hairs.

He was tempted to lie his way out of this, too. But he remembered what a previous president had told him sternly. Never, never personally lie to the press. You can have your press secretary or someone else lie for you, but never, never do it yourself. You won't win. The press will find you out and destroy you.

Underwood decided not to lie. Hasken had the goods on him, and he would have to handle it as best he could.

"Very enterprising of you, Mr. Hasken," Underwood replied with a forced smile. "I do not deny that I tried to throw everyone off my trail because I needed a private meeting with President Noy Sang to further explore facts on our alliance and our projected air base."

"But a leisurely sightseeing trip beforehand, Mr. President," Hasken persisted.

"Quite a natural thing to do," Underwood answered slowly,

groping for what he must say. "Although President Noy Sang had been in America long ago, she did not know much about our capital. Since she is eager to continue to model Lampang after our democratic principles, I felt it was vital to our relationship to give her an insight into how democracy really works in the United States." He paused. "On our little tour, I was able to do so. She was most impressed." He paused again. "As to what you characterize as our prolonged lunch—"

"About three hours, Mr. President."

"I could easily have used another hour," said Underwood smoothly, "but I was aware that this press conference had been planned and announced. Actually, I had prevailed upon President Noy Sang to stay an extra day to work with me in ironing out some key details of our agreement. To justify our loan to Lampang to Congress, I had to know how Madame Sang intended to spend the money and if it was in America's best interests. Further, I had to know more about the priorities for our new air base, and what guarantees I could get from Madame Sang."

From the corner of his eye, Underwood could make out Blake indicating the correspondent for United Press.

Underwood swung his head away from Hasken and nodded to the woman from United Press.

She was already on her feet. "Thank you, Mr. President," she called out.

He found Alice in the First Lady's Dressing Room on the second floor.

She was seated before the television set, watching the lead story on the evening news. She was watching Hy Hasken of TNTN recount his lengthy questioning of the president, and the president's less than satisfactory reply.

As Underwood walked in and Alice saw him, she came to her feet, turned off the television set, and planted herself in front of him.

"I'm surprised that you had the nerve to come up here," she said angrily.

He remained silent.

Then Alice exploded. "You lying son of a bitch! To think you'd throw me over, mess up my day, to sneakily take some South Sea chippy on a tour of the town! Who do you think you are anyway—not the president of the United States, I'll tell you that! . . . And who is this hula dancer, or whatever she is, to take precedence over your wife? When you're ready to tell me, tell me, and don't speak to me again until you're ready to stop lying and have come to your senses!"

FIVE

T HEY were all settling down in the small golden auditorium of Chamadin Palace in Visaka, the capital city of Lampang.

Approximately twenty reporters and newscasters were present to attend President Noy Sang's first press conference since her return from the United States.

Prominently, in the front row, were reporters from the Visaka *Journal,* the Lampang *News,* and *Red Banner,* the local Communist newspaper long shut down but reinstated by President Prem Sang before his assassination. *Red Banner* also appeared in Cambodia, Vietnam, and China.

Scattered in the rows behind them were reporters from Thailand, the Philippines, Taiwan, and Japan.

News of the results obtained by Noy in the United States had reached Lampang immediately; still the press was eager to hear her own account of her visit to Washington.

Marsop had come to the rostrum, and the press conference was about to begin.

Surveying the gathering, Marsop started to speak.

"Ladies and gentlemen of the press and related media," he began, "as you are aware, President Noy Sang returned from Washington, D.C., yesterday. Rather than attempt to catch up fully on her sleep and overcome the usual jet lag, she is eager to report to you the results of her visit with the president of the United States. Following her opening remarks, the president will take questions from the floor."

Marsop started off to his right, veering slightly to allow Noy Sang to come onstage and go past him. As Marsop stood aside, Noy Sang took a position behind the podium.

She appeared small, but her erect stance gave her impressive stature, and when she began to speak her voice was strong and without hesitation.

"It has been reported by all of you that I met with President Underwood twice, and at length, in the American White House and that we had a private lunch in a suburb of Washington known as Georgetown. As in all such meetings between two independent countries, it is expected that each side wants something from the other and in turn is prepared to give up something."

Noy Sang paused and looked out over the assembly.

"It was vital to the interests of Lampang that I obtain a sizable loan from the United States. I was forewarned this would not be an easy matter because the national debt in America is astronomical. The United States was prepared to be cooperative in lending Lampang money, but its idea of what they could make available and my idea of what we required were at considerable variance. President Underwood was prepared to approve a loan to us of one hundred fifty million dollars. I told him bluntly that his offer was generous, but not generous enough to help us solve our economic problems. We debated what he was prepared to give and what I desired to get at great length."

Noy Sang paused again and studied her audience.

"At last I was able to convince President Underwood that a substantial loan from the United States would do much to build an independent Lampang that could remain a faithful ally to America. The loan we settled upon was, in the end, almost twice the sum President Underwood was prepared to concede. The United States is lending us two hundred fifty million dollars, and the formal agreement will be signed in the next month or two."

There was a spattering of applause in the auditorium, and Noy Sang was surprised by it and stood blinking her pleasure.

"Now," she resumed, "let us get to what we in Lampang must give the United States in return. Very little, actually. The United States has long wanted an air base on Lampang, and it was inevitable that we would be cooperative in giving them one. The only factor at issue was the size of the air base the United States wished. To put it simply, they wished a formidable and large base for their fighter jets and cargo planes, and we wanted to lease them a reasonably smaller one that would not subtract too greatly from our land and be an invasion of our independence."

Noy Sang cast her gaze around the room.

"We won this point, too. We reached a compromise satisfactory to Lampang and to the United States. They will build an air base that will not take up more than ninety thousand acres. Within this reservation there will be a strictly American facility of ten thousand acres enclosed by a security fence. This city within a city, containing twenty-five hundred buildings, will be manned by thirty-five thousand people, of whom twenty thousand will be citizens of Lampang. This base will add one hundred million dollars to the Lampang economy annually, through goods, services, supplies, wages, and fifteen million dollars rental from the United States Air Force. For Lampang the lease of this base will cost us very little in sovereignty, and gain us very much, including a defense arm added to our military that could serve us well in a time of crisis."

Noy Sang scanned the audience once more.

"I sincerely believe we've achieved more than we could have imagined in this alliance with a democracy we all respect and admire."

She paused again.

"Now, if you have any questions, I will do my best to answer them."

The tall, thin reporter from *Red Banner* was immediately on his feet, arm upraised.

"Madame President . . ."

"Yes, please."

"You spoke of meeting twice with President Matt Underwood to debate and bargain over this trade. Did you find him outright anticommunist?"

"Not at all," she answered at once.

"Well, however he presented himself to you, the fact is well known that he has surrounded himself with warmongers who are eager to carve up territory for their imperialist cause. If he showed you one face, to deceive you, there must be another face he would not show you. Will you tell us what you perceive of that other face, which until now has looked with less than kindness on the poor and struggling of other nations? Tell us, in all honesty, what you can of that other face."

Standing there at the podium, she thought of how she could answer this reporter dedicated to communism in Lampang.

She was careful. She knew that every word she spoke would be read or seen by Matt Underwood or shown to him by Blake, Morrison, and his other aides.

Tread softly, she told herself. But then she told herself what was more important.

Be honest, she told herself. Speak your true feelings.

"In a short time, I came to know President Matt Underwood quite well," she began. "I can say this from the bottom of my heart. He is a good man. He is a true democrat in the broadest sense of the word, in the sense that democrat and democracy encompass all the best aspects of both capitalism and communism. Of course the United States is committed to a policy of offsetting advances made by the Soviet Union. Despite this, President Underwood is neither personally anticommunist nor a Red-baiter. He loves people. He loves freedom for them and security for them. He is exactly what I said at the outset. He is a good man, and a kind one. Except for my late husband, I have never met a better man."

The reporter from *Red Banner* did not hide his skepticism. "You can be sure of that after two meetings with him?"

"I'm positive of that."

The heavyset man from Visaka *Journal* was on his feet, hand upraised. "Madame President . . ."

"Yes, please," said Noy Sang.

"You ask us to trust your judgment. Does General Samak Nakorn trust it as well?"

"I think he may. I can't say for certain yet. I have not met with General Nakorn since my return. I will know more after this evening, when I will attend a dinner at the general's residence to welcome me home."

The man from Visaka *Journal* stared at Noy Sang. "Maybe I can give you some information that will help you this evening," he said.

"What's that?"

"I met with General Nakorn at breakfast this morning before this press conference. I questioned him intensively about the result of your meetings with President Underwood. General Nakorn seemed less confident than yourself in what you had achieved."

This was tricky, Noy Sang knew, and perhaps a trap, but she had opened the door to it and now she had to allow Nakorn's opinion to be heard.

"I'll be glad to hear what General Nakorn told you," Noy Sang said, weakly, since she was not glad to hear publicly what Nakorn had said. "Please continue."

"General Nakorn believed it was unwise to give the Americans less than they wanted for an air base," began the man from Visaka *Journal*. "He felt it would be wiser to give the United States the larger air base they wanted, not only for our future self-protection but to cement a relationship with an ally we may need to depend upon. As to the loan, General Nakorn was satisfied with that, feeling the money would be of great value in modernizing our army and strengthening it with conventional weapons when the time comes to wipe out the Communist opposition."

Noy Sang flushed at the last. "I have no intent to wipe out the Communists," said Noy Sang sharply. "I am prepared to spend part of the loan to modernize our air force as a defense against any external enemies, but I intend to spend most of the money on education for the young and help for the health and independence of the old."

"I think General Nakorn will be surprised."

"He shouldn't be," said Noy Sang. "He knows very well I've arranged for Minister Marsop to meet with the Communists, specifically Opas Lunakul, in an attempt to bring unity and peace to our country."

The man from Visaka *Journal* shook his head. "General Nakorn does not think that can happen. He believes that prolonged negotiation with the Communists can work against us and only antagonize our American allies."

Noy Sang stood firm. "I believe negotiations can be successful and that President Underwood will be satisfied with the result."

"Will you tell General Nakorn that?"

"Tonight," said Noy Sang. "I will tell him exactly that tonight." She glanced about the room. "Any further questions?"

Noy Sang did not like General Nakorn's dining room in Lampang's National Defense Building. Except for a full-length portrait of Nakorn wearing a uniform heavy with medals, and a smaller portrait of President Noy Sang, the decorations on the walls made it look like the museum of an armory. Along two walls were hung ancient swords, criss-crossed and gleaming, and on the facing wall were rifles belonging to the previous century.

An adjutant to the general had shown the guests to their seats at the long dining-room table. At the head of it sat Noy Sang as president of the nation. Directly opposite her sat General Nakorn as chief of the army and host for the evening. To one side of Noy Sang was placed her sister, Thida, and next to her Marsop, and after them several of her cabinet ministers.

Beside Nakorn were Colonel Peere Chavalit and a number of his military aides in full uniform.

Fingering his goblet, Nakorn addressed himself to Noy Sang. "Welcome back to Lampang, Madame President, after what I am told was a successful trip to the United States. Marsop kept me personally informed of the steps you took with President Underwood."

"Steps I gather you are not entirely in agreement with," replied Noy Sang.

Nakorn feigned surprise. "Why do you say that?"

"Because I have learned how you feel about my diplomatic activities," said Noy Sang. "I had a press conference this afternoon. The gentleman from Visaka *Journal* was forthright in stating he had breakfasted with you, and you made your views on my diplomatic efforts clear. You did not like them."

Nakorn frowned. "Surely there must be some misunderstanding."

"Let's find out," said Noy Sang, smiling. "For one thing, I'm told that you felt I should have been even more generous with the space I allocated to the United States for an air base."

Nakorn's frown deepened. "I'm not sure I voiced that dissent. But I'm prepared to voice it now, unless you prefer that we wait until after dinner."

"I prefer to discuss it now."

"Very well," said Nakorn. "The United States needs the large air base as a crucial matter of self-defense, and we need the United States as a powerful partner in our own self-defense. Why deny them what they require?"

"I have not denied them what they require," said Noy Sang. "The president of the United States is quite pleased with our arrangement. He grasped the point I was trying to make with him. That it was absolutely essential that Lampang not only appear—but remain—an independent state. That too many concessions to any foreign power, even a staunch ally, would weaken our position at home, here among our own people. If the opposition to our democratic ideals, in this case the Communists, could show that we were giving up too much precious land to foreigners, rather than to our own people, it would weaken us in our own country, where we must maintain control. You can see that, can't you?"

"Actually, the air base is not my main concern," said General Nakorn. "Give or take, a few thousand acres will not affect our future. Our future lies in the loan you obtained from the United States."

"So I've heard," said Noy Sang, wryly.

"Let me congratulate you on the size of the loan you managed to get from President Underwood. It was beyond my expectations."

"Thank you, General."

"It is something I dreamt about and hoped for," Nakorn continued. "With this money we can modernize our army and acquire new conventional weaponry to give us the best fighting force in this part of the world. Certainly, once the money is spent properly we will have the strength to attack and wipe out the Communist rebels in one concerted offensive."

"You want the loan to obliterate the Communists," said Noy Sang quietly.

"Absolutely. There can be no better purpose."

"You know I disagree with you, General."

"Disagree with me?"

"On how the loan is spent. I've discussed this with Minister Marsop at length. We are not allocating the money to murder Communists. We will be spending it on the health, education, and welfare of all our people on Lampang."

"But the Communist threat—"

"There will be no threat. Marsop is meeting with Lunakul to come to a peaceful agreement that will absorb the Reds into the mainstream of our society."

Nakorn half lifted himself from his seat. "Impossible. They cannot be trusted for one moment. Marsop is too soft for them. . . . Forgive me, Minister Marsop, but you are not a military man and you do not have my experience in these matters. Lunakul and his gang understand only strength, their own and ours. If our president still insists on your meeting with them, Marsop—"

"I do," Noy Sang interrupted.

"—then I should accompany Marsop. The Communists know they can't fool around with me."

Noy Sang shook her head vigorously. "That would never do, General. Lunakul knows your record and your desires. Your presence would only antagonize him." She paused. "Marsop is the only one with a possibility to reconcile both sides."

Nakorn shrugged. "Whatever you wish . . . I see that they are ready to serve our dinner. That calls for a toast. Colonel Chavalit, will you see that the champagne is poured."

The colonel rang a bell that summoned a wine steward. The steward was followed by a waiter carrying two chilled bottles of champagne in a glistening silver ice-bucket.

As the first course was being served, the waiter slowly made his way around the table, pouring the champagne.

When the first of the meal was on the table, and the champagne in its flutes, General Nakorn rose, glass in hand.

"Let me offer a toast to President Noy Sang and her remarkable success in America."

Noy Sang concentrated on General Nakorn as she brought

up her flute to return the toast. All other glasses were uplifted as everyone joined the toast and drank.

A moment later, Noy Sang heard a gasp and turned in the direction from which it had come.

She realized that the gasp had come from Thida, that her sister was pale and coughing, and swaying dizzily.

"Thida, what's wrong?" Noy Sang called out.

Thida had a wracking fit of coughing. "I—I'm choking. I feel sick. I'd better lie down."

General Nakorn was instantly on his feet. "What is it?" he wanted to know. He half circled the table to reach Thida.

"I—I don't know," gasped Thida. "I'm going to faint."

Nakorn grabbed her to support her, and shouted across the table, "Let's get her to the bedroom to lie down. Summon the residence physician!"

As Nakorn, with Noy Sang's help, brought Thida to her feet and half carried her out of the dining room, Colonel Chavalit was on the telephone with the military doctor. "Come at once!" he cried out. "The general's bedroom! An emergency!"

No sooner had he hung up than General Nakorn dashed in.

"Get an ambulance!" he shouted. "We must get her to the hospital immediately!"

Two hours and twenty minutes later Thida died.

There had been poison in her champagne.

While Noy Sang burst into tears, breaking down completely, Marsop tried to comfort her, and General Nakorn rushed off to begin his investigation into the death.

Noy Sang was dry-eyed and exhausted when, an hour later, General Nakorn returned. He was grim.

"I've got to the bottom of it," he announced. "I myself questioned everyone on the kitchen staff. At last I wrung the truth out of two of them. It was the wine steward who was responsible. He's a member of the Communist Party. I hate to have you learn it this way, but all the Communists will murder even the innocent to get their way."

Noy Sang blinked at the general. "But why Thida? What did she have to do with Communists?"

"I don't know. I only know you must have no further hopes of negotiations with them."

"We'll see," said Noy Sang. "I now want to question this Communist murderer."

General Nakorn raised his hands helplessly. "I'm afraid it's too late, Madame President. I ordered him taken right out and executed. He is better dead."

General Nakorn sent them back to the palace from the hospital in a military limousine.

Marsop closed the glass partition separating the chauffeur from himself and Noy Sang, who were both seated in the rear.

He wanted to speak to Noy in privacy.

"What are you thinking, Noy?" he began.

"It's terrible, just terrible. It's unbelievable."

Marsop sat quietly holding Noy's hand. At last he released her hand, and turned to half face her.

"Noy—"

"Yes?"

"Noy, it was an accident."

Her face expressed puzzlement. "What was an accident?"

"Thida's death."

"I—I don't understand you."

"Let me explain," said Marsop. "During the toast, did you see Thida and me join the toast?"

"I'm not sure. I don't think so. Since General Nakorn was offering the toast, I guess I was looking at him."

"Probably," said Marsop. "But had you been looking at Thida and me, you would know it was an accident."

"What do you mean?"

"Remember the old-fashioned way our parents used to toast?"

"I'm not—not sure," Noy said falteringly.

"During a toast they linked arms, or rather crossed them, and they drank not from their own glasses but from each other's."

"Are you saying—?"

"I'm saying Thida and I laughed and toasted in that old-fashioned way. She held her drink before me, and I held my drink before her. Then we drank each other's champagne. Her champagne was fine, and I was not affected. But when she swallowed my champagne, she swallowed poison, and she died."

It was beginning to dawn on Noy. "You mean—?"

"I mean the poison was meant for me. I was the one targeted for death, not Thida. By accident she drank my champagne and it killed her. I was supposed to be dead, not Thida. My drink was meant to eliminate me."

"My God! . . ."

"Yes."

"But, Marsop, who would want to kill you?"

"I can't say for certain. It could be someone who would not want me alive to bargain with the Communists. What do you think?"

"I shudder to think of it."

"Think of it," said Marsop softly, and he settled back in the rear seat to await their arrival at the palace.

* * *

The news of Thida's death reached Washington, D.C., not many hours later.

It came to Anuthra, Lampang's ambassador to the United States, and he hastened to visit the Department of State and call upon Secretary of State Ezra Morrison.

"I knew you would want to know as soon as possible of this grave development," said Anuthra, "since Thida was successor to Noy Sang for the presidency of Lampang. I felt it was an official matter, and that President Matthew Underwood would want to send a representative to the funeral."

"He certainly would," said Secretary of State Morrison. "Again, let me convey my deepest sorrow and condolences. I will instantly inform the president of this sad affair."

Matt and Alice Underwood were in the solarium on the third floor of the White House, having a drink before dinner and watching the television news when the call came from Ezra Morrison.

Underwood took the call and signaled Alice to lower the volume on the set.

"Some bad news from Lampang," Morrison began.

"What bad news? Does it have to do with Noy Sang?"

"No, not really. Her sister, Thida, was poisoned at a dinner party and died almost immediately. Noy Sang was right there."

Underwood exhaled his relief that Noy was safe, but then was incredulous. "Her sister? Tell me, Ezra."

Morrison reported what he had been told by the ambassador.

When he was done, Underwood said, "That doesn't sound like an accident. Are there any other details?"

"Not from the ambassador."

"How's Noy Sang taking it?"

"I have no idea, Matt. Not too well, I'd guess."

"I'd better find out for myself. Can you or Blake phone Lampang for me and get Noy Sang on the line? It's one in the morning there. If she's asleep, wake her. I want to speak to her as soon as possible."

"I can do it," promised Morrison. "Stand by. I should get back to you in two or three minutes."

Underwood hung up and sat staring at the telephone.

"What was that all about?" Alice called over.

"Noy Sang, the president of Lampang—"

"Oh, yes, the one you had so much business with."

Underwood ignored the jab. "She just lost her sister. Apparently intentional poisoning."

"They're really barbarians down there."

"I don't know the circumstances. I only know that the sister, Thida, was next in the line of succession. Obviously we'll have to treat it with seriousness."

"Another cozy trip for the vice-president?"

"Maybe. I don't know if Trafford is the right person."

The telephone rang, and Underwood grabbed for it.

There was a rushing sound that usually accompanied overseas phone calls. Then a male voice came on.

"President Underwood?"

"Yes, this is Underwood."

"I am Marsop here."

"Hello. I've heard the terrible news. How is Noy?"

"You'll hear for yourself. Here she is. Please hold on."

Even at the distance, Underwood could hear her voice, soft and clear. "Matt, is that you?"

"Noy, I've heard the awful news. Is it possible?"

"I know, it's incredible, but it happened in my presence."

113

"Tell me in your own words what happened."

"Well, it was at dinner in the dining room of General Nakorn's National Defense Building. He proposed a toast—"

Then she went on, brokenly, and told Underwood how Thida had died.

When she was through, Underwood said grimly, "I'm told the poisoning was not an accident."

"It was and it was not. The poisoning was intentional. But it was an accident that Thida was the victim. It was really meant for Marsop." She repeated the circumstances of how Thida and Marsop had drunk each other's wine.

"Who would commit such a murder?"

"Someone who did not want Marsop to sit down with the Communists and bargain for peace."

"We know how General Nakorn feels."

"He blames someone else, a wine steward on his staff who was secretly a Communist and did not want peace talks."

"Has the steward been interrogated?"

"Only by the general. He was satisfied the killer had been found. He had him executed immediately."

"Does that make sense to you?"

"I don't know." Noy broke down briefly. "I only know that Thida is gone." She paused. "I didn't mean to get you involved in this family affair, Matt."

Underwood protested. "It's more than a family affair. Thida was your successor. That in itself would be important to us." He hesitated. "Usually on these sad occasions we find someone to represent us. My vice-president or Blake or Morrison. But I feel this is more important."

"It is a small matter to the United States."

He leaned closer to the telephone. "It is a big matter to me, and a personal one." On impulse, he continued. "I intend to fly to Lampang and attend the funeral myself."

"Oh, I don't want you to go through that. . . ."

"It's something I wish, Noy. Something I want to do. I want to give you support. You'll need it. Take all you can get."

"You are so kind. I don't want you to take such a long journey over someone you did not know."

"I want to do it for someone I do know."

"If you insist."

"Yes, I insist. I want to be among those beside you."

"I will appreciate that. It would give me much comfort."

"Then, count on it."

As Underwood hung up, Alice tried to speak to him. But he already had the receiver back in hand.

"Get me Paul Blake," he commanded the operator. "Wherever he is, find him for me."

Alice tried to speak once more, but Underwood held up a hand, ordering her to be silent.

Seconds later, Blake was on the phone.

"Yes, Matt?"

"You know the news about Lampang."

"I do."

"Very well. I'm going there at nine in the morning to attend Thida's funeral. Have Air Force One ready."

"Do you feel this is a wise thing, Matt? I'm sure it is something Vice-President Trafford could routinely handle. You have a long schedule of appointments tomorrow. It would mean cancelling every one. And the press, what about the press?"

"They're welcome to come along in the press plane. But try to keep the package simple."

"I can't, Matt. First thing, I'll still have to dispatch a planeload of engineers from the White House Communications Agency to install the two special phone systems. And there must be the military backup plane to replace Air Force One if anything goes wrong, and to carry your national security adviser, your military aide, your physician, more Secret Service agents. You'll be very visible." He hesitated. "Won't you reconsider?"

"No, Paul. Do what you have to do, but I'm going. I intend to be in Lampang for the funeral. Get moving."

This time Alice was on her feet, and standing over him.

"Don't shut me up again," she said shrilly. "I heard it all, and I say you're crazy to fly halfway around the world to attend the funeral of someone you don't even know."

"I promised."

"Break that stupid promise. This is madness, chasing after some clever native woman who's trying to entice you. It'll look terrible."

Underwood glared at his wife. "Not if you come along. You're invited, Alice."

"That's ridiculous, going all the way to that hot dump over an affair of no consequence to you, to us, to the country. If you want to be a fool, then be one—alone!"

In the Press Room of the White House, Hy Hasken listened to the announcement by Press Secretary Bartlett. Before he had heard the finish of it, Hasken perceived what it was all about. He came to his feet, eased his body among the other White House correspondents seated behind him, and dashed for the nearest telephone in the rear.

Using his phone card, Hasken punched out the long-distance number from Washington to Sam Whitlaw's private line in the main editorial office of The National Television Network in New York City.

Whitlaw answered immediately. "Yeah?"

"Hy Hasken, boss. I'm in the Press Room. There's just been an announcement that the president is flying to Lampang tomorrow morning. It's the funeral."

"I saw the wire coverage," said Whitlaw. "Noy Sang's sister poisoned. You're saying Underwood's flying all the way there to attend the funeral? Why?"

"I don't know yet. Maybe to tighten our relationship with Lampang. Maybe the follow-up on his relationship with Noy Sang after their two meetings here. I truly don't know."

"It makes no sense."

"Whatever it makes," said Hasken, "Underwood is making a big deal of it. He's sending a press plane ahead."

"And you want to be on that plane, Hy?"

"I think I should be."

"It's not even a lead story," growled Whitlaw. "Why waste the time?"

"You said you wanted me to stay on Underwood's tail. You told me to ignore the White House and give my attention to the president."

"Well, yes."

"This is an odd trip. I feel I should be there. I want to know more about it."

Whitlaw was silent a moment. "It *is* odd for the Pres to throw everything aside to fly that far for a funeral for Noy's sister."

"Maybe he isn't going for Noy's sister," said Hasken. "Maybe he's going for Noy."

"What does that mean?"

"I'm not sure. I'll let you know when I find out. You can get someone to cover the White House for me. Let me stay with the president. What do you say, Sam?"

"I say wild-goose chase." He paused. "But I like this goose. Go get him."

SIX

AIR Force One came to Muang Airport on Lampang from Washington, D.C., in a haze of early-afternoon heat and humidity. It landed smoothly on the long airstrip, braked, and gradually slowed down. A jeep with three airport personnel curved in front of it, led it ahead, and then to a turnoff toward a spacious slot reserved for the plane.

On the field nearby, the eleven White House reporters and their crews, who had arrived an hour earlier on the American press plane chartered by the press pool, were roped off and kept in place by blue-clad Lampang security guards. Next to them the local and other foreign press had been similarly contained. Hy Hasken and his cameraman and sound technician had secured a front-row vantage point.

Hasken consulted with Gil Andrews, the cameraman. "Did you get a full shot of Air Force One landing?"

"Enough to cover three of your shows."

"Okay, now they're opening up. Next, President Underwood will appear. Pick him up medium close emerging and coming down the ladder. I can see a delegation at the foot of the ladder. When and if Noy Sang steps forward to meet him —and there is a good possibility that she will—I want a tight close-up of her greeting Underwood. That will be important. You got it, Gil?"

"Got it, Hy."

Just then the door of Air Force One opened, and attendants rolled the aluminum ladder up to it.

Hasken's attention was riveted on the open doorway. Several Secret Service men came out, surveyed the scene, and waited. Moments later President Underwood emerged and fell in behind the Secret Service. Underwood appeared rested and trim —no doubt he had slept on the crossing—and he was wearing a freshly pressed dark-gray cotton suit.

He came down the ladder, followed by more Secret Service agents.

"I've got him," said the cameraman.

"Just get him on the ground when Noy Sang, Minister Marsop, and the delegation meet him."

Hasken scanned the area below, and the official delegation, for any sign of Noy Sang.

He could not find her.

Someone, a youngish man, left the delegation and approached Underwood, hand outstretched.

Hasken thought that he recognized the greeter, but he wasn't sure.

"Where's Noy Sang?" the cameraman, Andrews, wanted to know.

"No idea," said Hasken. "She's certainly not here. Probably at the palace getting ready for the funeral."

Then Hasken heard a familiar high-pitched voice. It was that of Press Secretary Bartlett. "The president is off to the Oriental Hotel. All of you will follow in two buses. There can be no complaints from any of you. You're staying in the same hotel. You've got accommodations nearly as good as the president's. Once we get there, you'll be directed to your rooms. You'll have an hour to change and freshen up, and then back to the buses and off to the funeral. Try to preserve some decorum. After all, this is a funeral."

Troubled, Hasken turned for the bus. The fact that Noy Sang had not shown made his story a nonstory. Without more, he would suffer Whitlaw's wrath.

Heading for the bus, he prayed for something more.

In the lobby of the splendid old Oriental Hotel, crowded with the rest of the press corps among the rattan furniture, Hasken watched as the president and his Secret Service contingent were guided past the stairway toward a bank of elevators.

A Lampang official was guiding them, and once they were safely behind the elevator doors, the official spun away.

It was then that Hasken recognized him.

The official, the very one who had welcomed the president as he had left Air Force One, was Marsop, Noy Sang's minister of foreign affairs.

The members of the American press corps did not recognize him, and tended to ignore him, but Hasken moved quickly to intercept him.

"Minister Marsop," Hasken called out.

Marsop squinted uncertainly and halted.

Hasken closed in on him. "You may not remember me, sir,

but I'm Hy Hasken. I'm with American television. I covered you when you came to Washington last week with President Noy Sang."

A glimmer of recognition flitted across Marsop's face. "Oh, yes, I think I remember."

"I won't bother you now, but there are two questions I must ask. The first is relatively simple."

"Yes?"

"Can you give me some idea of what the president's suite looks like?"

"It is large, over three thousand square feet. It's called the Leader's Suite, with a living room, dining room, entertainment room, two bedrooms, and three baths. All windows are made of bulletproof glass. It's actually the penthouse. There's a corridor leading from the elevator to a stairwell for the Secret Service guards. At the top there's a metal detector protecting the penthouse. The two floors below it are for the president's staff and press."

"Thank you, Mr. Minister. One more question if I may."

"Please."

"President Underwood on short notice flew to Lampang to attend Thida's funeral. It was unexpected. I didn't realize that Underwood knew Thida that well."

"He didn't know her personally at all," Marsop said.

"You mean President Underwood never met her?"

"Never, at least not to my knowledge."

Hasken's surprise could not be disguised. "But then, why did he fly all the way here to attend her funeral?"

"Because he wanted to give support to President Noy Sang. He wanted to comfort her."

"No politics involved?"

"None whatsoever. This is personal. Your president is a compassionate man."

Hasken stared after Marsop as he disappeared into the crowd in the direction of his limousine.

Hasken, nibbling his lower lip, considered what he had heard.

President Underwood was here to see Noy Sang, and for no other reason.

He had not even known the deceased.

But apparently he knew the living very well.

Hasken smiled to himself.

Whitlaw would not be disappointed. There might be a story, a very good one, at Hasken's fingertips after all.

He determined to stay close to it, as close as was humanly possible.

For Hy Hasken it was another funeral, as funerals go. A little glossier, perhaps, considering the representatives of various nations—in this case mostly Asian ones.

From his vantage point at the crest of a small hill in the cemetery, five kilometers outside Visaka, Hasken had a good view of the graveside down the slope below.

There were, next to the coffin, Noy Sang, her son, Den, Marsop, and some elders, probably the parents of Thida and Noy. Among the foreign mourners, President Matt Underwood stood closest to the grieving family.

From the distance to which he and other journalists had been restricted by army guards, Hasken couldn't hear a word. He could see a Christian clergyman's lips moving.

Dust thou art, to dust returneth, he was sure.

The closed casket was edging toward a deep hole. Hasken

could see Noy kneel and place a bouquet of flowers on the top of the casket as it began to be lowered from view.

While respectful, Hasken was basically uninterested.

He had not known Thida. She had been a name to him, no more. But then, she had been no one to Underwood, except Noy's sister. Hasken tried to be attentive.

Suddenly, as the coffin disappeared, Noy seemed to break down. Her shoulders hunched and she crumpled. Marsop reached out to steady her as the ceremony continued to its conclusion.

Hasken was sure that Noy was weeping now, and then he saw President Underwood relax his solemn rigidity and step backward, out of line.

He could see Underwood ease past little Den and Marsop and squeeze in beside Noy. He could see Underwood take her limp hand, whisper to her, and draw her head against his shoulder.

Then he was startled to see Underwood bend his head and kiss Noy on the cheek, not once but several times.

What a shot, Hasken thought with excitement.

Je-sus, what a juicy morsel for the six o'clock news back home.

Hasken whirled around for Gil Andrews, and then realized that he was not there. No cameraman had been admitted to the funeral.

No cameraman, no picture. Hasken swore at his bad luck. This wouldn't play in a flat news-report. It was a visual. Yet, there had been no way to capture it.

Now the funeral was over, and they were all turning from the grave.

Underwood, his arm around Noy's waist, was leading her away.

"Where are they going?" he wondered aloud.

An American voice behind Hasken answered authoritatively, "They're going to a wake. It's a Lampang custom. Back to the palace. Noy Sang will be hostess at a buffet for invited guests."

Hasken half turned. "What about the press?"

"Special guests only, special people," the voice answered. "You know we're not people."

Hasken swore under his breath again.

Noy and Underwood would be alone, and he could not get near them.

Excuses wouldn't work, not with Sam Whitlaw.

But something had to go on. He tried to speculate what Noy and Underwood would talk about.

He hadn't the faintest idea, but he knew that sooner or later he would find out.

The wake took place late that afternoon in the Peacock Room, a smaller reception room of Chamadin Palace.

Matt Underwood had gone back to the Oriental Hotel to shower and change into a dark suit. Entering the crowded reception room, he could see Noy Sang at the far end of the room, and she had changed, too, into an ankle-length purple sari. She had also, he could see, recovered her composure and was introducing strangers among the guests, mostly Asians from sympathetic neighboring countries.

Underwood went directly toward her, got in line, and clasped her hand as she whispered, "Thanks, Matt. Let me introduce you to a few of our neighbors."

She did so, and Underwood greeted them graciously and moved on. Separated from the others momentarily, Underwood cast about for another familiar face. Besides his collection of unobtrusive Secret Service men dispersed around the dining room, he recognized only two other Americans. One was Bartlett, his press secretary, and the other was hunched, impassive Percy Siebert, whose pale-blue eyes were fixed on him now. Siebert was Director Ramage's CIA station head at the United States Embassy in Visaka, and had been waiting for him in his suite after his arrival on Air Force One. Before the funeral they had talked a little, enough for the president to regard him as a friend.

To one side, Siebert had taken note of the president's arrival and was making his way through the crowd toward him.

The CIA station head took Underwood by the arm and whispered, "There is someone you must meet, Mr. President, a good friend of mine and of the United States." He pointed the president to a stocky, older man in a crisp uniform bedecked with medals. Siebert made the introduction. "President Matthew Underwood, this is General Samak Nakorn, head of the Lampang Army. General, the president of the United States."

Underwood reached out and shook hands firmly.

After exchanging a few pleasantries, Underwood sought Noy Sang again, saw her not far away, and once more started in her direction.

When he reached her, he was pleased to see she was briefly alone and to see her face light up.

Taking her by the arms, he leaned over and—unembarrassed by the presence of others—kissed her on the forehead.

"How are you, Noy?"

"It's over. I'll survive," she said. Then added, "How kind of you, how very kind of you, to come all this way to express your condolences."

"It was something I felt I wanted to do, Noy."

"It did very much for me. I won't forget it." She pointed to a long table filled with food. "You must be hungry. Try the dish in that white bowl, *Gai Tom Ka.* It's chicken stewed in coconut milk. Truly delicious." She pushed him toward the table, lowering her voice to say, "We'll find time to talk later."

Underwood parted from her, dutifully went to the buffet table, took a large plate, a fork, and a napkin, and began to fill his plate with chicken, fried rice, curries, fish, and a tiny omelet mixed with herbs.

About to leave the table, he noticed that General Nakorn was coming toward him from the opposite direction, filling his own plate. Before Underwood could consider speaking to him, Percy Siebert, the CIA station head, stepped between them.

"Mr. President," Siebert whispered hastily.

"Yes?"

"I wonder if you could spare a moment to talk to General Nakorn. He's very anxious to have a further word with you."

"Any idea what that's all about?"

Siebert nodded. "I'd say it would be useful for you to hear him out. He's a great friend of the United States. What he has to say may be in our interest."

"Well, then, of course."

Underwood remained in place as Siebert reached out to bring General Nakorn to him.

"You wish to speak to me?" said Underwood.

"I hoped to," said Nakorn. "You are one of the reasons I came to this reception."

"Please go ahead."

"It concerns our Communist problem here on Lampang," said Nakorn. "Surely you are aware of it from your own State Department and your meetings with President Noy Sang."

"I think I have an idea of the situation," said Underwood coolly.

"Perhaps you do not know how grave it is," continued

Nakorn earnestly. "We have neighbors across the sea who are literally breathing down our throats. I refer to Vietnam and Cambodia. They are pouring guerrillas into our two adjacent islands, and they have armed them with the very latest weaponry. If they are allowed to continue this without intervention, they will soon become too powerful for my army to handle. Ultimately they will come to Lampang, overrun it, and oust President Noy. They will crush our democracy here and take full control. Lampang will become Communist, a satellite of the Soviet Union in the South Pacific. This must be stopped by force while there is still time, while we have military superiority."

Underwood had been listening closely, and it gave him a twinge of concern that if there was truth in this, Noy's regime and very life could be endangered.

"I've been told the Communists were willing to address themselves to some compromise," Underwood said.

General Nakorn shook his head vigorously. "Not possible," he said. "That is the belief of some of our liberals who have been deceived. In fact, it is President Noy's own notion that such a meeting of the minds can be formed. She has no real knowledge of the Communists' strength and intent. She is being lulled by sweet words, but if she admits the Communists to our system, she will be gobbled up."

"You're positive of that."

"Absolutely. Ask Mr. Siebert for his opinion."

Underwood faced Siebert, who had been listening in silence. "What do you think, Percy?"

Before he could reply, Nakorn interrupted. "I'll leave you two alone. Thank you for hearing me out."

Underwood watched Nakorn melt into the party, and then he faced Siebert again.

"Well?" he asked Siebert.

The CIA station head bobbed his head. "I'd say he's generally right. I'm not trusting the general's private sources alone. I'm trusting my own, based on what I know from our paid informants. No matter how any meeting between Marsop and Lunakul would turn out on the surface, it would lead to a takeover by the Communists in the end." Siebert paused. "You understand, Mr. President, I have no personal stake in this matter. My job is to report objectively to Langley, and to you. It is my opinion that it is best for the United States if Madame Sang does not allow the Communists to become a legitimate party in Lampang. Madame Sang does not realize that her action would give the Soviet Union a position they've never had in this part of the world."

Shaken, Underwood said, "You're certainly being unequivocal about this, Percy."

"I mean to be. We have no choice but to go along with General Nakorn. There can be no thought of a compromise. Lampang's army must drive the Communists farther into the jungle and strip them of their strength, and then eliminate them."

"Why are you telling me this now?"

"I think you must tell Madame Noy Sang exactly what I'm telling you."

"You're suggesting that I speak to her about matters of state without consulting our own Department of State? In fact, why aren't you taking this through regular channels?"

"Because if Madame Sang would listen to anyone, she would listen to you. You alone would have the greatest influence over her. You've just agreed to lend her millions to keep Lampang free and on our side."

Underwood sighed. "I'll see what can be done."

He dismissed Siebert and finished his meal, which had suddenly become tasteless.

After putting aside his plate, he scanned the room and caught sight of Noy Sang shaking hands and saying good-bye to some foreign dignitaries.

Finally, noting that she was alone, Underwood pushed past several groups and approached Noy.

She saw him coming and smiled. "I was hoping to see you again."

"I'm here. Do you have a little time for me? I must speak to you alone—well, as privately as possible in this room."

Noy wrinkled her brow, trying to understand his concern. "Marsop," she called over her shoulder, "President Underwood and I would like to have a few minutes together. Will you be a good fellow and see that we are not interrupted?"

"I will fend everyone off," Marsop promised.

"Very well," said Noy, drawing Underwood into a corner, almost hiding them behind a tall, leafy rubber plant. "Let's talk. Matt, I haven't seen you this serious before. Tell me what is on your mind."

"I just had a conversation with your General Nakorn."

"You know my opinion of him."

"I'm less concerned with what Nakorn has to say than with what Siebert, our CIA station head, had to tell me."

"What did he say, Matt?"

"Apparently you've arranged a series of talks between Marsop and the rebel head, Opas Lunakul. Your General Nakorn was strongly against it." He skipped a beat and then added, "And so was Percy Siebert."

Noy's delicate countenance had tightened. "Do you want to tell me what they told you?"

"I'll repeat every word." He hesitated. "It seems to make some sense."

Her voice was low. "Tell me, what makes some sense?"

As best he could, Underwood tried to relate everything he had heard from General Nakorn and everything that Percy Siebert had confirmed.

Noy listened emotionlessly.

When he came to the end of his recital, Underwood caught his breath and added, "You know I'm on your side, Noy. It was without hesitation that I approved of the loan you wanted for Lampang, indeed for a much greater sum. I intended that it be used for what you wanted, to make Lampang independent and its democracy strong. I saw that to be in my own nation's self-interest as well."

"But now you are less certain," said Noy stiffly. "Are you telling me there were strings attached to your offer?"

"Strings?" said Underwood, briefly bewildered.

"That your loan carries with it a demand that we break off with the Communists, suppress them, and prove we are an anticommunist country worthy of being a trusted ally of the United States?"

"Noy, you misunderstand. That loan is yours to do with what you think best for your people. But you should reconsider one thing: that you may be allowing yourself to be too lenient with the Communist insurgents who want to destroy you."

Noy was very quiet, eyes fixed on Underwood. When she spoke, it was with contained passion. "Matt, our Communists are not trained in Moscow. They are plain peasants, plain people, farmers, who want to eat three meals a day and to have a safe roof over their heads and their children's. My husband understood that when he ran for president. He felt these Communists who wanted land reform above all else could be integrated with all our peasants and learn to gain what they want more slowly and without bloodshed. I always stood with Prem in his belief. Today I stand by what he stood for. I don't want massacres. I want mediation. When the Communists hear my plans, see that these are exactly as their own without killing, I am certain they will put down their arms and come along with us."

In his own mind, Underwood retreated. She made as much sense as Nakorn and Siebert. Perhaps more.

He had one question. "Weren't your husband and your sister Thida murdered by Communists?"

She answered unhesitatingly. "I have not a shred of evidence of that. Naturally we were suspicious, and an exhaustive investigation was made, but we found no link to the Communists. Lunakul denies it without reservation. Maybe he lies. Maybe he is being truthful. Matt, we must give truth a chance before bullets."

Underwood said, "Well, you may be right. It might be worth giving truth a chance."

Noy touched Underwood's arm. "Matt, I must leave to say good-bye to our other guests. But before I do, I want to ask a favor of you. When I was in Washington you invited me to stay an extra day so that you could show me your capital city and get to know me better. I did so."

"And I appreciated it."

"Now I want you to return the favor in kind," she said. "I want you to stay an extra day in Lampang so that I can show you my people and how they live. Also, I want you to get to know me even better, so that you are convinced of my sincerity. Consider spending that extra day here with me. Don't try to answer now, but go back to the hotel and sleep on it. You can give me your decision at breakfast here tomorrow. I hope that you will stay the extra day."

"For political reasons?" asked Underwood.

"For personal reasons," answered Noy. "I want to enjoy a day with you alone in my environment. Please, please consider it, and whatever you decide, I'll understand."

Matt Underwood had returned to his suite at the Oriental Hotel. Refusing to see Siebert or the press, he had dined alone, then tried to sleep, but tossed restlessly in his hotel bed. In his mind he reviewed Noy's invitation, wanting desperately to accept it but still uncertain.

At last, jet lag caught up with him and he slept soundly.

Awakened by a servant, he showered, shaved, and dressed, and was driven to the Chamadin Palace before eight A.M.

In the dining room, sipping orange juice, were Noy, her son, Den, Marsop, and of his own party only Press Secretary Bartlett.

"Good morning, Mr. President," said Noy somewhat formally. "Did you have a good night?"

"Eight or nine hours and dreamless," said Underwood. He addressed Bartlett. "What time are we scheduled to leave for Washington?"

"Air Force One will take off at eleven. The press plane goes at noon," said Bartlett.

Underwood concentrated his attention on Noy Sang, who was beside him. "I've been thinking of your offer, Noy," he said. "Does it still hold?"

"Of course, Matt."

"Then, we're on."

"I've put everything else aside for this," she said. "I'm just delighted. First we'll tour Visaka and the suburbs. Our destination will be my summer place, Villa Thap. It has a lovely beach where we can cool off. We can change and swim there."

"I wasn't prepared for that."

Noy smiled. "I was. We have swim trunks in all sizes. You can have your choice. I'll arrange for us to take a basket with a light lunch. How does that sound?"

"Perfect," said Underwood.

Bartlett looked puzzled. "Is there something I should know?"

"Yes," said Underwood. "You can tell the press I'm on schedule. Have their plane leave at noon. But I'm not going to leave an hour earlier. I'm going to pretend to and spend an extra day here, and probably leave at midnight."

"That's going to upset a lot of plans, Mr. President. Is this stay-over imperative?"

"Officially, I'm taking the extra day to delve into the Communist situation on Lampang with the help of Madame Noy. That's what you can tell the press when you land back in Washington and I don't follow until the next day."

Bartlett remained troubled. "Is there an unofficial reason?" he inquired.

Underwood smiled at Noy and then at Bartlett. "There is one, but not for publication. Just for your information."

"Very well," said Bartlett.

"I want the extra day for some rest, and to get to know our Southeast Asian ally a bit better."

"Thank you, Matt," Noy said in an undertone.

"Soon as breakfast is over," Underwood added to Bartlett, "you can leave and arrange everything. Inform the Secret Service that I'm staying the extra day and I expect them to remain, too. I don't want to get into trouble with those leeches. But for yourself, you herd the correspondents on the press plane and take off with them. Tell them I've gone already. That'll get rid of any suspicions."

"What do I tell the first lady?"

"The official version," said Underwood with a small wince.

Leaving Chamadin Palace, Press Secretary Jack Bartlett stopped to speak to the first Secret Service agent in the hallway.

"Smitty," he said, "there's been a change of plans. The president won't be leaving at noon but closer to midnight. Also, you'd better plan to be mobile this afternoon. I know the president is taking a tour of the city and suburbs after eleven thirty. I think his destination—he's accompanying President Noy Sang—is Villa Thap, her summer place. Where's your boss?"

"The last I heard, Lucas went down to the palace gate to talk to the captain who's the Lampang security chief."

"I'd better find him," said Bartlett. "I want to tell him the president's new schedule."

Bartlett left the palace and walked toward the gate, where he could see Lucas in conversation with a Lampang security officer.

Bartlett interrupted. "Frank, I need you for a minute."

The gate was open, and Bartlett waved the Secret Service head outside.

There were two pillars, and Bartlett brought Lucas to the nearest one, out of earshot of the Lampang officer.

"Frank, the president is sending the press on after he leaves. Only he isn't leaving here on schedule. They are not to know that he's decided to stay the rest of the day and see some of the city with President Noy Sang. Then he's going to drive into the countryside with Noy. She has a summer home called Villa

Thap. She wants the president to have a swim before lunch, and to cool off before he leaves for Washington."

"Thanks for telling me," said Lucas. "I'll run out to this Villa Thap and look it over before the president gets there. He'll be coming around two o'clock?"

"Just about," said Bartlett. "I'll be leaving the president entirely in your hands."

"You needn't worry."

"Keep the local press at a distance. Our own press will be on their way home. But the locals can be troublesome. I want the president to have some privacy."

"He'll have all the privacy he wants," guaranteed Lucas.

After that, Bartlett took a Lampang staff car back to the Oriental Hotel, and Lucas went through the gate and strode into the palace to notify his agents.

No sooner were both out of sight than Hy Hasken stepped from behind the pillar.

Lighting a cigarette, he considered.

Villa Thap was now his own destination.

But where in the hell was it?

He decided to go to the gate and inquire of the Lampang security officer.

So President Underwood wanted this extra day in Lampang with Noy Sang alone.

Hasken grunted. Not quite. Not if he had anything to say about it.

Villa Thap was thirteen kilometers outside Visaka.

With his rented car, Hasken collected his photographer, Gil Andrews, and the sound man at the Oriental Hotel, and then he followed the directions he had been given.

Once he had found it and parked, he and his crew surveyed

the layout. Like most of the summer homes, Villa Thap was an airy, elegant mansion built into a hillside. Presumably because it was shady and cool there.

Hasken stood on the edge of the hilltop and peered down at Noy's summer home. He could see a fair portion of it, even the steps leading to the front door. There was a path that led to a crest from which stairs dropped out of sight to a private beach below.

"You want to get the president and his lady," said Andrews. "You won't see anything from here, especially if they go down to the beach for a swim."

"You're right," agreed Hasken. "It's a blind spot. You can bet the Secret Service will keep us up here with the local press. We won't be able to see a damn thing." He turned around and then added, "Maybe."

Behind them, across the road, was a row of modern beach apartments five and six stories high.

"The one right behind us," said Hasken. "It's six floors. The top floor must have a perfect view of the beach. Let's find out."

The three of them crossed the road to the six-story apartment building and rang the bell, summoning the landlord.

In less than a minute the landlord appeared. He was a gruff, elderly man no more than five feet tall, olive-skinned, with a flowing gray moustache.

"Yes?" he asked.

"We'd like to rent an apartment," Hasken said.

"All taken," the landlord rasped.

"Just for a few hours," said Hasken. "The top floor facing down toward the beach."

"It's taken, too. Rented by a banker from Visaka. He always comes here from the city by six o'clock."

"We'd be out by five o'clock," said Hasken. "Not disturb

137

anything. Just want to take some photographs from the sixth-story window."

"I don't know," said the landlord. "It's his apartment. . . ."

"But you rent it to him," said Hasken. He opened his jacket and took out his brown wallet. "You could sublet it for three or four hours." Hasken removed some bills. "I could pay in American dollars."

The landlord eyed the bills greedily. "American dollars?"

"One hundred of them," said Hasken, beginning to count out the bills. "For just a few hours."

"I don't know," said the landlord. But by then he knew. "You would disturb nothing?"

"Not even a speck of dust," promised Hasken, handing over the greenbacks.

Minutes later they were inside the sixth-floor apartment.

Gil Andrews went directly to the window and narrowed his eyes. "Perfect," he murmured.

"The beach," said Hasken.

"Every inch of it. Clear as can be. With my zoom lens I'll be able to count the grains of sand."

Hasken grinned. "Set up your equipment."

Matt Underwood and Noy Sang were seated comfortably in the rear of her Mercedes sedan, and her pockmarked chauffeur, Chalie, was driving them, circled by a motorcycle escort.

"Are we near the main street?" Underwood asked.

"You mean downtown, as in America?" Noy said. "Visaka has no downtown. For that matter, it doesn't have streets either. Just roads and numbers on buildings."

Underwood peered out of the car window once more. "I

think what confuses me is the mix of temples and churches. How did that happen?"

Noy laughed. "I can see our history is not so well taught as yours. Let me explain. Just two hundred years ago my ancestors, everyone's predecessors, lived in Thailand. There the king had decreed Buddhism as the prevailing religion. However, there was a large sect of Thais who had been converted to Christianity by missionaries. They decided to move out of Thailand and establish a new home with greater religious freedom on Lampang. That's how the churches came to be. When Lampang prospered, others on Thailand wanted to move to Lampang and they followed. They were still Buddhists, and so they built the temples. In general, Thai influence is very great over here. Many Christians were eventually impressed by the democracy in the United States, and democracy became yet another influence. Everyone speaks English here and the government is patterned after the very system Jefferson created and would have approved. Matt, look off to your left."

"Yes?"

"The National Museum. Founded in 1784, it is the largest museum in Southeast Asia. We can go inside if you wish, but I'm sure you've seen enough of museums everywhere."

"Thanks, I'll pass," said Underwood. "But it is a stunning building."

"There's something just as stunning not far from here. Unlike anything you have in Washington."

Soon the entourage arrived at the Dusit Thani Hotel, and Noy led Underwood, surrounded by security guards, to a moat-like arena.

"Our Snake Farm," said Noy.

Underwood looked down the steep walls. The center was

braided with a mass of snakes, every species from king cobras to Russian vipers.

"Every morning," said Noy, "our scientists go down into the pit and extract venom from the reptiles to prepare antitoxins against snakebites in more primitive areas outside the city." She studied him. "Your shirt is clinging to your body, and soon your coat will, too."

"Well, it is hot and muggy."

"Yes, and you've had enough of sightseeing. Come along to the car. In twenty minutes or so you can be at Villa Thap and on the beach. Does that appeal to you?"

"I can't wait."

"You can get into swim trunks."

"And you into a bikini."

Noy smiled. "Lampang is not quite ready for a bikini. Will a sarong satisfy you? It doesn't cover any more than a bikini."

"You'll wear a sarong?"

"The minute we get there."

He tried to picture her. "I certainly can't wait."

Noy had him by the forearm. "Then let's not waste another minute."

From a side window of the sixth-floor apartment that over-looked the street below and the Villa Thap beyond, Hy Hasken surveyed the scene.

The street immediately below was crowded by now with the local press, which was held back by the Lampang security guards. Behind them were the curious residents of the neigh-borhood.

President Underwood and Noy had arrived a half hour ear-lier and immediately been escorted down a steep stairway to the villa.

Hasken with his naked eye and the cameraman with his zoom lens were alone to witness what would come next. The sound man had no longer been needed—there would be no voices to be picked up from the beach at this distance—and Hasken had sent the man back to the Oriental Hotel to pack for all of them and to arrange the earliest commercial flight to the United States—by any route, as long as its final landing place was Washington, D.C.

"You've got a closer view than I have," said Hasken to Andrews. "Have our presidents come out of the villa yet?"

"Not yet."

"You couldn't have missed them?"

"With this lens? It's got everything in close-up. Besides, there's no one on the beach except two American Secret Service men."

"Not what I'm looking for," said Hasken. "Keep your eye on the steps leading down from the villa."

They both watched silently a minute, and suddenly the cameraman spoke.

"They've just come out of the villa," he announced. "She's wearing a red sarong and he's got on tight white trunks."

"Great! I see them all right, but without your lens they're not completely clear."

"They're descending to the beach. They're in the sand. Christ, that sarong—"

"What do you mean?"

"She could have concealed more with a bikini."

"Is your camera going?"

"It's going all right. My lens is practically pop-eyed."

"Hey, relax," said Hasken.

"Let me concentrate," said Andrews breathlessly. "They're going into the water."

"Stay with them," said Hasken excitedly.

After a few minutes the cameraman said, "They're playing around."

"Playing around?"

"Well, swimming, leaping up and down like porpoises, rolling in the water." He paused. "I think they're coming out now."

"Keep that camera tight on them."

"Never mind. Wow!"

"You sound like a wolf," said Hasken.

"I'd like to be one and get a piece of that. Noy, I'm talking about, in the sarong. It's clinging to her body like it's pasted on, and you can practically see her body like she's naked all over. Jeez, one boob is practically hanging out. I'm sure I can see the nipple, it's big and brown—"

"You can *see* it?"

"Je-sus, what I'd give to be in his boots."

"You're not. He's president of the United States."

"Well, she's more than that. Would you believe me—he's wiping her off with a towel. What an ass she's got, the biggest, softest, best I've ever seen."

"Contain yourself, buster. She's president of Lampang."

The cameraman shook his head incredulously. "The president of Lampang has got the biggest and roundest ass in the South Seas."

Impatiently Hasken stepped over and pushed the cameraman out of the way. "Let me have a peek through that lens."

What Hasken saw was Noy standing in profile facing Underwood. Andrews had been right. One breast was partially exposed, and the wet sarong had slipped up higher over a cheek of her buttocks. Hasken sucked in his breath. She was an object of art.

Noy was seated now on a bright yellow towel. Underwood had dropped down beside her. She was feeding him from a basket. Underwood was speaking to her.

"I'd give anything to know what he's saying," murmured Hasken. "They're conversing now." He stepped back. "Some summit conference. You better take it over. The camera may need a slight adjustment."

Andrews was at his lens and adjusting his eyepiece. "That sarong gets me," he said, mostly to himself. "Could she be wearing anything underneath?"

"She'd better," said Hasken, "or Underwood will be on top of her in a minute."

"He practically is now," said the cameraman. "He's leaning against her. He's got his left arm around her waist. I swear he's covering her breast."

"I doubt it," said Hasken. "Not with Secret Service men on the beach, too."

"It looks like it. Now, he's—"

"He's what?"

"Kissing her!"

"Passionate or chaste?"

"On her cheekbone. She just jumped up." He reset the camera once more. "She's starting back for the steps to the villa. Our Pres is on his feet not far behind her."

"They're leaving?"

"They've left."

Hasken stirred himself away from the window. "Then it's time for us to leave, too. Let's beat it back to the Oriental. Your boy should have a plane reservation for us by now. I want to get right on it and get back to Washington before Underwood returns. This is a hot one, and I want to air it as soon as possible."

Andrews began to repack, first his camera and lenses, and then his tripod.

When he was all set, he met Hasken at the door.

"Hy," the cameraman said, "do you think he's humping her?"

"Don't be crazy. Presidents don't do that."

"Oh, no? Harding? Cleveland? Kennedy?"

"Of course. But otherwise, absolutely not. Presidents don't boff presidents."

"You're sure of that, Hy?"

"Positive. Don't even think of it. We're going to give old Matt enough trouble without it. Now let's get home and get on the air."

When President Underwood returned to Washington and the White House, he sought his wife before going to his bedroom.

Alice was in the First Family Bedroom, seated on a sofa, legs crossed, staring at the blank television set.

"Well, here I am," said Underwood. "It was a helluva long trip."

He crossed the room to kiss her, but she averted her face.

"No, thanks. You've had enough of that."

"What are you talking about?"

"You mean you haven't seen television or a newspaper?"

"Why? Should I have? I just got off the plane. Alice, what's this all about?"

"About your extra day in Lampang, about your living it up."

"You know I needed the day with President Noy."

"Discussing the Red Peril?" She glared at him. "The Communists. Or her sarong?"

"What's got into you?"

"The same thing that got into all the newscasts and the press. Which leads to a better question. What got into you?" She took up the remote control. "Hy Hasken was on the air a few hours ago with a full report on your extra day in Lampang."

Underwood was bewildered. "He couldn't have been. He went back on the press plane a full day ahead of me."

"That's what you think. Would you like to have a look at what he saw in Lampang? Hasken stayed behind and got it all. And now I've got it all on videotape to show you what a stupid and lecherous fool you are. Sit down and watch the screen."

Confused, Underwood edged into a chair, eyes fixed on the television screen as Alice pressed a remote-control button.

Hy Hasken's face filled the screen. He was holding a microphone and standing in front of the White House.

"This is Hy Hasken back on the Washington beat. I returned from the island of Lampang two hours ago, where I remained with President Underwood during his unscheduled extra day on the island. While the president had intended to return to the White House earlier, and even sent the press back ahead of him, I learned that he was remaining in Lampang one more day for a secret meeting with President Noy Sang. After his meeting with her, which I was unable to attend, the president drove with Madame Noy to her summer villa outside the capital city of Visaka. Our cameraman was able to find a point from which we could cover him. Now, exclusively for you, a glimpse of President Underwood and President Noy Sang on the beach in front of her villa, enjoying a few minutes of relaxation."

There were shots of Underwood and Noy cavorting in the water.

There were shots of Underwood and Noy emerging from the water.

Underwood heard Alice's voice. "What's that she's wearing? She might as well be naked."

"Alice, it's a sarong. It's what all the women wear in Southeast Asia."

Alice fell silent.

The screen was filled with shots of Underwood toweling Noy dry.

More shots of them sitting on the beach.

A shot of Underwood with his arm around her.

"What's your hand doing on her breast?" Alice demanded.

"I had no idea it was there."

A shot of Underwood kissing Noy on the cheekbone.

"And you're discussing communism," Alice said bitterly.

Underwood swallowed. Hasken, that dirty bastard. Underwood swallowed again. "I'm trying to console her about losing her sister."

Alice pressed the remote and shut off the television set.

Calmly, Alice stood up. "She was still grieving, was she? Bullshit, Matt. The worst kind. She was trying to use you in any way she could. I won't let you get sucked in like that again. It looks bad, very bad, for both of us. After Hasken released his exclusive tape to all the television stations and press, it ran in prime time on the three major networks, made the front pages of every paper I've seen, and Blake tells me both news magazines are using Noy on their front covers. Matt, for God's sake, you're the president of the United States. Around you the whole world is falling apart, but you're uninterested and unavailable because you're too busy diddling around with the accidental head of some ridiculous two-bit island out in nowhere. If you ever spend another second alone with that woman, I'll leave you, Mr. President. Don't you forget that. I'll leave you. So you keep your britches buttoned up and behave yourself. Otherwise, you're in real trouble."

SEVEN

THE call, on the private line, was from the Department of State to the White House.

Secretary of State Ezra Morrison was speaking to President Matthew Underwood.

"Matt," he said urgently, "something has come up. I must see you immediately."

Underwood was irritated with the call. "I have a lot going on today, Ezra. But I suppose I can squeeze you in if it's really that urgent."

"It's urgent," Morrison assured him.

"Give me a clue to the problem."

"It's in two parts," said Morrison. "Part one is that you're set to address the United Nations on Friday after General Secretary Izakov does."

"What's urgent about that?" Underwood mentioned. "This speech has been on the agenda for months."

"Well, you're going to discuss the roles the United States and the Soviet Union have in Third World countries. To make our summit pact possible, it has to be guaranteed by both sides that we are not interfering with other countries. We're not promoting democracy by force or use of our weapons and the Communists are not doing the same."

"Of course. We've talked that out a dozen times."

"But we haven't allowed for subsequent events."

"What events?" asked the president.

"It's just come to my attention that the Soviet Union is actively interfering with another country. It is something you may want to include in your speech."

Underwood frowned. "I certainly might want to. Who is this other country the Soviet Union is messing around with?"

"Lampang," said Morrison.

This was a jolt for Underwood. "You're joking."

"I have it all straight from Visaka."

"What happened?"

"I'd prefer not to do this on the phone. I'd prefer to discuss it with you in person as soon as possible."

"Come right over."

"A half hour," said Morrison.

"I'll make room on my schedule," promised Underwood. He blinked with disbelief at the telephone. "Trouble in Lampang, is it?"

"Sit tight. I'll tell you all about it."

"Yes, Lampang," Morrison repeated, taking the chair across from the president's desk.

Underwood impatiently pushed aside the papers on his desk. "Get to the point."

Morrison had opened a folder and was reviewing several memorandums. "The Communists moved out of their stronghold on that second island, Lampang Thon, and invaded Lampang itself last night. I don't know the strength of the invasion yet. It may be a company, several companies, or even a battalion. I do know that they overran and conquered three villages before General Nakorn could be fully alerted and rush his troops down there."

"Is it still going on?" Underwood wanted to know.

"Yes, but I think it's a mop-up at this point. Even though the Communists were better equipped than ever before, and inflicted considerable casualties, the Lampang army was able to stand them off and even repel them."

"I'm surprised," admitted Underwood, "truly surprised. Madame Noy assured me a compromise meeting had been scheduled between Marsop and Lunakul."

"The meeting was a sham," said Morrison. "The Communists had no intention of compromising. They meant to take Nakorn off guard and resolve the situation by force."

"Incredible," Underwood said. "Who gave you this information?"

"General Nakorn. I tried to speak to our CIA headquarters, but Siebert and his aide were off in the hill country. Everything comes from Nakorn. He's eager to press ahead and subjugate the Communists once and for all. I told him not do to so until he had direct instructions from you."

"That was wise."

"You may want to work it into your speech at the United Nations. Certainly, after we have more complete information. I think you must confront the Soviets head-on with this one."

Underwood was lost in thought. "Let me think about it. Keep me up-to-date. Then I'll decide what to do."

Even during his conversation with Ezra Morrison the president had decided what to do.

Now he did it.

He brought in Paul Blake. He said, "There's some trouble down in Lampang."

"I've heard."

"I want to get a call through to Madame Noy Sang. Locate her for me and put her on."

It was ten minutes before he heard her voice.

"Noy, how are you?"

"Fine, Matt, perfectly fine now. You've heard of our trouble here?"

"I've heard from Secretary of State Morrison. He spoke to General Nakorn. Here's what I heard." He told her briefly, and then asked, "Does that sound right, Noy?"

"Yes and no," said Noy. "I'm not sure. It's still unclear. We're basing everything on General Nakorn's report. We were attacked by Communist aggressors. We fought them off. On the other hand, Marsop talked on the phone to the Communists, to Lunakul, and Lunakul denies it categorically. He insists it was the other way around. His version is that Nakorn and our troops crossed over to strike a Communist garrison, and that the Communists retaliated and fought them back to the mainland. I don't know yet who's being honest in this affair."

"Is it possible Nakorn is right?"

"Oh, yes. After the final skirmish, after the Communists retreated, we found many of their weapons. Their arsenal was almost totally Russian."

"Weapons from the Soviet Union?"

"I doubt if they came directly. I think they came through Vietnam and Cambodia."

"You know I'm going to address the United Nations at the end of the week along with the general secretary on our hands-off policy and their own."

"I know about that."

"Morrison wants me to mention this possible breach of faith. What do you think?"

"You'd be safe to mention it."

"My instinct tells me not to." He hesitated. "Noy, I think it would be wiser to have the report come from you."

Noy sounded uncertain. "From me? You want me to protest to the United Nations?"

"I could easily arrange it with the president of the UN General Assembly. You'd speak of the battle, the aggressor unclear, but one thing clear, the Lampang Communists have Soviet weapons. I could touch on it, too, afterward. Your speech would make mine more effective because I could chastise the Soviets for breaking a verbal agreement to back no more local Communists anywhere."

"I don't know, Matt."

"I know," insisted Underwood. "My staff will arrange your hotel in New York and schedule your speech to the General Assembly. It would be very helpful for both of us."

She hesitated. "Maybe I could do it."

"This must come out in the open. The sooner, the better. It'll force the Communists to be more restrained, and ease the path for your peace talks with them on Lampang."

"All right, I'll do it. Will I see you?"

Underwood chuckled. "What do you think? At the United

Nations, more formally. And informally, dinner together when the General Assembly is adjourned."

"I'll be there," said Noy.

Once the announcement of Noy Sang's appearance at the United Nations had been made, the Soviet ambassador to the United States, Berzins, lost no time in calling on Morrison at the Department of State.

"Is your president actually supporting this Noy Sang woman's address to the General Assembly?"

"That's my understanding."

Berzins was indignant. "Your president is seeking trouble. We have gone to so much difficulty to arrange for General Secretary Izakov and President Underwood to speak to the United Nations as a step toward a pact guaranteeing no further aggression from either side, and now your president decides to meddle with it by inviting Madame Noy to make accusations against us. No good can come of it."

"Well, the problem here, Mr. Ambassador, is that President Underwood believes, as does Madame Noy, based on an ongoing investigation, that the Soviet Union did take aggressive action through its Lampang Communists against the government of Lampang."

Ambassador Berzins's indignation did not abate. "Utter nonsense. We are not supporting local Communists anywhere to make aggressive moves against any government, least of all that of Lampang. There is no evidence that the skirmish on Lampang was instigated by Communists. It could very well have begun with General Nakorn and forces within the Lampang government."

Morrison shrugged helplessly. "That may be true. On the

other hand, Lampang has discovered evidence that the latest Soviet weapons were used against it."

"The weapons could have come from anywhere," Berzins snapped. "They could have been bought from Syria, from a hundred marketplaces that deal with Soviet weapons, just as they deal with American weapons."

"The president may want you to prove that."

"It requires no proof. Only logic and good faith." Ambassador Berzins stood up. "I have a message for you to take to your president. Our government wants him to rescind the effort to get Madame Noy to address the General Assembly. It is the only way to continue the progress being made by our two nations toward a peace plan."

Morrison came to his feet. "I'll report your request to the president. I can't promise anything. I am merely the secretary of state, not the president. It will be up to him to decide. But I will do my best."

"Thank you," said Ambassador Berzins coolly, and he left the room.

Once he was by himself, Morrison put through a call to Chief of Staff Paul Blake and requested that they both meet with President Underwood in an hour, if possible.

Blake called back shortly. It was possible, and Morrison was expected at the Oval Office in one hour.

Fifty minutes later Morrison was in Blake's office in the White House, quickly filling him in on the Soviet ambassador's protest and request.

Soon Morrison and Blake were seated opposite the president in the Oval Office.

"What's on your mind?" demanded Underwood.

"I'm concerned about a visit I had a short time ago from the Soviet ambassador."

Morrison then proceeded to lay out Berzins's protest and his demand.

The president listened in stony silence. "In short, what it comes to is that he wants me to cancel Madame Noy's appearance before the General Assembly?"

"He feels that as an ally of Lampang, you can do it. There are two points to be considered here, Mr. President."

"Go ahead."

"First," said Morrison, "Berzins feels the grounds for Madame Noy's appearance are shaky, at best. Evidence that the Lampang Communists instigated the attack is questionable and possibly unfounded. Evidence that the Communists used Soviet weapons is also questionable, since the weapons could have come from many sources other than the Soviet Union. The ambassador feels Madame Noy's appearance will certainly chill any peace negotiations between you and the Soviet general secretary. That's the first point."

"What's the second?"

Blake intervened, to give Morrison a hand. "The second point involves our own self-interest. We've stated our position before, and it's apparent we should state it again."

"Madame Noy," said Morrison, "wants to condemn the Lampang Communists to force them back to her own peace table."

"And that," added Blake, "is something we don't want."

"I think it's an admirable idea," said Underwood.

"Forgive me, but it's a terrible idea," said Morrison, "especially from the point of view of the United States. Madame Noy is imbued with impractical, idealistic notions, possibly obtained from her late husband. But these are notions that don't work in the world of reality."

Blake lent support once more. "They can't work, Matt, because the Communists will walk over Madame Noy in any meeting or series of meetings. They're tough and good at that. She isn't. Matt, we have a big investment in Lampang. We're just beginning the process of constructing a giant air base there. We can't take chances with the local Communists. They are capable of infiltrating under the guise of a democratic party and then trying to weaken the American position. Madame Noy's speech at the United Nations will serve the Communists in two ways. Obstruct our own peace talks with the Soviets. Obstruct our own strength in Lampang." Blake was silent a moment. "Matt, consider what Ezra has told you and what I have said. You must get on the phone to Lampang and speak to Madame Noy. You must inform her there's been a change of policy here. You must tell her in the strongest terms that she cannot speak at the UN. Will you do it?"

Underwood stared at Blake, then shifted his unwavering gaze to Morrison.

At last he spoke. "The answer is no. I will not tell Madame Noy she is unwelcome at the United Nations. I think she should speak there. I'm all for it, and let's not have any more on this subject. Good day, gentlemen."

The following day, late in the afternoon, Matt Underwood had been seated in the Oval Office with Blake, going over his United Nations speech, when his secretary buzzed him.

"Yes, Emily?"

"A call from your daughter at Wellesley. Can you take it or should I have Dianne phone back?"

Underwood was immediately enthusiastic. He hadn't spoken to Dianne in almost two weeks, and he was eager to hear her voice. Moreover, a call in the afternoon was surprising. She usually telephoned Alice or him in the evening in the family quarters upstairs.

"Of course I'll take it. Put her through."

Blake came to his feet. "I'll let you speak to her alone," he said. "I'll be next door if you want to go over the speech once more."

"Thanks, Paul."

After his chief of staff had left, Underwood took the call on the telephone rather than on the speaker. "Dianne, what a treat."

"Hi, Dad. How are you?"

"Dianne, where are you calling from?"

"Right here in the dorm," said Dianne.

Underwood could see her the moment that he heard her voice. She had long, flowing blond hair reaching to her shoulders, a sweet face with an upturned nose as tilted as Alice's own. There was no doubt that she took after Alice. Underwood never thought of himself as good-looking, although perhaps Dianne had inherited a certain warmth and openness that was in his own countenance.

"How are you, Dianne, honey? Is everything all right?"

"Couldn't be better, Father. I'm working hard, and I'm still spending some evenings out with Steve."

"Great."

"I wanted to tell you I got my senior thesis subject okayed. 'Great Female Leaders in the Twentieth Century.' How do you like it?"

"I like it very much. You mean Margaret Thatcher, Indira Gandhi, Golda Meir, and the like?"

"And how they affected their countries and the world in ways male leaders might not have."

"I'm feeling a little put down," said Underwood cheerfully.

"You've had enough attention. I think women should get their share."

"Couldn't agree with you more, Dianne."

"That's why I'm calling. I need a favor."

"Shoot."

"I know, of course, you and the Russian are addressing the United Nations at the end of the week. But I saw in this morning's *New York Times* that Madame Noy Sang of Lampang will be on hand to speak to the General Assembly."

"That's right."

"Is she a friendly sort of person?" asked Dianne.

"Very. You'd like her."

"Well, that's it," said Dianne. "I want to come down to New York and interview her. Can you lend a hand?"

Underwood hesitated momentarily. "Possibly. I don't know her plans except for the UN address. What do you have in mind?"

"It would be a real scoop for me, meeting her," said Dianne excitedly. "Not only because I admire her, but talking to her firsthand would give me a perfect windup for my senior thesis on modern women leaders."

Underwood agreed that was a good idea.

Dianne said quickly, "I mean, if she'd take the time to talk to me."

Underwood thought of Noy and knew there would be no problem. "She'd talk to you, all right," said Underwood. "But there is another obstacle. As I pointed out, I don't know what she's planned for after the UN when—" Underwood interrupted himself. "What am I saying, Dianne? Of course I know what she'll be doing after the UN. I invited her to dinner—she and several members of her staff are dining with me at The

Four Seasons—and she accepted. You can join us there. I'll seat you right next to her."

"You would? That would be memorable."

"Count it as done," said Underwood, pleased. "Say, Dianne, how'd you like to hear your old man speak at the UN? You can be there for Madame Sang's address, too."

"I'd love it!"

"I'll reserve a seat for you in the gallery. When the UN session is over we can meet in the Delegates' Lounge and then move on to the United Nations Plaza and talk a little before dinner."

"No, you'll be busy after the speeches," said Dianne. "I have a few friends to see in New York. I'll meet you at The Four Seasons. How's that?"

"Fine. Make it eight o'clock."

"How should I dress, Father?"

"How do I know about such things, Dianne? You're beautiful in whatever you wear."

"Never mind. I'll be there all duded up, and with a notebook. You sure you don't mind?"

"I'm sure," said Underwood. "And I'm sure that Madame Noy will be pleased. See you, then, on Friday."

Underwood summoned Blake and worked for another hour on his UN speech, and when he was satisfied, they called it a day and he headed for dinner with Alice.

He walked from the Oval Office across the L-shaped colonnaded terrace to the ground floor entrance, and rode the elevator upstairs.

He found Alice having her vodka martini in the Family Dining Room.

"I'll have one of those, too," said Underwood, speaking to the valet, and sitting across from his wife.

"I just had a call from Dianne," said Alice. "She wanted to know what to wear when she joins you and that Noy woman for dinner in New York after your speech."

"Of course you're invited to join us, too."

Alice ignored this. "I told you when you made a fool of yourself on Lampang that I won't have you seeing this Noy woman again."

"Alone, you said."

Alice shrugged. "That's true."

"You know I am not going to be alone with her. Madame Noy will have some of her staff. I'll have my daughter. Do consider coming along."

"Count me out. I'd like to see Dianne, but I can see her anytime. As for the Noy woman with her political blabbing, that would be intensely boring. So no thanks, I'll wait for you to tell me what happened."

"If you insist. But won't you reconsider, Alice?"

"Sounds dreary," she said. "No, thanks again." She finished her drink and came to her feet. "Let me dress for dinner. And see if you can be as amusing with your wife as I'm sure you'll be with that sarong lady."

She left the room, and Underwood's eyes followed her, sadly.

Dianne Underwood was already at The Four Seasons when her father arrived with his chief of staff, Paul Blake (Morrison was occupied at a reception given by his Soviet counterpart), Noy Sang, Marsop, Secret Service agents, and Noy's personal security guards.

Underwood kissed his daughter, and quickly brought her into the group to make the introductions.

"Your speech was very good," Dianne said to her father.

"You're kind of prejudiced," Underwood said to his daughter. "My speech wasn't half as good as Madame Noy's. . . . You really impressed everyone, Noy. It was your directness and sincerity. It gave a good deal of validity to my own words."

"You flatter me, Matt," said Noy. "But I admit the speech was a high. Me, up there alone at the speaker's rostrum in the General Assembly Hall, standing between the two Léger murals in that giant domed place. Addressing two thousand persons, who were hearing my speech in six languages. I admit it was thrilling."

As the maître d' led them down the steps to the lower level of the restaurant toward the central fountain, Dianne overheard Noy say to her father, "Your daughter, Matt, she is perfectly exquisite."

"Thank you, Noy. If she is as beautiful as you, I would be more than pleased."

When they arrived at the main table, Blake took over the seating. He helped Noy to her place, directed Dianne to one side of her and Underwood to the other, and then set chairs for Marsop and himself.

After they had been seated, the sommelier collected their drink orders and Blake conferred with the maître d' about their dinner.

Underwood heard Dianne's voice.

"You're truly wonderful to let me be here and question you," Dianne was saying to Noy.

"I'm flattered to be part of your thesis," replied Noy.

Dianne leaned toward Noy. "My father already congratulated you about your speech today, but let me do so again. I watched the faces of the people you were talking to. I could see they were impressed."

Noy laughed. "All except the Russians, I'm afraid."

"Your grasp of politics is remarkable," Dianne went on.

Noy at once became serious. "If I have any such grasp, I owe it to my late husband. And, of course, in the time since, to Marsop."

Underwood intervened, to speak to his daughter and Noy. "Don't be fooled by her modesty, Dianne. Of course she owes much to her husband and Marsop. But I have never met a woman with such a perfect political instinct—yes, instinct, as well as logic and good sense. She's a marvel. You may quote me, Dianne."

Her notebook on the table before her, Dianne had her pen in hand and was already scribbling information.

She glanced up. "I'm not going after facts," she explained to Noy. "I have pages and pages on you from other sources. What I'm interested in is what I can get only from you." Her eyes met Noy's. "I mean your feelings about everything."

Noy seemed startled. "My feelings?"

"For example, take Wellesley," said Dianne. "Not many years ago you were there. I'm there now. Of all schools, what made you choose that one?"

Noy smiled. "Since I was growing up in a democracy, I wanted to study in the leading democracy in the world. I told my parents, and there were no objections. My mother sent for dozens of university catalogues. Wellesley seemed the most attractive."

Once more, Underwood intervened. "Not quite, Dianne, not quite. Noy is being deliberately evasive and even frivolous. Again, her modesty. I happen to know, from discussing it with her, that she chose Wellesley because she had made an almost scientific study of the courses there and saw they were superior to others."

"Oh, Matt—" Noy interjected.

"Don't deny it, I know it's true," said Underwood. "It was your sensibility, your brain power, Noy. I've known many high-powered women, but never one with the kind of head you carry around."

"Were you happy at school, Madame Noy?" Dianne wondered.

"Yes, why do you ask?"

"Well, I'm comfortable there," said Dianne. "But I'm an American. It's where I belong, home. But you came from a long distance, a foreigner from Southeast Asia. How did you feel about that?"

Noy was thoughtful, remembering. "At first, I felt alien, isolated," she said. "Scared. Soon I made friends. I found we were all people, with much in common. I began to feel comfortable, American, much as you do today."

"Dinner is being served now, Dianne," Underwood interrupted. "Save your questions for later."

"Let her go on, Matt," Noy said. "Dianne, you can continue asking questions while we eat. I really can do two things at one time."

"Just one more question for right now," Dianne said.

"Please go ahead."

"Another to do with your feelings, Madame Noy, much, much later, just recently."

"Whatever you wish, if I can answer."

"You're the only one who can answer," Dianne said. "It's about after your husband was killed and you became the president of Lampang."

"Is that question necessary, Dianne?" Underwood asked.

"No, it's quite all right, Matt," Noy said to Underwood. "Let your daughter go on." She half turned toward Dianne. "The question you want to present?"

Dianne was having a little difficulty, but at last she formulated what she wanted to say. "Your husband, once you lost him and were alone, did you ever have any desire for another man?"

Noy stared at the girl seriously. "Another man," she repeated. "Do you mean for sexual needs or for companionship?"

Dianne seemed taken aback by her frankness. "I—I guess I meant companionship. Maybe I meant both. Let's speak of companionship."

Noy nodded. "In the year and a quarter since the assassination, I have never met another man I wanted to spend time with, except one. At the risk of embarrassing him, I am speaking of your father."

Dianne blinked, and glanced at her father and back to Noy. "Really, you enjoyed being with my father?"

"Don't take Madame Noy seriously," Underwood said quickly. "It's really the other way around. Dianne, you can take me seriously when I say that of all the women I've met since I've been in the White House, Madame Noy has been far and away the most congenial. On each occasion we met, I requested additional time to be with her."

Dianne looked at Noy, thought she might be blushing, and then she fixed on her father. "Why?" she asked.

"Why I wanted to spend more time with her?"

"Yes, I want to know. I want to know how she appears to someone like you."

"There are obvious reasons," said Underwood. "She's intelligent, for one thing. Interesting, for another. Also, she possesses certain qualities that can't be exactly defined."

"Like what?" Dianne pressed her father.

"She's warm, she's attractive. Then there's something indefinable. A magnetic quality."

Noy smiled and addressed Dianne. "That's the very way I see your father. Now I think we really must have our dinner. Try your salad, it's delicious. That sweet thing is a mango. We have them in Lampang."

"I know," said Underwood. "I had The Four Seasons arrange to have them sent from Lampang. To make you feel at home, Noy. Now let's eat."

By this time they were all hungry and they ate.

There was little talk except from Dianne, who continued to interject questions, which Noy tried to answer as honestly as possible.

Throughout, Underwood listened to the exchange between his daughter and Noy.

When the dinner was over, as if fearing to lose the opportunity, Dianne continued to pepper Noy with questions.

"You're overwhelming her, Dianne," Underwood protested mildly.

"Am I?" Dianne asked Noy. "Am I asking too much?"

"Not at all," said Noy.

Dianne saved one question for the last. "You may think this nervy of me, Madame Noy, but I wonder if you'd have the time to visit Wellesley tomorrow and allow me to show you around the campus? There have been a few changes."

"I'd enjoy that very much," said Noy instantly. "It's a matter of timing. I could be in Boston tomorrow morning, and then take a stroll about the campus with you for an hour or two. Then I must prepare for my return to Lampang. Yes, I'd love this little excursion. I'm even excited about it."

When the dinner was over, Underwood came to his feet and helped Noy with her chair. "You should get some rest tonight before going to the school and then back to Lampang tomorrow."

"I will," said Noy, gathering up her purse.

"Dianne," Underwood said, "we'll drop off Madame Noy at the Pierre and then I'll take you back to school."

"You don't have to come along," said Dianne. "You've got to be getting back to Washington."

"I want to," Underwood insisted.

Blake stepped forward. "Mind if I join you?"

"If you wish," said Underwood.

Then, taking Noy possessively by the arm, Underwood led the party out of The Four Seasons.

Having dropped off Noy Sang and Marsop at the Pierre Hotel—unconcerned about his daughter's presence, Underwood had given Noy a farewell kiss and accepted her thanks—Underwood, Dianne, and Blake were driven out to John F. Kennedy Airport. There they boarded Air Force One for the flight from New York City to Logan Airport in Boston.

At Logan, another presidential limousine was awaiting them, as well as two cars filled with Secret Service agents.

Then they drove to Wellesley College.

Underwood did not have much opportunity to speak to his daughter. Mostly, he had conversation with Blake, who was trying to help the president catch up on his backlog.

Entering the 400-acre Massachusetts campus, Underwood tried to imagine what it had been like when an eighteen-year-old named Noy, with her eager face, lissome body, and dedication to democracy had been an undergraduate so long ago. He decided it had not changed. Tonight there was an air of serenity among the bright-faced students taking late walks.

Approaching Dianne's dormitory, Underwood told the chauffeur, "Stop here. I'll walk with my daughter the rest of the way. I want a bit of exercise."

When Blake started to leave the limousine with them, Underwood held up his hand. "Wait for us, Paul. I have a few things to discuss with my daughter." Underwood turned to the two Secret Service agents preparing to follow them. "Jim, Ed, give us some distance as long as you feel it's safe. My daughter and I have a few personal things to talk about."

Underwood took Dianne by the hand, and they started up one of the campus walks.

"I'm sorry we didn't get a chance to talk, Dianne. Blake is always so full of business."

"Don't worry, Father. I had a memorable time. All those things that Noy told me. They're bouncing around in my head."

"Wonderful. I'm pleased you got what you wanted."

"And more," she said enigmatically.

They had arrived at the entrance to Dianne's dormitory.

Underwood lingered briefly with his daughter.

"I'm curious," he said. "What did you think of her, Dianne?"

"Madame Noy?"

"Yes, Noy."

Dianne met her father's gaze directly. "Never mind what I think of her. You know what I think of her. The real question is, What do you think of her?"

"That's easy," said Underwood. "I like her, too. I did from the start, and even more so now."

Dianne shook her head. "That's the understatement of the year. You don't like her. You care for her deeply."

Underwood appeared to be taken aback. "Well, that's pretty extravagant. I still hardly know her."

"Father, I'm going to tell you something you may not want to hear. Especially since you're a married man. I don't think you care for her deeply. I don't even think you have affection for her." She took in her breath. "I'm going to say it right out." She said it. "I have an idea you're in love with Noy."

She had never seen her father look more startled. He could hardly find words. When he found them, he said, "That's ridiculous, Dianne. Love her? My God, I haven't loved anyone since your mother and you. Dianne, this woman is practically a stranger to me. How could I possibly love her?"

Dianne was adamant. "You do."

"Whatever gave you such an idea?"

"Knowing you so well," said Dianne. "Nice as you are with Mother and other people, you are basically uninterested in them. But you came to life with Noy. You were younger and livelier. You were interested in her and in everything she had to say."

"But that's usual whenever I meet with the president of another country."

Dianne would not have it. "She's hardly a president to you. She's a young woman. She's breathtakingly beautiful, delicate, warm, smart, very smart, and almost everything she says is interesting. I can't blame you if you've fallen in love with her."

"Foolishness!" Underwood exclaimed. "What's got into you? Let's not discuss it anymore."

"If you don't want to, we won't," said Dianne. "But I watched you with her, Father. You hung on to every word she spoke. And when you spoke to her, each time it was like a caress. . . ." She paused. "If you don't want to discuss it further, I won't. Just one thing. When you have time, give it some thought. I mean your true feelings about Noy. You may think of me as young and inexperienced and hostile to Mother and troublemaking. Forget all those things. Just give some attention to what I've been telling you. Do turn it over in your mind."

"To what end?"

"To know that you're still young and alive, and can be moved. I think it's invigorating and I think it's healthy."

Underwood tried to be firm. "I told you it is utter foolishness. I don't want you ever again to bring this up. Me in love with Noy Sang? It's crazy. Forget it. I certainly intend to."

But on Air Force One, heading from Boston to Washington, he pretended he was asleep to keep Blake quiet, so that he could think about it.

Eyes closed, he thought about it.

Much as he respected his daughter, and her intelligence and perceptions, he knew that she was far off the mark here.

He had told her that she was crazy, and to forget about it, because he certainly would.

But try as he might, he couldn't.

In his mind's eye he saw Noy, and then he heard her, and his heartbeat quickened.

Could his daughter be right?

Could he *possibly* be in love with the president of Lampang? That just couldn't be.

But most of the way back to Washington he thought about it, and he wondered.

In the morning, having questioned Matt the night before about the United Nations and The Four Seasons, and having heard his version of the day and evening, Alice Underwood decided to hear her daughter's version of the last night's dinner.

Still lying in bed, Alice put through a call to Wellesley College, and was pleased to catch Dianne in her room before she left to meet Noy Sang.

"Hello, Dianne. I just felt like touching base with you. How are you? Did you get some sleep?"

"I slept perfectly, Mother."

"I was asking Dad about his speech at the UN. He told me it went well. But you know how he plays everything down. So I thought I'd ask you. What did you think of his speech?"

"Forceful. Never better. He laid it into the Russians."

"That's wonderful. I'm delighted he rose to the occasion."

"I assure you, Mother, he did."

Alice approached the next question cautiously and proceeded in a casual way. "The dinner afterward at The Four Seasons. How was it?"

"Couldn't have been better. I lucked out, thanks to Father. He seated me right next to Madame Noy Sang."

"I'm glad. Did you get what you wanted for your thesis?"

"Everything and then some, again thanks to Father."

"What do you mean—thanks to Father?"

"I mean he was so helpful and kind," said Dianne. "He got Madame Noy to speak from her heart. She did. Father was wonderful with her, and she responded. She treated me as if I were her daughter."

"I see," said Alice. "So you were impressed by the way Dad handled Madame Noy."

"He was darling."

"Darling?"

"Mother, what can I say? He knew just how to handle her and he did."

"How was that?"

Alice sensed that Dianne had heard her tone and was retreating slightly.

"He—he handled her warmly, made her comfortable with

me. It was a break for me. And Madame Noy's visit here today is a bigger one. I couldn't be happier."

"Then neither could I," said Alice.

After hanging up, Alice was anything but happy.

She had heard what Dianne had said, and she had read between the lines.

Matt had played up to Noy.

That stupid goat.

That son of a bitch.

Alice was suspicious now; she couldn't let this one go.

She'd better nail it down, she told herself, and fast.

She liked being first lady, and she intended to keep it that way.

EIGHT

ALICE Underwood reviewed what Matt had told her of the meeting with Noy and then what Dianne had told her of the same dinner.

Alice did not like the sound of it.

Every word pointed to the fact that Matt was being overly attentive to the sarong lady. Further, he came to life whenever he was in her presence. It spelled something that added up to trouble. In the last year he had been cool toward her, Alice reflected. Maybe that was too strong. Put more accurately, he had been uninterested in her. But there was no doubt he was interested in a younger woman named Noy from Southeast Asia.

It was impossible to conceive. Yet there it was.

Fully awake, Alice realized that she had been too casual about the other woman. It was time she learned more about Madame Noy Sang, and the kind of threat she represented.

Immediately her mind went to Paul Blake.

He would be her best informant. He knew as much as anyone did about Noy. He had met her in the White House. He
had even been with her and Matt and Dianne at The Four
Seasons last night.

Alice considered how she might approach Blake.

Actually, he would present no difficulty. Alice had known
for a long time how Blake had felt about her. She could wrap
him around her finger. He had an almost childish crush on
her.

She would invite Blake up to the First Lady's Dressing
Room next door. She would be as attractive as possible. She
would dress for him. Better, she would undress for him, meaning she would wear evening lingerie.

Stepping out of bed, she showered and sprayed her body
with a light cologne. Then she searched through her lingerie
closet and selected a filmy, deep-cut peach-colored nightgown
and a robe that matched, and put them on. Moving to her
dressing table, she carefully applied her makeup. Satisfied, she
turned toward her full-length mirror and practiced how she
could best be seated to give Blake as much leg and thigh as was
decently possible.

Reassuring herself that her legs and thighs, full, shapely,
pink, were quite a sight, and irresistible to every man but her
husband, she decided that she was ready to receive her visitor.

She telephoned the chief of staff's office, reached his secretary, and seconds later had him on the line.

"Good morning, Paul. It's Alice."

"What a pleasant surprise. Good morning to you, Alice."

"Do you have any free time right ahead?"

"If I didn't have, I'd make it, if it's for you."

"It's for me. Try to make it."

"When?"

"Now," said Alice. "It's a personal matter, and I'd rather the president didn't know you were seeing me."

"I understand."

"I'll be in the First Lady's Dressing Room. We'll be alone."

Alice imagined that she could feel Blake quiver.

She walked into the sitting room, ordered some tea, waited until it was served, then sat on a low sofa and postured. Her gown and nightdress fell to one side, and her exquisite left leg and part of the thigh were bare and exposed. Then, remembering Noy with Matt on the Hasken videotape, she recalled how a bit of one of Noy's breasts had been clearly visible. Effective. A real come-on. She loosened her satin belt, and then loosened her neckline further. She bent forward to see what happened.

What happened was that both of her magnificent breasts sprang free. Firm but free. She knew that if Blake kept his eyes there, he could see her nipples.

Well, why not? She had something to find out, and she would use almost any means to find it.

Sipping her tea, pleased with herself, she waited.

In minutes Paul Blake was at the door and then inside. He eyed her with an intake of breath that she knew was more than amorous.

Alice remained seated, inviting him to cross the room to greet her.

As he approached she bent toward him, extending her hand. She could feel her breasts drop forward. She was sure he had a glimpse of the nipples.

Certainly, taking her hand, his eyes almost came out of his head.

"Much too formal," she said, offering her cheek.

Blake palpitated, bent forward, and kissed her dryly on the

cheek. Then, licking his lips, he pecked another kiss, a wet one, and she smiled.

"That's better, Paul," she said. "Why don't you pull up a chair?"

As he began to do so, she knew he would be confronted by her leg and thigh throughout their conversation.

He sat down. "You're looking wonderful," he said. "Absolutely ravishing."

"Thank you, Paul, dear, thank you. It does a lot for a woman to hear that."

"You must hear it a good deal."

"Not enough," said Alice, pouting. "Thank God for you and some gallantry." She changed the subject. "There are a few things I want to talk to you about. You must understand that they're personal and that this is confidential."

"Between us," said Blake. "You have my word."

"I've always known I could trust you. Paul, when something confusing comes up, especially when it relates to Matt, there's no one to turn to—except you of course."

His eyes shifted from hers downward to her décolletage.

"Say anything you wish, Alice," he said quietly. "Speak your mind."

Alice nodded. "About last night at dinner in New York. You were there with Matt and Dianne, and that—what's her name? —Noy Sang woman, weren't you?"

"Throughout the dinner, then on the plane with them to Boston."

"I'm interested in the evening," said Alice. "I've heard two versions of it. Matt, of course, tells me nothing. I mean, as if there weren't a thing to report. Dianne, on the other hand, was more forthcoming, so I have some idea of what went on. I was hoping you could tell me more."

"Like what, Alice?"

"I want to know if the president behaved."

Blake was bewildered. "Behaved?"

"Specifically, I want to know how he behaved with Madame Noy Sang. Did he gush over her? Was he attentive to her? Dianne says he was attentive. I have the impression he was more than routinely so. Do you agree?"

"Yes, I suppose you could say he was attentive."

"There are two ways of being attentive to a woman, Paul. Politely or specially."

Blake considered this. At last he answered. "It was more than politely. In fact he praised her a good deal to Dianne."

Listening, Alice felt she wasn't getting enough from Blake. She could get more. She could stun and excite him by taking him into the bedroom, into bed; but it was unthinkable, even though she had thought it.

"Let me put it to you another way," Alice said. "Do you think my husband's interest in Madame Noy is only political? Or is it something other than that?"

Blake had been staring at Alice's exposed knee and thigh. He tried to keep his mind on what she had been saying. It was elusive, but he fastened on to it. "Truthfully," he found himself answering, "I don't think Matt is the least bit interested in Lampang."

"Then you're saying he's interested in Madame Noy?"

"I can only guess, Alice. But yes, I'd say his interest in Lampang has to do with Noy. Not politics. Noy."

"You feel certain of that?"

"Consider the evidence," said Blake. "From the start, when she first came here, when he met her, he broke all commitments and his entire schedule that opening day with her. He was supposed to give her a limited loan. He gave her a huge loan. He was supposed to get a large air base from her. She wanted to allow only a small one, and he gave in to her wishes. She was to go home that night. He cancelled everything and spent yet another day with her. When her sister died—someone Matt didn't even know—he dropped everything to fly all the way to Lampang to attend the funeral. Then I'm sure you watched television and saw him go swimming with her—"

"I saw," said Alice stiffly. "I saw her in that sarong."

"Wouldn't that indicate his interest in her is personal and special?" His eyes were once more on Alice's thigh. Then he said indignantly, "You don't deserve that, Alice."

"Well, then, what it comes down to is Noy herself. I suppose I should know more about her, and what there is about her that interests him."

"I'm sure there's little I know that you don't know."

"She's beautiful, isn't she?"

"In an exotic fashion, I guess. But certainly not as beautiful as you, Alice."

"Thank you, Paul." She paused. "This Noy, she's a widow, isn't she?"

"She's a widow all right."

"If this nonsense with my husband goes on, I may be regarded as a widow also. As a loner, at least. Paul, how did Noy's husband die?"

"He was shot in his office by persons unknown. The Communists were supposed to have done it."

"How could that have been?" Alice wondered. "I remember Matt saying her husband was friendly to Communists."

"Not quite," said Blake. "Prem Sang had been trying to accommodate them, absorb them into his government. Many people were impatient about that."

"Paul, that doesn't sound right to me. I'd like to know how he really died. Every detail."

"I don't think anyone has that information fully, Alice. Although I could try to find out what's known to date."

"How?"

"Ezra Morrison should know. Do you want me to speak to him?"

"Could you be a dear and do that? Question him confidentially of course."

"I'll do that at once."

"When?"

"Now," said Blake, regretfully taking his eyes off her and rising. "I'll be in touch with you as soon as I know something."

Once he had his appointment, Blake decided that it would be safer to see Ezra Morrison at the Department of State.

In Morrison's vast office, Blake found it difficult to settle down. He paced about, waiting for Morrison to sign some papers, and when Morrison was done, Blake dropped into the leather chair across from him.

"What can I do for you, Paul?" Morrison inquired. "Is this for the president?"

"It's for the first lady."

"Oh?"

"It's a personal matter. Confidential. A favor."

Morrison snorted. "I'd do her any favor, if she'd do one for me. I'd love to fuck her."

"Who wouldn't?" said Blake.

"You, too? Not that I care for her that much. I just have a hunch she'd be fun between the sheets."

"Well, you can forget it, and so can I," said Blake. "Alice has her mind on her husband."

"Meaning?"

"She wants to keep him," said Blake. "She wants to be first lady, not second lady, and she's a little nervous about the time he's spending with Madame Noy Sang."

"The Madame's not bad either," Morrison said. "If I could get there, I wouldn't mind a tumble with her."

"I'm afraid that's what is on Alice's mind concerning Matt."

"You think he'd do something?" said Morrison.

"He's done plenty already," said Blake.

"So the first lady is worried about Madame Noy. What's any of this got to do with you?"

"Alice wants to know more about Madame Noy Sang," said Blake. "I guess the way a football coach scouts and wants to know more about the opposition."

"What's to know that the public doesn't already know?"

Blake came forward in his chair. "How Noy's husband, Prem, died, how he really died."

"That's not my cup of tea, Paul. He was shot by assassins."

"That seems to be a fact. The missing fact is, How did he really die? Alice wants to know who was behind it." Blake paused. "Maybe she wants to know if Noy was implicated. Although that's doubtful. Still . . ."

"Official word is the Communists."

"Also doubtful," said Blake. "Who really?"

Morrison shrugged. "I honestly don't know. If anyone here knows, it would be someone in Langley. Ask Director Ramage. The CIA is supposed to know everything."

"Would Ramage tell you?"

"No. Not on your life."

"Is there any way you can find out?"

Morrison twisted uneasily in his swivel chair. "There might be ways. Maybe." He stared at Blake. "Level with me, Paul. How important is this to you?"

"How important is the first lady to us?"

"I see, it's like that," said Morrison.

"Alice wants to know," said Blake. "She insists. I told her I thought I could find out. Could I?"

Morrison was thoughtful. "Possibly."

"Will you pursue this further, Ezra?"

"I can try."

"Is that a promise?"

Morrison laid his arms on the desk and met Blake's anxious eyes.

Morrison pushed himself to his feet. "Give me a few hours."

Not long after leaving Paul Blake, Ezra Morrison let himself into the luxurious apartment on Wisconsin Avenue in Georgetown that Mary Jane O'Neil owned.

At first glance, it was difficult to associate her with Alan Ramage, the CIA director. For a deputy director for operations, one would have expected a young lady who was brisk, efficient, somewhat masculine in manner. While Mary Jane might have been efficient on the job, she was neither brisk nor masculine. At five feet two, she was entirely feminine, playful, fun, although intense in her lovemaking.

Morrison found her in the lacy bedroom, as he expected to. She was in a soft chair next to the bed, watching television. Today there were, as there had been every week, two glasses of Scotch and soda on a table beside the chair.

"Hello, sweet," Morrison greeted her, bending to kiss her fully on the lips. The lingering kiss induced an immediate erection, which rarely happened with his wife, and reassured him now as he reached for his drink.

They both drank, making small talk, and the moment that Mary Jane's drink was finished, she came to her feet and threw off her silk bathrobe. Already undressing, Morrison was mesmerized by her small, firm breasts and the thick patch of pubic hair between her legs.

She went straight to the bed, and Morrison finally undressed, followed, and dropped beside her on the cover. Foreplay was brief. He wasted no time on preliminaries. He was ready.

Mary Jane was as active and energetic as ever, and Morrison was pleased with his endurance.

When they were through, he lay on his back, panting, and Mary Jane, satisfied, curled against his body. "You're good, Ezra, very good. You're the best I know. You're spoiling me for all other men. Happy?"

"Ummm."

"Why don't you leave your wife and move in so we can do this every day?"

"Mary Jane—"

"I'm just kidding. You know it." She fell back. "I wish I could do something as special for you."

Until then he had not given a thought to his earlier conversation with Blake. Yet it had been in the back of his mind as something he should bring up. Now, pleasured, his senses returning, he remembered Blake and what he must find out for him and for the first lady.

"Something special for me?" Morrison repeated. "You already have, my love. Hey, wait, there is something else you can do."

"Name it."

"Uh, Mary Jane, I'm involved in a situation where I've got to know more about Madame Noy Sang."

Mary Jane was puzzled a moment. "That Lampang woman?"

"Exactly."

"I can't imagine there's anyone who'd know more about her than you do."

"This is something specific," said Morrison. "I must find out how Prem Sang was murdered. Exactly who killed him and why."

Mary Jane sat up in bed, wrinkling her brow. "Even if I had the answer, I can't discuss such things, you know that."

"I'm not asking for some top, top official secret."

"The best I can do is make an educated guess, from what I've heard," said Mary Jane. "The United States was worried about President Prem and his relationship with the Communists. I think the feeling was, at least at Langley, that if someone could get rid of Prem, his wife would become president. But she's an amateur, helpless, useless, inexperienced. When she runs in the next election, it seems a certainty that General Nakorn, a tough customer, could easily beat her. As far as the CIA is concerned, Nakorn is our man."

"Yes, he'd make life easier for us."

"He'd do our bidding," said Mary Jane. "He'd go right at it, wipe out the Communist insurgents, and give us the biggest and best air base and defense in the South Pacific. So I'd say the strategy, the strategic wishful thinking, was to get rid of Prem, let Noy take over, then beat her legitimately in an open election."

Morrison was sitting up. "Very good. Yet someone had to take the risk of getting rid of Prem."

"Even if I knew, Ezra, I couldn't discuss it. So let's forget that part." She stared at Morrison. "You're looking chipper. Ezra, can you get it up again?"

"It is up."

She reached out between his legs. "That'll do nicely. Now's the time to use it. I can think much better when I'm relaxed."

"Think about what?"

"About whatever you've been asking."

"I want you to give it another try."

"After we have another try," she said.

"Lie down, Mary Jane. Enough talking."

Immediately, she was on her back. Morrison kissed her breasts and then got up between her legs.

This was an extended one, better than the first, and noisy. They both came loudly, a few seconds apart.

"How was that?" he asked, falling off her.

"A winner," she gasped. "I'm yours. You can have anything you want from me. You still want to know who killed Prem?"

"It would be helpful."

"I'll tell you, you rapist. I'm at your mercy. I'll tell you anything you want to know."

"Who killed President Prem?"

She steadied her breathing. "The boss knows. Ramage knows. He set the whole thing in motion. It's nothing he did or that the CIA would do. I'm fairly certain he sent the word along to Percy Siebert, our CIA station head in Lampang."

"And Siebert?"

"I don't know positively. Logically, I would think that Siebert transmitted our wishes to General Nakorn. Probably told him it was President Underwood's idea. Now, you seducer, does that help?"

"It does, sweet."

"Where did you hear all that? Not from me. A little birdie told you. Don't dare get me involved."

"I don't even know you."

"Good. . . . Have you got one more left in you?"

He wasn't sure, but he was grateful. "Maybe. Give me twenty minutes."

"I'll give you another drink and twenty minutes. Don't forget, I'm counting the time on the clock."

Still somewhat exhausted from his acrobatics with Mary Jane O'Neil, Ezra Morrison prepared to call Blake.

He hesitated briefly before picking up the phone to reassure himself that Mary Jane had it right. He had to remind himself that she was the CIA deputy director for operations under Ramage, and she would have it right.

He had Blake on the phone at once.

"Paul, are you alone?" Morrison wanted to know.

"Relatively."

"I don't mean your staff. I mean the president. Is he within earshot?"

"He's gone up to the Hill with the treasury secretary. He won't be back for a while. What's up? Have you got something for me?"

"I do. I may have it all."

"Your source?"

"About as high up as you'd want at the CIA."

"Can you tell me?" Blake was eager. "I want to know as soon as possible."

"Not on the telephone," Morrison said. "I'd suggest you come over and have a quiet chat with the secretary of state."

"I'm on my way."

"I'll be here and I'll be alone," said Morrison.

Forty-five minutes later, Blake was in Morrison's office.

Morrison buzzed his receptionist's office. "No calls, Suzie," he said. "I'll let you know when I'm free."

Morrison walked over to the sofa and sat down beside Blake.

"I have as much as we'll ever get," said Morrison.

"And you're sure of your source."

Morrison smiled. "I couldn't be closer to my source unless I fucked them."

"I'm listening, Ezra."

Slowly, choosing his words carefully, Morrison told the chief of staff what he had heard from Mary Jane O'Neil— without mentioning her name.

When he was through, he said, "There you have it, Paul."

"But you don't know exactly who was responsible."

"You mean, who sent the hit men? That's unimportant. It's enough to know that somehow they were assigned to get Prem with the full knowledge of Ramage, and with a clearance from the president. After all, the CIA notifies the president of everything in progress in its morning briefing book."

"Suppose Underwood didn't know?"

Morrison grunted. "I choose to think he did know. In any case, the president bears the prime responsibility."

"Incredible."

"What are you going to do with this information?"

Blake got off the sofa. "I'm going to tell the first lady. I don't know if it will make her happy enough." At the door he considered what he would say. "It might," said Blake. "Thanks, Ezra. I owe you one."

Having received Blake's call, Alice Underwood readied herself for his momentary arrival in the First Lady's Dressing Room.

She posed in front of the full-length mirror, wearing only sheer black bikini panties and a lacy half-bra. Then she pulled on a black dress that she knew would slither above her knees when she sat down. She stepped into high-heeled pumps and sat to await Blake's coming.

When he came in, she signaled him to the chair immediately opposite her.

After greeting her, Blake settled down low in the chair and made no pretense of looking at anything above her neckline.

Her hemline was up high, and when she uncrossed her legs, he thought he could make out the wisp of panties at her crotch. He was certain it was her panties, and there was a dark triangle behind them between her legs.

Alice quietly allowed him to enjoy himself.

"You have something for me, Paul?" she said softly.

What he wanted to tell her was that he had something better than talk. He had an embarrassing erection. He wondered if she was disgusted enough with her husband to give her husband's chief of staff a chance. Then, reluctantly, he dismissed his erotic fantasies and tried to concentrate on the news Alice was waiting for.

"I have an idea who might have been responsible for the death of President Prem," Blake said.

"Who?"

"Your husband, Alice. In a sense he's responsible."

Alice showed her shock. "That's impossible."

"Hear me out, and then decide."

"Matt?" she said. "He's not that kind of person. You'd better tell me the whole thing."

"Sit tight and listen," said Blake. "Prem didn't want a United States air base in Lampang. But he did want to compromise with the Communist insurgents. He wanted to bring them into his government. As you know, that was contrary to United States policy."

"I'm aware of that."

"The idea grew at some level of the CIA that if Prem could be removed, Noy would replace him, and that since Noy was not up to the job, she would be manipulated by General Nakorn, who is a friend of the United States."

"So someone made the decision to get rid of Prem."

Blake nodded. He reeled off the names of the players. First Ramage. Then Siebert. Still, he explained, the go-ahead had to come from the president of the United States. "Matt sees all the CIA reports in his daily briefing book. Nothing gets past him."

Alice's incredulity remained. "I can't imagine him okaying an assassination. I mean, I know Matt. He's too soft for that. Maybe he never saw the CIA report."

Blake lifted his shoulders. "The odds are he did, in some form or other. I can't see anyone going over his head."

"You're sure of the source for this?"

"I'm told it's the best."

"So Matt's responsible?" Alice suddenly lighted up. "Noy's a widow because of him."

"Yes."

"That's wonderful!"

She fell back, laughing, the string of bikini between her legs plainly visible. Blake's eyes bulged and he became breathless.

"What," Blake mumbled, "what's so wonderful? What are you going to do about it?"

"I'm going to tell Noy Sang."

"You're what?"

"Why not?" said Alice. "Noy is still in the United States, at Wellesley, in fact. I want you to get Morrison to locate Noy, and say he wishes to see her for late afternoon tea here at the Department of State. To discuss further details of the air base, or whatever. She's to have this meeting with Morrison, but she won't, really. That'll be a pretext for Noy's meeting with me. Yes, with me, Paul, face-to-face. I'm going to level with her. When I'm through, I think I will have put an end to my husband's little flirtation with Prem's widow. Will you arrange it?'"

Noy Sang had been reached at Wellesley, and she had been agreeable to coming back to Washington and to delay her return to Lampang for a meeting with Secretary of State Morrison.

She had met with Morrison over tea and finger sandwiches in his office at the Department of State, and he had discussed the possibility of enlarging the American air base on Lampang. She had resisted it, and to her surprise he had given in rather easily.

Suddenly he had risen and said, "Madame Noy, I have a meeting with the Egyptian foreign minister and I must step outside and talk to him. But I have someone else who must speak to you, and I'd appreciate it if you would remain here for another ten minutes."

"Whatever you wish," said Noy.

She was puzzled by Morrison's abrupt departure, about being left alone, and about whom she was expected to see next.

She sipped her tea and waited, when the entrance door opened and a rather tall, very striking woman appeared and approached her.

Noy thought the woman looked familiar.

The woman said, "Madame Noy Sang. Let me introduce

myself. I'm Alice Underwood, the wife of President Underwood. May I join you?"

"Of course," said Noy, bewildered.

Alice sat across from Noy. "Let me freshen your tea and
pour some for myself." She began to pour. "I wanted the
opportunity to meet with you myself. There is a matter I wish
to discuss that concerns you in a personal way."

Noy sat dumbly, wondering what was going on, wondering
what personal matter Alice Underwood could possibly want to
discuss. It was obvious to Noy that this had all been prear-
ranged. Morrison had not actually wanted to talk to Noy; had
only wanted an excuse to bring Noy to the White House to
meet with the first lady.

Sitting there, following the first lady's movements as she
finished pouring the tea, Noy appraised her. Noy felt uncom-
fortable about having thought that President Underwood had
any special interest in her when he had such a perfectly attractive wife. To Noy, Alice's face was a Grecian cameo, every line
and feature symmetrical. Alice appeared poised and apparently
fully at ease.

By contrast, Noy felt physically inferior. She felt small, diminished, with nowhere near the pale beauty and lithe figure
that the first lady possessed.

Watching the first lady, Noy tried to imagine why this meeting was taking place. Noy could not find a single clue.

But now Alice Underwood was speaking. "I wanted to see
you alone," Alice was saying, "because by accident I came
across some information about the assassination of your late
husband."

"You know something about Prem I don't know?"

"It's something I feel I should tell you, as one woman to
another."

Noy's bewilderment had increased measurably. "What possibly—?"

"I can tell you the truth about your husband's death, and why he was murdered."

This was totally unexpected, and Noy blinked. "You're speaking of Prem's murder? You know something about it?"

Alice put down her cup. "The truth. I happen to know the truth. How—how it came about."

"If I couldn't find out, how could you, over eight thousand miles away?"

"This will be clear to you in a few minutes," said Alice. "You deserve to know how you were widowed. I don't mean to upset you, but I'm sure you don't want mysteries."

"I want the truth if you know it," said Noy.

"Very well, then brace yourself for it," said Alice. "You've been spending a lot of time with my husband, and I'm sure he has impressed you."

"He seems a very decent man."

Alice hardened. "He is, but don't be fooled. He's been pleasant, even kind, to you because he feels guilty and it bothers him. To know my husband, you've got to know that he loves his country above all else and will do anything for it. Even if it means sacrificing someone who stands in his way."

Noy was plainly shaken. Her face flushed. "You are implying—?"

"I am telling you, Madame Sang, that your husband was one who stood in my husband's way. President Prem was against the air base that is a necessity for us. Worse than that, President Prem wanted a reconciliation with the Communist insurgents in your country, which was even a greater concern to President Underwood. When the CIA decided that your husband should be silenced, and that it could be arranged by liquidation, Matt did not try to prevent it. As you know, the CIA can do nothing without an American president's consent. In whatever way it happened, actively or by averting his eyes, President Underwood approved the CIA's plan—and your husband was eliminated. He was eliminated to pave the way for you, who were seen as naive. Part of the plan is that you will be succeeded by someone more compliant with United States policy."

Noy was stricken. "I can't believe that."

"Do believe it, Madame Noy Sang."

"How do you know such a thing?"

"Our secretary of state learned it from the CIA, and saw that it was passed on to me."

"But after such horrendous behavior, why was I invited here, why has your husband been so kind to me?"

"I've already told you. Guilt. Matt's behavior may sound harsh, but he has a weakness, beneath everything else. Matt Underwood is essentially soft. He does something unspeakable, and then he backs up and is sorry about it. He can't change what he's done, but he's sorry. He's been trying to make it up to you."

Noy sat in silence a long time.

At last she spoke up. "Why have you told me all this?"

Alice did not reply at once. She studied Noy. "Not out of any guilt of my own. I haven't done anything wrong. I'm sorry about what happened, naturally, but I can't bring your husband back. There's another reason. . . ."

"Yes?"

"You're an extremely beguiling young woman, most attractive, and very warm and sympathetic to men, I'm sure. You have many characteristics I don't have. At least for my husband." She was quiet a few seconds, and then she stared at Noy squarely. "My husband appears to have some childish crush on you. In the beginning it was guilt, and then he came to know you and was attracted to you. This concerns me, of course. Matt *is* my husband, and I want to keep him. I want to remain his lady and first lady of the United States. I want no childish or adolescent interference. If my husband is momentarily impressed by you, Madame Sang, I don't want you to be foolish enough to be impressed by him. I want you to know what he can really be like. He can be heartless and selfish, even to the point of sacrifice of human life. I wanted you to know that, what Matt is really like. I was sure that once you knew fully about your husband's assassination you would no longer encourage Matt's advances. I intend to put a stop to any relationship between you. If what I've told you will bring that about, painful as it is to you and to me, then I will not be sorry. I hope that this will end anything between you and my husband, except on the most official level."

Noy stared back at Alice. "You've been very frank and revealing."

"It was the only way I knew to bring this to an end."

Noy came to her feet. "It is at an end," she said quietly. "Will you be kind enough to show me out?"

When President Underwood dropped off the secretary of the treasury, and came down from the Hill to the East Wing of the White House, he was surprised to find that Hy Hasken had emerged from the press room and was waiting for him.

"I'm too busy for talk," snapped Underwood.

Hasken did not budge. "You may not be too busy to tell me what Madame Noy Sang has been doing at the Department of State."

Underwood stopped in his tracks. "She's in Washington?

She was supposed to be at Wellesley with my daughter. Then fly from Boston to Lampang."

"She's here," Hasken persisted. "At least at Foggy Bottom, or had been a short time ago. Do you intend to see her?"

"Since I had no idea she was coming here, how could I intend to see her? Thanks for the information, Hasken. Now I've got to get back to work."

But when the president reached the Oval Office, he did not get back to work.

The moment he reached his desk, the president buzzed Paul Blake and ordered him to come right in.

When Blake arrived, Underwood did not bother to have him sit down.

"What's this I hear about Madame Noy Sang?" the president demanded.

"What did you hear, Matt?"

"That she's in the city. Is that true?"

"True," said Blake. "Secretary Morrison wanted to see her and asked me to find her at Wellesley. I did so. She delayed her trip home to come straight here. I got her over to the Department of State."

"A head of a state here and I wasn't notified?" said Underwood unbelievingly.

"You were locked up on the Hill, lunching with all those senators. I didn't want to disturb you."

"Did she see Morrison?"

"Yes, I picked her up and took her there myself."

"What did Morrison want with her?"

"As far as I know, it had to do with further clarification about our air base on Lampang."

Underwood frowned. "That was settled long ago."

Blake shuffled uneasily. "I also believe the first lady wanted to meet her and have tea with them."

"Alice met Noy Sang?"

"So I'm told."

Underwood knitted his brow. "What was that all about?"

"I wish I knew, Matt. I haven't the faintest idea."

"Okay. Thanks, Paul, you can leave. I'll find out for myself what's been happening."

The instant that Blake had left the Oval Office and Underwood was alone, he buzzed his secretary to reach President Noy Sang at Blair House.

A minute later he was on the telephone with Noy.

"I heard you were here," said Underwood. "I was quite surprised. According to my chief of staff, you met with my wife."

"I did."

Underwood was aware of Noy's uncharacteristic stiffness. "I'd like to see you briefly. I want to know what happened between you and Alice. Can you see me now?"

"No, I can't. I'm having a snack, and then Marsop and I are leaving for Lampang. I'm very busy."

"Too busy to see me," said Underwood, trying to sound hurt. "Surely you can find a minute."

"I can't," said Noy flatly.

Underwood was taken aback. "This isn't like you, Noy. You sound upset."

"I am upset."

"About what? Is anything wrong?"

"There's a great deal wrong."

"Aren't you going to tell me?"

There was a silence at the other end. Then Noy spoke again. "Yes, I think you should come over. I'll tell you exactly what's

wrong. I think you'd rather hear it from me than from someone else."

After ordering his Secret Service men to remain outside,
surround Blair House, or do whatever they did on sudden visits
like this, President Underwood waited to be admitted.

It was Marsop who opened the front door and let him in.
Neither by speech nor expression did Marsop give anything
away. He merely said, "Come in, Mr. President. Madame Sang
will be with you in a minute."

Underwood entered the large living room, which was unoc-
cupied, cast around for a place to sit, and finally sat at the edge
of a leather armchair.

He had cooled his heels only briefly when Noy came in,
unsmiling, grim-faced. Underwood jumped to his feet to intercept and greet her in their familiar way, with a peck on the
cheek. But she would not have it. She did not offer even a
handshake, and went past him to another chair that would set
some distance between them.

"I see something is wrong," Underwood said, returning to
his seat. "Noy, believe me, I have no idea what's going on or
how it concerns me."

"I'll tell you," she said, and lost no time in doing so. "It
concerns the assassination of my husband. I've finally found
out who was responsible for Prem's death."

All this was unexpected, and Underwood could only gather
his wits together to say "Who?"

For a person with so much natural warmth, Noy was an
icicle. "You pretend not to know?"

"I don't know. I don't know what you're talking about." He
tried to find some clue in Noy's countenance, but her expres-

sion gave nothing away. Underwood pressed her. "Who was responsible for Prem's death?"

"You!" Noy burst out. "You, Mr. President, were responsible for my husband's assassination."

Underwood was positive he had not heard her right.

"What—what are you saying?"

Noy repeated her accusation. "You, Mr. President, were responsible for my husband's terrible death."

Underwood was aghast. "I've heard you twice. I've never heard anything more mad."

"It's a fact."

"It's absolutely crazy. Noy, do you know what you're saying?"

She sat erect. "I know exactly what I'm saying, Matt. I have it on the best authority that you arranged through the CIA to get rid of my husband—because he was too conciliatory with the Communists. You passed the word down for his enemies to eliminate him."

Underwood was on his feet. "Noy, I don't know who put that utter falsehood in your head. Where did you hear such a wild story?"

Noy refused to flinch. "I heard it from your wife. I met with her today. She told me this face-to-face. Do you consider your wife a liar?"

"She's not a liar. But on this accusation she is. What she told you is absolute insanity."

"Is it?" said Noy. "Well, she got it directly, firsthand from your secretary of state. She was upset by it, and she wanted to be sympathetic to me. She also wanted to warn me of any future dealings with you. She said not to trust you because you'd put your position, your country, ahead of human life, anyone's."

"Noy, I don't know what she's talking about. It's not true about Prem's death. Not a word of it is true. She was crazy to tell you that, and you're crazy to believe her for one minute." He went on helplessly. "What could be her motive in telling you such a lie?"

"She was frank about that," said Noy. "She felt that we were getting too close, and you were showing too much interest in me. She wanted me to know what a selfish and cruel person you really are."

"You know better than that," Underwood protested.

Noy shook her head. "No, I don't. I really don't know you down deep. I can find no reason for your first lady to reveal all that unless there was some truth to it. Matt, I do believe her. I also—now I'll be up-front about it—believe you may be lying, because this has shaken you. If you're not lying, then you're ignoring the fact that you were in charge, the president of the United States, and that the CIA keeps you informed of its plots. Through neglect, you may have let this assassination get past you, let it happen because you were inattentive, which is equally horrible. In either case, you were culpable. My husband is in his grave because of you."

Underwood moved nearer to her. "Noy, be fair—"

"How can I be fair?"

"Give me a chance to look into this. I'm going to talk to Alice. I'm going to talk to Alan Ramage. I'm going to prove to you that what you heard was a pack of lies. My wife is a jealous woman, and she's not too fond of me either. When I'm through I'll be able to prove to you—not merely tell you, but prove to you—that you've been misled. I wasn't to blame for Prem's death, and, to the best of my knowledge, no one under me was responsible."

Noy pushed herself to her feet, glared at him, then walked

past him to the inner door. "Matt, you needn't bother to prove anything to me." Her hand was on the doorknob. "I choose to believe you are to blame for this terrible tragedy in my life, and —and I never want to see you again."

With that, she opened the door and was gone.

NINE

WHEN he had left Blair House and been driven back to the White House, Matt Underwood's mind was in turmoil.

Reaching the Oval Office, his first impulse was to find Alice and go after her until she told him where she had obtained the false information about him, and why she had passed it on to Noy. His next thoughts were to locate Blake and Morrison, and learn more about this whole mess.

Sitting at his desk, he considered his loss. He had been unable to convince Noy that he was innocent in the matter of her husband's death, and he was bereft at the realization that she might never again speak to him.

Why these feelings about Noy? Underwood's mind went back to Dianne, to his daughter's certainty that he was in love with Noy. That couldn't be, he continued to tell himself. He was a sensible married man. He was president of the United States, with a hundred other matters to occupy him.

But now the loss of Noy outweighed everything else.

There was only one thing to do. He must get to the bottom of the falsehood about his involvement with Prem's assassination. He must dig for the truth, and once he had it he would finally be able to prove to Noy that he'd had no part in Prem's murder.

That Alice would pin responsibility on him in order to turn Noy against him was not the whole story.

The missing part of the story was how Alice had got her hands on the information accusing him.

He must start with Alice and work backward until he arrived at the source of the malicious falsehood.

Glancing at the clock on his desk, he saw that it was close to midnight, and Alice might already be asleep. Anyway, he would find out and start with her.

Shoving aside the papers on his desk, he rose and went outside, where he was followed by a Secret Service agent. He strode along the colonnaded walk into the White House once more, and entered the small elevator, waving off the Secret Service agent.

Alice would be in the Queens' Bedroom, he knew.

Entering quietly, he saw that she was stretched under the blanket of the canopied bed.

He went to see if she was awake. He sat on the edge of the bed and leaned over her.

She stirred. Her eyes were shut, but she opened them briefly, and said drowsily, "Hello, Casanova."

It was the kind of stupid remark she would make after she'd had her sleeping pill and was on the brink of sleep, and he was determined to contain his anger and try to speak to her before she was gone and unreachable.

"Alice, I'm back. Can you hear me?"

"A little."

"I know you had a meeting with Madame Noy today."

"Who?"

"Madame Noy," he repeated.

Alice awakened slightly, but was fuzzy and hesitant.

"Yes," she finally said. "I saw her. She came here. We had tea."

"Why did you see her?" Underwood persisted.

"Your friend . . . I wanted to meet her." A lapse, a struggle for wakefulness. "She—she's pretty, all right. Don't blame you."

He tried to withhold his impatience. "There's nothing to blame me for."

"Oh, no?"

"Nothing," he said firmly. "But I have something to blame you for."

"What?"

"Alice, can you hear me?"

"Don't shout."

"Alice, why did you tell Madame Noy such a ridiculous story? You know I'm not responsible for her husband's death. You know that's not true."

There was a long silence. Alice moved under the blanket. "I heard it," she said.

"You heard I killed Prem Sang?"

"Never said you killed him. You're too—too far—too cowardly to shoot anyone. I said you were responsible for the assass—whatever."

He fought her sleeping pill. "Where did you hear that cock-and-bull story?"

"Heard it," she whispered.

"From whom?"

"Can't tell you. State secret. Please go away and let me sleep."

Underwood grabbed her shoulder and shook her a little. "I've got to know the truth. Who gossiped such tripe? You'd better tell me. I'm not going to let you sleep until you tell me."

There was another long pause. "Blake," she muttered.

"Blake told you that? He's only chief of staff. He doesn't know a damn thing I don't know. Where did he get his information?"

"Secretary of—" She sighed. "Morrison. Ezra. He told Blake."

"What was Morrison's source?"

"Dunno. Please leave me alone."

He shook her slightly once more. "Alice—"

"What?"

"It's a lie, and you must know that. I know nothing, not a thing, about Prem Sang's death. Why did you lay that on Noy? What an awful thing to tell her—and worse, that it was my fault."

She was half conscious. "Maybe . . . your fault."

"It was not my fault," he said loudly. "I had nothing to do with it, yet you believed the first thing you heard and carried on with it. Why, Alice, for God's sake, why?"

There was a shred of consciousness left, and Alice made an effort to grasp it, although her voice was indistinct. "I—I wanted that sarong woman to stop coming . . . on to you. She's a troublemaker. She's a widow and wants me to be a widow, too, by taking you away. Won't let her, specially since she's a widow because of you. It's you who did it to her, not me. Ask Morrison. Now go away and let me—let me have some peace."

It was early morning in the Oval Office, and Underwood, showered, shaved, neatly dressed, was ready to do battle as Ezra Morrison came inside in answer to his stern summons.

Underwood waited for his secretary of state to be seated.

Once Morrison was settled in, Underwood lost no time. "Ezra, you've given me a helluva lot of trouble. I should fire you."

Morrison was all innocence. "My God, Chief, that's tough talk for this hour. Especially when I don't know what in the devil you're talking about."

Underwood fixed angry eyes on him. "You've given me trouble with Madame Noy Sang. You've given me trouble with the first lady. You've accused me of an assassination. What in the hell haven't you done?"

Morrison slumped backward in his chair, as if relieved. "Oh, that," he said. "I'd half forgotten." He sat up. "It's simple, and I don't mind being honest about it. As far as I know, for some reason unknown to me, Alice wanted to know every detail of how Noy had become a widow. She laid it on Blake to find out. Blake came to me; said the first lady was very persistent about this. He wanted to know the truth about Prem's death for Alice. Blake was so anxious for the full story that I contacted the most discreet person I know at the CIA. I spoke to someone and found out what I could find out."

"Someone?" asked Underwood.

"Privileged, Matt. Some things are privileged. Anyway, it's not important who the someone was. Someone who presumably knew what was behind the killing. I learned it was a CIA scam. I'm not saying anyone there did it personally. It was just something to put on their agenda. Something that would benefit the USA. Hell, you get the CIA's NID and FTPO reports daily. I was certain you were aware of it."

Underwood controlled his indignation. "Well, I was not aware of it. Liquidate Prem? No, that was never in any report I saw."

"Maybe the CIA role was secondary, not important enough to trouble you with."

"Bullshit, Ezra. An assassination, even a hint of one, too unimportant to report to the president of the United States? The plan was never reported to me. I received no word from the CIA. Are you telling me they deliberately bypassed me and acted on their own? They made me responsible when I had no responsibility? Dirty pool, dirty poker, plain dirty everything. Ezra, I'm going to get the answers to all this, and fast. I'm going to have Ramage in here within the hour, and I'm going to get the truth out of the director of the CIA."

"Good luck," said Morrison, rising. "You know, Ramage runs his own shop out there."

Underwood stood up. "Maybe he does, but I'm the landlord, and don't you forget that."

After Morrison had left, Matt Underwood sat at his desk awhile, avoiding all calls, to see if he could determine how to handle Alan Ramage.

Soon enough, he realized there were no options. The only way to approach the director of the CIA was to do so directly and frankly. But this was not for a telephone conversation. This had to be done man to man.

At last, Underwood put through the call to Langley.

When he had the director on the phone, he said, "This is Matt Underwood."

"So your secretary announced. How are you, Mr. President? To what do I owe this pleasure?"

"Alan, I want to see you here in the White House."

"Sounds urgent."

"It is urgent, Alan. I want you to get your ass over here immediately."

"Give me twenty minutes," said Ramage.

For Underwood, taking calls again, the twenty minutes went swiftly.

Finally Ramage was announced and was in the Oval Office.

"Good morning, Mr. President."

Unsmiling, Underwood gestured to a chair across from his desk. "Sit down, Alan."

Taken aback by the president's aloof manner, Ramage lowered himself into the chair and waited.

Underwood said, "This has to do with Lampang."

"Lampang," said Ramage. "I thought that was all under control."

"Not quite, not quite," said Underwood. He leaned forward on his elbow, eyes set on the director of the CIA. "There's one bit of unfinished business I want to discuss."

"Sure, whatever that can be."

"It concerns the assassination of President Prem Sang."

Ramage squeezed back in his chair. "What do you want to know about that?"

"Who did it?" Underwood asked harshly.

"Who did it?" Ramage echoed. "The Communists, of course. General Nakorn investigated it, and that's what he came up with."

"General Nakorn is a liar."

"He is?" said Ramage, appearing surprised.

"I know who did it. We did it."

"We? You mean the United States? You can't possibly mean that."

"The CIA," said Underwood. "I guess that's still part of the United States."

"The CIA? You're on the wrong track, Mr. President. We're not in the business of assassination, and you know that."

"You're into some kind of nasty business in Lampang," said Underwood, "and before you leave here I expect to know all about it."

"You'd better clarify what you're after."

"I know some of it, Alan, so no more ifs or ands or buts. This is straight-arrow time. I've been informed we had a hand in liquidating President Prem Sang. Now I want to know if that's true, half true, or not true at all. No more ducking. This is your president you're speaking to. Now it's my turn to listen."

Alan Ramage did not disguise his discomfort. His eyes avoided the president's as they went from one flag to the other behind the president's desk.

He chose his words carefully. "The Company had some involvement, of course," he said. "Whatever you've heard may be partially true, but I assure you it's not completely true. I'll give you the real scenario, as far as I know it." He took a pack of cigarettes from his jacket pocket and held it up. "Mind?"

The president did not mind.

Ramage flushed out a cigarette and put a lighter to it. "All right," he said. "All right," he said again. "We knew we had some enemies on Lampang. We knew that Prem would not give us the air base we wanted, and, more important, that he would not eliminate the Communist insurgents. We knew that if Prem should somehow be put out of office—"

"What does that mean?" Underwood interrupted. "What does 'put out of office' mean?"

"Not killed, if that's what you're thinking. No, rather, forced to resign. Maybe something debilitating that would make him resign. Then he would be succeeded by his wife, Noy, and she would be weaker, easier to handle. There would be an election coming up, and if she ran, she'd be running against General Nakorn, a proven friend of our country. He'd win in a walk and we'd get what we want from him. So I consulted with our station head in Visaka—Percy Siebert, whom I believe you've met—"

"Yes, I've met him."

"—and I told him, I had no choice but to tell him after numerous meetings with Morrison, that we were unhappy with the president of Lampang and would much prefer his wife as president."

"But there were no instructions about assassinating Prem."

"None whatsoever. I told Siebert we had to find a means of getting rid of Prem Sang in an acceptable fashion. I told Siebert to ask around and find out anything he could about Prem that would make Prem throw in the towel."

"Why was I not informed about this in your daily briefing book?"

Ramage squirmed uneasily. "It was a covert operation in a preliminary stage. I don't like to involve you in covert operations until I know for certain what the CIA will do. I thought it was better to tell you about it after we had a direction, knew it could work out, and knew General Nakorn would soon be in the driver's seat."

"What happened next?" asked Underwood.

"I know that Siebert went to General Nakorn and requested his cooperation in finding a means to remove Prem from office."

"And Nakorn chose the quick route—assassination."

Ramage held up a hand. "Easy, Mr. President, we don't know that for a fact."

"We know the assassination happened. That's a fact. Who else but Nakorn could have done it or ordered it?"

Ramage was less certain. "Any of a dozen or more men under him. He may have suggested they investigate Prem, and someone may have taken it upon himself to get rid of Prem. For all I know, Nakorn may have gotten the word to the Communists, and they did it."

"They wouldn't have touched Prem. You yourself said he was on their side."

"Not totally. He was willing to talk to them, but not necessarily give in to their demands. They may have wanted to clean the slate for an easier, softer mark, namely Noy Sang."

"I doubt it. I doubt it very much. I don't think the Communists were responsible."

"Then I don't know who was," said Ramage. "I don't know where the responsibility lies, and I'm not sure that Siebert knows either. The assassination brings us to a blank wall."

Underwood was turning it over in his mind. "Not quite. It was a Company decision, and I'm responsible for all CIA decisions." He scowled. "This was done in my name. I simply was never informed. Had I heard what you were up to, I would have restrained you. I'd have been suspicious that your gang would let it get out of hand and lead to murder. This was done behind my back."

"Forgive me," said Ramage. "I don't know how to put this to you. . . ." He wavered to his feet, and paced back and forth before the president's desk. Then he halted and held his gaze on Underwood. "Mr. President, I must be blunt with you. I'm not sure you'll like it—"

"Go ahead," said Underwood.

"I think it all has to do with how you've been handling your office. You've been delegating matters of state and defense to others, to National Security and people under them. I was aware of this. For that reason, I did not send you our report in its tentative outline. It was something I had every reason to believe you'd delegate to someone with less competence than the CIA to act on."

He returned to his chair and gripped the back of it. "Anyway, Mr. President, it's all too late to change. It's ancient history. There's simply nothing that can be done about it anymore."

The president stood up. "You're wrong about that, Alan. There *is* something that can be done about it, and I'm going to do it. I'm not delegating this one. Good day, Alan. We'll not discuss this further."

Alone at his desk in the Oval Office, chewing away at the hamburger sandwich his waiter had brought in for his lunch, Matt Underwood considered what could be done about the mess he was in with Noy Sang.

There was only one way out, he saw, and he must act on it.

When his chief of staff returned to his own office an hour later, Underwood buzzed him and told him to come right in.

Paul Blake entered, a question on his face, and Underwood gestured him to the same chair that Ramage had vacated this morning.

Once Blake was seated, Underwood picked three sheets of paper off his desk and ran his forefinger down each one in silence. At last he looked up. "Your tentative schedule for the highlights of the next four weeks . . ." Underwood said.

"I hope it's all satisfactory, Matt."

"Fine. No problems." He found what he was searching for on the second sheet. "Except for one change."

"Yes?"

"The invitation to China. It says here I've been invited to attend an anniversary festival in Beijing and meet with the heads of the People's Republic of China." He raised his head. "Is that still in the works?"

"It is and it isn't," Blake said. "The invitation stands, of course. But when I first brought it up with you—well, you turned it down. You felt it was too far to go to watch some dancing and to talk with the Chinese leaders again about nothing of moment. You suggested we send the vice-president in your place. I haven't revised that yet because I felt you should have more time to think it through."

Underwood nodded. "You were right, Paul. I did need more time to think it through, and I have."

"Well, sir, what are your feelings now?"

"I've changed my mind."

Blake sat up. "You're going to China?"

"Definitely. The vice-president doesn't have enough clout to handle a meeting like that. As for the festivities, I don't want to insult our Chinese friends. We must remain on the best of terms."

"Good. I'm glad you see that, Matt."

"You can schedule me for two days in Beijing."

"I'll arrange it."

"Another thing, Paul. Something just as important to me personally." He could see from the expression on Blake's face that his chief of staff had already anticipated what he would say next. Nevertheless, he said it. "I want to get an early start to Beijing. En route, I want to stop over in Lampang for two days to straighten out the misunderstanding with Madame Noy Sang."

It was what Blake had expected, but he offered no reaction.

"I want you to inform Madame Noy Sang that I'll be in Visaka for the express purpose of meeting with her privately. Will you arrange the meeting?"

"At once."

"But before my meeting with Noy Sang, I want you to allow time for me to have another conference, also in privacy, with Percy Siebert, the CIA station head at our embassy in Visaka. I want him to report to my suite at the Oriental Hotel as soon as possible after my arrival. Tell him he is also to accompany me to an engagement I'll have after that."

"I'll see that Director Ramage makes the arrangement for Siebert immediately."

"Thank you, Paul. Get on with it."

After Blake left, Matt Underwood stood up and stretched and felt better. It was a rocky road ahead, he knew. Siebert wouldn't be easy and Noy might be even more difficult.

But it had to be done.

Damage repair, it might be called.

Damage from the first lady.

Or the CIA.

A week later, President Underwood in Air Force One was en route to the People's Republic of China, with a detour first to the island of Lampang.

Having landed in Visaka, Underwood, with Marsop beside him as an escort, was driven to the Leader's Suite in the Oriental Hotel. Marsop had been sent by Noy Sang to meet him and escort him as a matter of formality. Marsop had volunteered nothing about Noy except to say that she expected to comply with his request for a meeting in her office at Chamadin Palace.

Unable to get anything more promising from Marsop, Underwood separated from him at the Oriental Hotel, and, surrounded by his Secret Service detail, he entered for a meeting even less promising and more difficult—one with the CIA station head in Lampang, Percy Siebert.

The meeting with Siebert was as difficult as Underwood anticipated. Only by invoking the power of his office was he able to overcome the CIA agent's reluctance to cooperate. In the end, Underwood won the strenuous confrontation, and after an hour and a half of persuasion—actually of command —he was able to force Siebert to accompany him to the meeting with Noy at Chamadin Palace.

Underwood and Siebert were waiting in Noy's office when she entered.

She acknowledged Siebert and she greeted Underwood coolly. "I'm surprised to see you here again so soon," she said to Underwood. "Please, be seated."

After Underwood and Siebert sat down, Noy went around her desk to her chair.

"Why are you here?" she said directly to Underwood.

"You had accused me of being responsible for your husband's death," said Underwood. "I told you I would investigate the accusation and get to the bottom of it."

"I really think there's no more to discuss about that," said Noy.

"There is much to discuss," said Underwood, "especially when you are not in possession of all the facts. Will you please hear me out?"

"Of course," said Noy wearily, "if you have something to add."

"I had told you I would uncover the truth about your husband's assassination. I had been wrongfully blamed for it. I tried to tell you I don't like blood on my hands, especially when it doesn't belong there. Now I want to straighten all this out. Percy Siebert is a member of our embassy and, as you no doubt know, station head for the CIA in Lampang."

Noy moved her head. "I'm aware of that, Mr. President."

"Well, Mr. Siebert, in a secondary way, was involved in your husband's death, and after learning that I came here to see him, talk it out, and I am now forcing him against his will to let you know what really happened."

Noy's attention swiveled to the CIA agent. "Yes, Mr. Siebert?"

"You understand, Madame Sang, that I am not the main player in this unhappy affair," Siebert began. "I had a role because I was in Lampang. But the orders came from Alan Ramage, the director of the CIA. He informed me that President Prem Sang was obstructing United States policy in Southeast Asia. I was told to find a means of making him a closer ally to the United States—"

"He was an ally," Noy blurted.

"Not quite, Madame. The United States and Lampang had different goals," Siebert replied.

"And assassination was the means of achieving your goals?" Noy wanted to know.

"I never heard that word in my instructions. I was advised to find a nonviolent means. Perhaps a scandal. It is important for you to know that President Underwood had no knowledge of this undertaking, none whatsoever. He was totally innocent of my orders. They were not shown to him. Not even in the

FTPO—For the President Only—report. It was anticipated that he would object. Director Ramage urged secrecy, and I followed the director's orders."

Noy turned her head toward Underwood, and for the first time since they had parted at Blair House, the expression on her face softened and it was friendly.

"It's—it's good to hear that, Matt."

Underwood said nothing to Noy, but gestured to Siebert. "Go on, Percy."

"I tried to imagine whom I might turn to, and finally I chose General Samak Nakorn. I met with him. I briefed him on the wishes of my government. I did not tell him to harm President Prem, certainly not to kill him, but to find some means of shutting him up or driving him from office as soon as possible. I may even have used language like trying to find out if President Prem was involved in some government scandal. General Nakorn promised me that he would see what he could do. He would, he said, find some of his army intelligence staff to look more deeply into President Prem's affairs. In any case, he would see that Prem's resistance to American policy would be taken care of." Siebert caught his breath. "The next thing I knew, several weeks later two men had entered this office and shot your husband. It was not our design or wish. The president was totally unaware of what had been going on. He was not inattentive. He simply did not know."

Noy's gaze settled on Underwood. "I'm sorry, Matt, to have blamed you. I apologize."

"That's all I wanted to hear from you," said Underwood. "That you are satisfied I had no part in this."

"I am assured of that now," said Noy.

Siebert concluded. "The assassination was not the CIA's wish. But it happened. That's all I know."

Noy eyed Siebert closely. "Do you believe it was done on orders of General Nakorn?"

Siebert shrugged. "Possibly. I haven't an iota of proof."

"Nevertheless," said Noy, "I think General Nakorn should undergo a public investigation. He may be the only one who can tell us how the assassination took place. Mr. Siebert, will you cooperate?"

Siebert shook his head slowly, regretfully. "I cannot cooperate, Madame Noy, as much as I'd like to. I've given my allegiance to the CIA and taken an oath of office. I cannot tell my story in public—and I can't be made to. As a member of the United States Embassy, I have diplomatic immunity. I simply cannot reveal what is done in the CIA. I hope you understand that, Madame Noy."

Underwood interceded. "Perhaps an exception can be made in this case, Percy."

Siebert shook his head again. "You know that is impossible, Mr. President."

"Never mind, Matt," Noy interrupted. "I understand his position. Without a trial, a hearing, I will have to do the next best thing."

"What's that, Noy?" asked Underwood.

"Tomorrow, I am going to announce that I plan to run for election on my own against General Nakorn. He announced his candidacy one week ago. The United States believed that if I replaced Prem in office, I would be too weak to beat Nakorn in an election. That has been proved to be wrong. There have been no objections to the air base. It is looked upon as a protection of our democracy. And people are willing to let me meet with the Communists, fellow Lampangians after all, and bring them into our system. As a result, the latest polls show that I am far more popular than General Nakorn. I'll run against him, and I'll defeat him. That is my one ambition now. To retire our ambitious general from public life. Do you approve, Matt?"

"I approve, Noy. I heartily approve."

Noy rose and came around the desk to take Underwood's hand in both of hers. "Forgive me, Matt. I should have known we were on the same side. Have a success in China. Thank God you came here first, and be sure to come here again soon, as soon as possible."

When Underwood returned to his suite in the Oriental Hotel, Paul Blake was already there, packed and ready to leave with him for China.

As Underwood changed into a fresh shirt and a gabardine suit, and watched his valet repacking for the last leg of the journey, Blake stood behind him to question him.

"From your cheerfulness, I gather you had a satisfactory meeting with Madame Noy Sang," Blake said.

Underwood smiled. "Very. With Siebert there I was able to clear up the whole thing, and Noy apologized for blaming me for anything."

"Does she blame General Nakorn?"

"She suspects him," the president said. "She can't prove he was responsible for Prem's death, but she does want Nakorn out of the way. In fact, she's decided not to retire after this term. Tomorrow she goes on national television to announce she will run for election. She expects to beat Nakorn, and, if she is elected, she'll get him out of the way."

Blake watched in silence as the valet finished repacking.

At last Blake spoke. "Matt—"

"Yes, Paul."

"You know, Nakorn is our man in Lampang. We can depend on him."

Underwood locked his bag and lifted his head. "I don't trust him," said Underwood. "I trust Noy Sang."

"Ezra Morrison is already in Beijing. He won't be happy."

"I'm his commander in chief," said Underwood. "I'm the only one who should feel happy." He paused. "And right now I do."

TEN

THE Great Wall Hotel rose imposingly at the outskirts of Beijing. Arriving at its entrance, President Underwood had been impressed by the hives of Chinese heavily cordoned off along the way, their bicycles lined up neatly in row upon row of chromium racks. When he and his retinue entered the hotel he was even more impressed by the size and glitter of its vast lobby.

The hotel manager and Chinese Politburo members tried to lead Underwood to the glass elevators, but when he saw the broad, richly carpeted staircase nearby, he insisted upon walking up to the third floor, where he and Ezra Morrison would occupy adjoining suites. Underwood wanted to walk because he was tired of the cramped feeling he had from the airplane flights, and he wanted the exercise and resultant energy it would induce.

He was feeling somewhat more limber and invigorated

when he reached the third floor. Half of his contingent of Secret Service men had come in earlier with Morrison on the press plane, and they were already in position.

Underwood was shown into his suite, and his valet had gone directly into the bedroom to unpack.

Dutifully, Underwood allowed himself to be led about the suite.

When this was done, the manager said, "Sir, Secretary of State Morrison is in the adjoining suite awaiting your arrival."

"Good," said Underwood. "I'm eager to see him."

Tactfully, the manager and Chinese officials withdrew, and once his valet had left also, Underwood knocked on the connecting door between the two suites.

The door opened and Morrison appeared. They shook hands.

"Good flight?" asked Morrison, coming into the president's suite.

"Perfect. What have you been up to?"

"This morning I went first to T'ien An Men Square. It's still spectacular—and then I had a preliminary meeting with Premier Li Peng in the Great Hall of the People, and we reviewed tomorrow's program. There will be several speakers, but you will be the principal one. Peng will introduce you in the Great Hall, and you'll address the nineteen hundred delegates, and then Peng will close down the ceremony. That's tomorrow. This afternoon is photo-session time around the city. You'll be taken around to see all the sights you've seen dozens of times before. The Chinese press and the American press will love it."

"Sounds easy enough. Let's have a drink."

They were both standing at the small bar before Morrison resumed. "How was your detour to Lampang? Did you get to see Noy?"

"I did, and brought Percy Siebert with me. We were able to resolve everything. Noy and I are on friendly terms again."

"I gather that," said Morrison. "I just saw Noy."

"You saw her?" asked Underwood, startled.

"On television. On Chinese television. I could understand her because she spoke in English. The Chinese used subtitles for her speech."

"How was she?"

"Very effective, I thought," said Morrison. "She announced that she was running for election. I figured you might have had something to do with it. Until now only General Nakorn had announced. Up till now Noy had denied any intention of running. Then you drop in and see her—and suddenly she is going to run."

Underwood nodded. "I may have had a little to do with it, but the decision was her own. After Siebert had finished his explanation of events, she was just about convinced that Nakorn was responsible for her husband's death."

"Surprising, but possible."

"She can't prove it, Ezra. So she wants to crush him in an election, remove him as head of the army, and reduce him to a nobody."

Morrison busied himself with a cigar. "Understandable." He had the cigar ready and lit it. "At the same time, Matt, you know General Nakorn is our man."

"Of course I know. Blake reminded me of that in Lampang."

"We wouldn't want to see him defeated," said Morrison. "We know he's dependable. He believes in the Stars and Stripes."

"So does Noy Sang," Underwood said earnestly. "I'm sure of it."

"I'm not," said Morrison abruptly. "Your feelings about her may be colored by—by her personality. She's soft on Communists. We need someone who is hard on Communists."

Underwood snorted. "You see Communists under every bush. Joe McCarthy is long dead. Let him rest."

"It's my job, Matt. I'm your secretary of state. I don't trust them here, there, anywhere."

"I'm your president, Ezra. I trust them more than I ever did now that we're in a world where we can obliterate each other."

Morrison persisted. "I'd feel safer, much safer, with Nakorn in office."

"Noy's ahead in the polls. I'm certain she'll be in office on her own. We'll have to trust her, and I assure you that we can."

Morrison sighed. "I hope you're right. We can't afford to be wrong. We need strength in Southeast Asia. Which brings me to another thing. I've read the Chinese speech the staffers wrote for you. I presume you have, too."

"You know I have. Carefully." He hesitated. "I toned it down a bit."

"Why did you do that? I liked it the way it was."

"The Chinese are moving toward capitalism and democracy. I'm betting on that. I don't want us to forever treat them as enemies."

Restlessly, Morrison stepped away from the bar. "I hope you're not making a mistake, Matt. We don't know where China will be in the long run. In the short run, right now, China is a Communist state. And the way you're playing it, Lampang could be, too."

"You're too pessimistic, Ezra."

"Maybe yes, maybe no," said Morrison, sucking on his cigar. "My real immediate concern right now is Lampang. At the risk of offending you, Chief, I'd hate to lose a sure thing because you're smitten by someone with great tits in a sarong."

Underwood grinned. "You aren't offending me, except that you sound like my wife. You're absolutely right. Noy is something in a sarong. And yes, I'll bet she has great tits without a sarong. I'd rather bet on tits than on someone who carries—and rattles—a saber."

"I'm not sure love conquers all."

Underwood joined Morrison. "I'm not sure this has anything to do with love. Only that, historically, love does conquer all. Let's give it a chance, Ezra. Let me do it my way. I know what's at stake, but let's do it my way."

Noy Sang had not anticipated that her announcement on television that she was running for election would cause such a furor. General Nakorn had announced the week before, after a convention of the National Independent Party, and there had been little excitement. It had been taken for granted that Noy would not run, and therefore Nakorn had the presidency almost as an automatic matter.

Noy's own unexpected announcement of her candidacy had exceeded every expectation she'd had. Phone calls, press support, and cheering demonstrations throughout the country had followed it.

She had been so caught up and occupied by the excitement that by this morning she'd had a feeling of guilt that she was neglecting those around her. The one she had been neglecting the most, she felt, was her six-year-old son, Den.

Normally, Noy breakfasted with Den before he was driven off to attend his classes at St. Mary's School. From the beginning Noy had made it a point to see that Den was raised, as much as possible, like any other child in the city. She refused to send him to a private school but chose to send him to a public one. This decision gave him an opportunity to get to know average youngsters of his own age, and not just the offspring of wealthy families. Also, Noy had been insistent that he go off to school every day in her personal Mercedes with her own chauffeur, Chalie, driving him. She was aware that if she herself accompanied him it would mean fuss and fanfare, with at least half a dozen security guards preceding and following them. Noy did not want this. She did not want to have Den think that he was something special. So she sent him off daily to St. Mary's with Chalie chauffeuring him in the Mercedes sedan.

But this morning, spurred by her guilt, she had accompanied Den and Chalie to the school. She was suffering a sense of guilt at her time away from the boy, and she wanted to take advantage of every opportunity to be with him and show her interest in him and his classes.

She walked with Den to the main entrance of the school playground, where his three friends—Toru, his best friend, and two others—would be waiting. Den kissed his mother hastily, leaped out of the car, and raced across the sidewalk to greet his friends.

A quick wave and then he was with them in the graveled yard facing the school building.

Satisfied, she sat silently in the Mercedes while Chalie drove her back to the front gate of Chamadin Palace.

Leaving the car, she called back, "Chalie, you pick Den up at two o'clock alone as usual. I'm going to be busy the entire afternoon. Will you do it?"

"As ever, Madame," called back Chalie.

Starting into the palace, there was only one person Noy wanted to contact on the outside with a report of the great reception the televised announcement of her candidacy had received. That person was, of course, Matt Underwood. Glancing at her wristwatch, she reminded herself that about this time Underwood would be in the Great Hall of the People in Beijing, and unavailable for any frivolous call.

She promised herself she would call him in a few days when he was finished with his official business in China and back at his desk in the Oval Office in Washington, D.C.

Over her shoulder she could see Chalie go off in the Mercedes toward the underground garage, where he could leave the Mercedes until it was time to fetch Den.

Driving down the garage ramp, Chalie parked the sedan in the area reserved for the presidential cars.

He opened his door, stepped out of the Mercedes, and turned away from it. As he did so, he heard the scrape of a movement behind him.

Twisting to see what it was, he had only a glimpse of a thick baseball bat in someone's hand. It came smashing down on his head before he could avoid it or defend against it.

The bat struck him full and hard on the back of the skull. His knees buckled and he blacked out.

The Mercedes sedan was waiting outside the St. Mary's School at two o'clock when Den and his friends scampered across the yard toward the exit.

"There's your car," called Toru.

"It's always there," Den called back. "Chalie is on time every day. He's afraid of my mother."

"What's to be afraid of?" Toru wanted to know. "Just because she's president?"

"I suppose so," said Den. "Hey, that was a dumb geography class."

"Not as bad as history," said Toru.

"See you tomorrow morning," Den called back. "Don't forget the movie on television tonight. *Casablanca.* I read it was the most popular one on American television. We'll talk about it tomorrow."

Den dashed out of the yard, leaving his friends behind, grabbed the front door of the Mercedes, yanked it open, and flung himself in beside the driver. His eyes were still on his friends as he waved to them, and the car drove off.

They drove on a half minute with Den looking straight ahead through the windshield. Lost in thought, Den said, "Cripes, another boring day in school, except for arithmetic."

"Ummm," said his driver.

They had come to the end of the block when the car veered sharply right.

"Hey, what are you doing?" Den cried out. "You always turn left here."

He twisted in his seat for Chalie's reply. Only there was one thing wrong.

It wasn't Chalie in the chauffeur's seat.

Chalie had a pockmarked face. This driver had a smooth, plump, brown face with a long, pointed nose.

"You're not Chalie," Den said accusingly. "You're someone else. What are you doing here?"

"Chalie got sick," said the driver. "He asked me to pick you up."

"But this is the wrong way."

"No, it isn't!" a voice said from the rear. Den whirled in his seat to look behind him. He saw a moustached man crouching there, someone who must have been hiding down low on the car floor during the pickup. Den saw that the man was holding a silver gun, just like the ones in the movies. He put the barrel of the gun against the boy's head. "Now, you be quiet, young man, if you don't want a hole in your head. . . . Shove over. Move closer to the driver and make room." He gave Den a push. "Now, move!"

Den began to tremble, which never happened in the movie.

The moustached man was short and squat. He climbed over the back of the car seat and squeezed himself down beside Den in front. Den was in a vise between them.

"Now shut your eyes, because I'm going to blindfold you," the moustached man ordered.

Quickly the man had something over Den's eyes and secured it behind with a double knot.

"I want to see my mother." Den's voice quavered.

The man tested the blindfold and was satisfied. "You're going to see your mother. Unless you make trouble. Then you won't ever see her or anyone else again. Now, keep quiet. We'll get you where you're going in a hurry."

Marsop was in Noy's presidential office, standing at her desk, riffling through her papers for a document he needed.

He was startled by the shrill ring of one of the three telephones on her desk. The ring, and subsequent rings, came from the white telephone, the phone Noy permitted to be used only for calls from members of her cabinet, or for emergencies.

The telephone was clearly for Noy, and Marsop shouted for her. There was no answer. Wherever she was, she was out of earshot.

As the telephone persisted with its urgent ringing, Marsop decided that he could answer it.

He lifted the receiver off the hook. "Hello. President Sang's office."

The voice on the other end was a deep rumble. "Who is this?"

"This is Minister Marsop."

"I must speak to President Noy Sang."

"I'm sorry. She's not in her office."

There was a pause. "You can get a message to her?"

"Of course."

"Immediately?"

"Why, yes. Who is this?"

"I am on the staff of the army."

Marsop thought he recognized the voice. It was a strong bass that had impressed itself on him at cabinet meetings and military meetings. It was a voice that sounded like that of Colonel Peere Chavalit, second in command of the army in influence and Nakorn's closest deputy. Although Marsop could not be sure.

"Are you Colonel Chavalit?" Marsop wanted to know.

"That is of no importance. I wish to speak to President Noy. If she is not there, I will speak to you. You can convey my message to her."

Marsop nodded at the phone. "I'll do that." The tone of the voice, what it was saying, had begun to sound ominous to Marsop. "I am ready to give her any message. Tell me what it is."

"It concerns her son Den Sang."

This was definitely ominous and Marsop held the receiver tightly. "Is anything wrong? Is he all right?"

"Perfectly well."

This was puzzling. "Are you calling from his school?"

"He left St. Mary's half an hour ago, as you can see from your clock."

Marsop sought and found the time on Noy's desk. The time was 2:32 in the afternoon. Den had been scheduled for pickup —was always scheduled for pickup—at two o'clock by Chalie, Noy's driver.

Marsop swallowed hard. "Den—where is Den?"

"With us. With friends."

"Where are you?"

"We'll get to that."

"How do I know Den is there?"

"You wish to hear his voice?"

"I do," said Marsop.

There was a whispered consultation at a distance from the telephone, then footsteps, then Den. "Marsop," Den said shrilly, "I'm here. I am—"

Abruptly he was off the phone. Marsop envisioned that it had been snatched away from him.

The deeper voice was on the phone once more. "You have heard him."

"Is he safe?" Marsop demanded.

"Perfectly, if you attend promptly to the message I wish you to pass on to President Noy."

"Yes, I promise," said Marsop. "What is the message?"

"I want to see President Noy at once."

"You can come to the palace—"

"Don't be a fool. I want to see her on my terms, right where I am."

"If it can be done—"

"It must be done if President Noy wishes to see her son alive."

Marsop's heart tripped. He tried to keep his tone even. Take this seriously, he told himself, but do not panic. "What—what is your message, sir?"

"Listen carefully. Do you have a pencil? Write down what I tell you."

"I have a pencil."

"Very well. Get this right . . . President Noy Sang must come to the corner of—the southwest corner of—Khan Koen Road and Bot Road, and she must come alone. Do you have that? Read it back to me."

Marsop choked. "Southwest corner of Khan Koen Road and Bot Road. Alone."

"Exactly. Have her do that within the hour and she will see her son alive and safe."

Marsop stuttered. "It—it—it may be difficult for the president to leave the palace alone. She has a security guard that follows her every move. I don't know if she can manage this."

The voice on the other end was deeper and angry now. "She will find a way. She must come alone or the boy is dead."

"Wait! Do you have her car—?"

"Her car is in the palace garage."

"Let me drive her!"

"No. She must come alone in a taxi, and no one must follow her. She's to be dropped off three blocks away. Do you hear me?"

"Yes. . . ."

"I repeat. Alone. Or the young boy will be dead."

The hang-up was loud and reverberated in Marsop's ear. He held the silent receiver a moment and then he, too, hung up.

This was shocking. The first thing he must do was find Noy, and then reason with her.

He remained at the desk, hurrying through her papers until he found her day's schedule.

She was in a meeting with a half-dozen of her agricultural staff in the Rama Room.

He went to find her, opened the door of the room, and saw that she was seated at a round table, listening to one of her advisers read to her from a report.

Marsop crossed the room until he reached her, and then, beckoning, he bent down closer to her ear.

"I must see you immediately," he whispered. "This is an emergency."

She met his eyes fearfully.

"Outside," Marsop said.

Excusing herself, she rose from the table and followed Marsop out of the room.

In the hall, Noy grabbed at Marsop's arm. "What is it?"

"Don't get too upset—"

"What is it?" she demanded again. "Tell me."

"Den—" he began.

Her hand went to her mouth. "Is he hurt?"

"No," said Marsop quickly, "as far as I know he's all right. Noy, he's been kidnapped. The word was never used, but there's no doubt it is kidnapping. They're ready to free him, but there's a ransom demand."

"What do they want?"

"You," said Marsop. "I'd guess they're ready to exchange Den for you."

Noy was astounded. "Me? What do they want with me?"

Marsop was uncertain. "They want to talk to you."

"Who are they?"

"I don't know, Noy. The man who called on the telephone —he was actually calling you; I answered the phone—he had a deep voice, but not one I recognized."

"Marsop, tell me exactly what was said to you on the telephone."

He tried to recall every word for her. Then he handed her the slip of paper.

She narrowed her eyes to read it. "Khan Koen Road and Bot Road," she read. "Go three blocks down to Uhon Square, then walk back to this corner." She raised her head. "Are you certain it was Den's voice you heard on the phone?"

"Yes, he was able to say very little. But it was Den."

"It could be a hoax."

Marsop was hesitant. "I doubt it, Noy. Den isn't home from school yet."

Noy pulled at Marsop's arms, and her voice choked. "Let's get to the garage!" she exclaimed.

Preceding him down the stairs, entering the garage, Marsop heard her gasp. "Chalie!" she called out.

Crumpled on the floor beside the Mercedes was Chalie. Noy rushed to him and kneeled, taking his pulse.

"He's alive," she said over her shoulder. "My God, look at the blood on the back of his head. Call my office and have someone get a doctor. Wait here for him."

Back in her office, Noy waited restlessly for Marsop to return, trying to imagine what had happened, and what she herself should do next. In minutes, Marsop was back.

"Chalie is all right," he reported. "A minor fracture, but he'll be on his feet by tomorrow."

Noy listened, and then shook her head. "I guess it's not a hoax. They have Den. I must go along with their demand."

"I'd like to come with you," Marsop begged.

"You quoted the man as saying that unless I come alone, Den is dead. Didn't you?"

"That's right."

"Then I must go alone, Marsop. I can't take chances with those lunatics."

"It could be dangerous."

"I have no choice. It's me or it's Den. For me, Den is everything." She wagged her head at Marsop. "How do I do this alone with six security guards following every step I take?"

Marsop was at a loss. "I don't know."

"Well, I know. Follow me to the kitchen." As they walked through the dining room, she went on. "The cook, Juliellen, she's just about my size. Every day"—Noy glanced at her wristwatch—"just about this time, she goes out to the market. This time she will not go out. But I will."

As they went into the kitchen, Juliellen, who had been reading a newspaper, threw it down and came respectfully to her feet.

"Juliellen—"

"Yes, Madame President?"

"That sweater and skirt and apron you're wearing, is that what you wear when you go to the market?"

"It is, Madame."

"Do you have another set I can wear?"

"You, Madame? Of course I have more, but—"

"Never mind, Juliellen, I need your clothes—instantly. Don't say a word to anyone. I want to wear what you wear to the market."

"I also wear a shawl around my head."

"All the better. Go fetch your clothes. I'll wait for you in the pantry."

Fifteen minutes later, when Noy emerged from the pantry, she was wearing a gray sweater and blue denim skirt identical to Juliellen's. Taking the shawl from Juliellen's hand, she tied it over her head and tried to conceal her face in its folds. "How do I look?"

"Not very presidential," Marsop replied.

"This should get me past the front gate. Where do I get a taxi?"

"A block south of the palace. There are always several in front of the church."

"Then, I must hurry."

Marsop was at her heels as she started to leave. "Noy," he pleaded, "I can't let you go by yourself."

"You must. Anything else will endanger Den."

"This may endanger you."

"Never mind. Just remain at my desk. I'll get in touch with you. Can you give me some money?"

Marsop reached into his jacket pocket. "What if you don't call?"

"If you don't hear from me in an hour, contact the police. They'll be familiar with the area." She started to leave. "Marsop, you stand by, and pray for both of us."

After the taxi brought her to Uhon Square, she hastily paid her fare and left the cab.

She surveyed the area, confused, then intercepted a young man carrying some packages and asked the way to Khan Koen Road and Bot Road.

The boy pointed west. "Three or four blocks that way."

Checking her watch, Noy saw that she was still within the designated time. She began to walk as fast as she could. The walk seemed interminable. Suddenly she realized that she had arrived at her destination. She crossed Khan Koen Road to the southwest corner and stopped, and stood with her back to a cluster of trees, apprehensive and wondering if Den's captors would deliver him.

Realizing she was wearing Juliellen's clothes and might not be immediately recognizable, she untied her head shawl so that her well-known face would be instantly identified.

She waited five minutes and was becoming more and more nervous when she heard light footsteps behind her. She whirled about just as Den, unwrapping a blindfold, stumbled toward her, calling out, "Mother!"

Noy ran to him with an exclamation of relief, and fell to her knees as he came into her arms. She hugged him as tightly as possible.

"Den!" she cried out. "You're safe. Are you all right? Did they hurt you?"

"No, Mother, I'm fine, but you must look out—"

But by then, when she looked up, there were two others looming over the pair of them. They were both husky young men wearing sunglasses and attired in army fatigues. Around their waists, through their loosely hung khaki jackets, she could see holstered guns.

One soldier tapped Den on the shoulder. "Let her go, kid. You can get going. She will stay."

"No—" Den protested.

The nearest soldier tore Den out of her arms. "Go, while you can!"

"But where? . . ."

Noy had risen upright. "Do as they tell you, Den. Walk in that direction. You will find a taxi. Have it take you to the palace." She dug into her skirt pocket for some change. "Take these to pay the taxi. When you get to the palace, go directly to my office. You will find Marsop. Tell him I will try to see him soon."

"Enough talk," the second soldier said harshly, fingering his revolver. With his free hand he gave Den a shove. "Go, leave, at once!"

Den turned away and began to run.

Noy watched him, her eyes filling with tears of relief.

The soldiers had flanked her now. Each had her by an arm. Roughly they swung her around toward the trees.

"Come, Madame," one said.

"Where are we going?"

"To have a talk with someone waiting for you," the first soldier answered. "Now, get going, faster, faster!"

Den Sang had found a taxi and taken it straight to the palace. Inside, he had hurried to his mother's office, where Marsop was seated on a corner of her desk with his eyes fixed on the phone.

The second that Den entered, Marsop rose and embraced him.

"What happened?" Marsop wanted to know. "Where is your mother?"

"They took her, two men took her. They sent me out to see her on the corner, and then they followed and grabbed her and let me go. She told me to find a taxi and come here."

"But where did they take her?" Marsop begged the boy.

"I don't know. They made me run away for a taxi. Then they started taking her toward the trees—"

"What trees?"

"Trees at the edge of the park. I could see them after they took off the blindfold."

"You were blindfolded?"

"Yes, then they untied it and there she was. Then they grabbed her."

"They had guns?"

"Yes, Marsop, each of them, under their army uniforms."

Marsop had been standing over the boy, and now he bent toward Den and took him by the shoulders.

"All right, Den, now tell me about yourself from the start. You were in school. You left—"

"With my friends. I ran to the car and went inside."

"That wasn't your car. Your car is still here."

Den lifted his hands. "It was the same car, Marsop."

Marsop understood. "They substituted another just like the Mercedes. Then what?"

"I didn't see Chalie at first. I was busy waving to my friends. The driver started the car away, and then I saw that he wasn't Chalie."

"No, he wasn't. What happened next?"

"We drove away from the school. A big man who must have been hiding on the floor in back jumped up, crawled over the front seat, and pushed me to the middle. He took a handkerchief and blindfolded me."

"Did he say anything? Did the men speak?"

"No. They drove on and on and then stopped."

"How long did the drive take you?"

Den was lost. "I don't know."

"Guess."

"A long time. Maybe fifteen minutes. Maybe more."

Marsop tried to analyze the drive, the distances beyond Khan Koen and Bot Roads, but it was impossible.

"Then what happened?" Marsop asked.

"It felt like we went down in a garage like ours. They pulled me out of the car. We went through a door to stairs. They helped me go up the stairs."

"One flight? Two?"

"Two flights. I counted the steps. They pushed me into a room. When I was inside they took the blindfold off."

"Tell me what you saw." said Marsop. "Try to remember, Den."

"Four men in the room, in uniforms."

"Did you recognize any of them?"

"No."

"Did they use each other's names?"

"No, they were quiet, except for one of them. He asked for Mother's private number. He said he'd kill me if I didn't give it to them. I gave it, and he went into the next room to call."

"Yes, I answered the call," said Marsop. "It was for your mother to go to see you alone."

"Then they tied the blindfold back on and took me down the stairs to what I guess was the garage. We drove around many corners. Then we stopped, and they dragged me out and put me behind some trees, until the blindfold was untied. Then I saw Mother."

Marsop sighed. "And they took her away. And made you run off."

"Yes. Why did they want Mother?"

Marsop stared at the telephone on Noy's desk. "I expect we'll know soon enough."

They sat talking about inconsequentials, about school, Den's classes, and soccer football—although Den was worried about his mother.

When the white phone on Noy's desk rang, they both started.

Marsop went quickly behind Noy's desk, perched on the front of her swivel chair, and lifted the receiver.

"President Noy's office," he said.

"This is Noy," the strained voice on the other end said.

"Thank God it's you!" exclaimed Marsop. "Are you all right?"

"I'm fine. The important thing is Den. Did he return safely?"

"He's with me now. Unharmed."

"Tell him I love him."

Marsop called over the telephone to Den. "Your mother sends her love. She says she's all right. Noy, is anyone listening to you?"

"Yes and no. In the room, not on an extension."

"Do you recognize anyone?"

There was a silence.

Marsop pressed on. "Is Colonel Chavalit one of them?"

"No."

"You're kidnapped?"

Noy hesitated. "I'm told I'm being held in custody."

Marsop could hear an indistinct male voice from somewhere beyond Noy.

Immediately she said to someone, "Yes, yes, I will hurry. Marsop—"

"I'm listening."

"I'll be released," said Noy, "but there is a condition. You must do what they want you to do. With my approval, of course."

"Go on," said Marsop anxiously.

"You must announce on television and to the press that I will not run for election," said Noy. "Because of poor health," she added. "You will inform General Nakorn that as president I have ordered a special election to be held a week from today. Do you have that right?"

"I'm afraid so," said Marsop dully. "You will not run for election against Nakorn because of ill health. I am to call him and tell him it is your wish that a special election be held in one week. When am I to do this, Noy?"

"Now," said Noy. "Call General Nakorn right now about the election. Arrange to appear on prime time on television tomorrow evening with a short statement that I am in the hands of my physicians."

"When will you be released?"

"The day after the election," said Noy.

Marsop wondered if he dared say more. "Is there anything else you want me to do?"

"It would be good if you could get someone from the out-side to visit the palace and confirm to the world that"—she paused—"that I am sick."

"Someone?" Marsop echoed. "Who?"

That instant the telephone rang off.

Marsop put down the receiver slowly.

He was on his own and afraid.

There were calls he had been instructed to make, but there was one he must make before any of the others.

Because he had understood Noy. He knew who the someone was. The person who must come visiting.

Immediately he picked up the telephone again.

In Beijing, President Underwood sat in the front row of the Great Hall of the People with members of the Chinese Polit-buro Standing Committee.

He had just finished delivering his speech, a successful one, he thought, when he saw Ezra Morrison hastening along the front row toward him.

Morrison came before him, knelt, and said, "Mr. President, there's a long-distance call for you."

"Washington?"

"No, Lampang."

"Who's calling? Noy?"

"It's Minister Marsop. He says it is extremely urgent."

Underwood came to his feet immediately, worried. "Where do I take the call?"

Apologizing to those around him, he followed Morrison out of the Hall to a side door where a Chinese official was waiting for them.

The three hurried to a small room, empty except for a table and chair, with a telephone on the table. The receiver was off the hook. Underwood picked it up. "Marsop?"

"Yes, Mr. President. I'm sorry to interrupt, but I must speak to you. About Noy. She—"

The telephone went dead.

Underwood showed his irritation. "Disconnected."

The Chinese official took the phone, punched a button, reached someone, presumably the operator, and began to speak in Chinese.

At last he hung up. "If you will wait here, Mr. President, the operator will try to get you the caller in Lampang again."

"Je-sus," Underwood said to Morrison, "what can that be? Well, not a thing to do but wait."

"I'm sure it'll only be a minute," said Morrison.

It was five minutes more than a minute when the telephone pealed again.

Underwood snatched up the receiver. "Marsop?"

"I am here again."

"You were beginning to mention Noy." Underwood waved Morrison and the Chinese official out of the room, and when the door was closed, he clutched the phone tightly. "Marsop, is anything wrong?"

"Something is wrong, yes."

"We are not on a safe line. Does it matter?"

"I cannot go into details. But I have spoken to Noy. She could not speak freely, except one thing. She wanted me to get in touch with you. I was afraid to interrupt, but—"

"You did the right thing," said Underwood. "Noy can't speak to me, yet you spoke to her. It makes no sense."

"You will understand when I can explain."

"You want me to come to Lampang?"

"If possible, before you return to Washington. I will be here waiting in the palace for you. When you are here, I will explain everything in person. It is better."

Underwood felt a constriction in his chest. He did not like the sound of the call. He was gripped by anxiety.

"Is this a matter I can do something about?"

"I don't know, Mr. President. At any rate, Noy seemed to think so. She feels you can be helpful."

"Then I'll come there at once."

"When can I expect you, sir?"

"Overnight," said Underwood. "I was going to leave China this evening. I still will. But I'll come straight to Lampang, before going to Washington."

"We would be most grateful," said Marsop.

"I gather this is really urgent."

"Yes, it is."

Underwood inhaled and then exhaled. "I'll see you sometime in the morning."

He was immobile for half a moment, trying to imagine what was going on. He had a suspicion, yet he wasn't certain. But he was certain what was to be done next.

He rose, left the room, and went into the corridor of the Great Hall, where Morrison was restlessly pacing.

Morrison came to him at once. "What is it, Matt?"

"I don't know exactly. But something is wrong down there."

"Something urgent?"

"Marsop left no doubt about that. I'm needed there as soon as possible."

"You mean you're going to take Air Force One to Lampang before going to Washington?"

Underwood took his secretary of state by the arm and moved him down the corridor.

"I must do this," said Underwood. "I have no choice. It's something I wanted to do anyway."

Morrison showed his dismay. "It's a drastic move, Matt. It screws up a lot of things. You're expected in Washington."

"I'm also expected in Lampang. That gets top priority in my book."

"Well, you have an idea what is going on, and I don't. So whatever you say."

"That's what I say, Ezra. Lampang first. Look, you oversee our scheduled return. You and Blake get on the press plane and take off. Just go on as if nothing has happened. I'll take Air Force One after that along with the Secret Service."

"There will be a lot of questions," Morrison said gloomily. "You insist on this, Matt?"

"I insist on it," said Underwood.

ELEVEN

HY Hasken had taken a taxi back to the Great Wall Hotel in Beijing, and in the privacy of his single room he put through a call to Sam Whitlaw at the offices of The National Television Network in New York City.

Still suffering a hangover of jet lag from his endless flight to China, Hasken was mixed up about the time difference between Beijing and New York.

When a night editor made him aware that he had the time backward, and that Sam Whitlaw was at home, Hasken consulted his pocket address book and found Sam's home number in Manhattan.

Once again Hasken put through his long-distance call, and after a handful of seconds Whitlaw answered it. He did not sound sleepy, but then Hasken remembered that his boss was rarely sleepy. He was accustomed to being awakened at any hour of the morning, and always alert for some sudden-breaking news.

"Hello."

"Sam. Is that you? This is Hy Hasken in Beijing. It's seven tomorrow evening where I am. Can you hear me all right?"

"Where?" said Whitlaw, less alert, momentarily befuddled, so that Hasken knew that he had been sleeping.

Hasken raised his voice. "I'm in China. Beijing, China."

"Oh, yes. With the Pres. How did his speech go?"

"Excellent. He's good at that, you know."

"So he impressed them," said Whitlaw. "No news there. What are you calling me about at these prices?"

"The Pres," said Hasken. "He's doing it again."

"Doing what again?"

"Changing his itinerary without telling anyone. He was supposed to leave Beijing for Washington tonight. He's sending the press plane ahead, and he's pretending he's already left for Andrews Air Force Base. Only he hasn't. He's making a detour. He's going to Lampang instead, before proceeding to Washington."

"To Lampang? On a schedule he hasn't announced?"

Hasken confirmed it. "Like he did last time. Remember when he came to Lampang for the funeral of Noy's sister? Remember he gave himself an extra day to go sightseeing with Noy and went swimming with her? You remember the super pictures I got?"

"I certainly remember. That was great," said Whitlaw.

"Only because I stayed over; refused to take the press plane back. Well, I'm doing it again. I'm dogging the president's footsteps. I'll have to take a commercial plane back, but I'm sure you'll agree it's worth the investment. Maybe it'll cost a little more, but it could be worth it."

Whitlaw didn't speak a moment. Then he spoke. "Why is Underwood going to Lampang out of schedule?"

"I don't know, Sam. But I'm suspicious."

"How did you get onto this?" Whitlaw asked.

"I saw Ezra Morrison come into the Great Hall. He had a whispered consultation with the president. Then they both left. I slipped out of the press section and followed them. Actually, I was only hoping for an exclusive interview on the results of the China trip. I figured if I couldn't see the president alone, I could corner Morrison. The two of them went into a room, apparently to take a telephone call. I got out of sight and ducked into a phone booth, leaving it partially open—"

"A phone booth in China?"

"The coming of democracy. When Underwood and Morrison came out of the room, they walked up the corridor together, talking. I could hear them. That's when I heard that the president was diverting to Lampang, and sending the press plane ahead to Washington. I heard the president tell Morrison to accompany the press and to take Blake with him. Afterward, Morrison announced that the president was too busy for a press conference, and that he himself would hold a press conference on the press plane. He promised to answer all the questions about the president's China trip. The press accepted that as routine. But not me. I knew about Lampang, and I figured there might be a better story there."

"So you're letting the press go ahead, but you're not going to be with them."

"I want to go to Lampang."

"With no idea what's up."

"No real idea," said Hasken. "But it has got to have something to do with Noy. Everything that involves the president in this part of the world does. And way back, at the start, you told me to stick to the president, wherever he went, whatever he did."

"I said that? I guess I did."

"So now that he's unexpectedly heading for Lampang, I believe I should be there to greet him."

"Will he see you?"

"It all depends on why he's there. If he won't see me, I can hang in close."

"If you think you can . . ."

"You know me, Sam."

"So why are you calling me?"

"No press plane," said Hasken. "I have to do this on my own. That means TNTN pays."

"An ordinary commercial flight shouldn't be much."

"There's no commercial flight until later this evening. I'd get into Visaka after the president arrived. It would be harder to see him."

"What are you suggesting?"

"A charter flight from China to Lampang. If I left soon, I'd be there to welcome Underwood."

"Hey, that could be a helluva lot of money."

"True," admitted Hasken. "If it leads to something, it's a bargain. If it adds up to nothing, it's a loss. What do you think?"

"I don't know what to think. You have a feeling something is going on in Lampang?"

"A gut feeling," said Hasken.

There was a silence on Whitlaw's end of the phone. "I'm mulling it."

"Whatever you say, boss."

A longer silence. At last Whitlaw found his voice. "All right, one word."

"Say it."

Whitlaw said, "Go."

President Underwood arrived in Visaka on Air Force One late in the evening.

He had tried to nap on the flight from Beijing, but he was kept awake by a turmoil of speculations. Marsop, a quiet, conservative man, had requested that he come to Visaka at once. That meant an emergency of some sort. The fact that Marsop had made the call instead of Noy meant that she was not available—unless she was ill—and that something drastic was afoot.

Fully awake, Underwood tried to imagine what could be going on. Without a real clue, it was impossible to guess. He would simply have to be patient and wait for an explanation from Marsop.

Would Noy be on hand to do the explaining? If she hadn't telephoned him herself, it was unlikely that she was available.

If she wasn't available, where was she?

When Air Force One landed and rolled to a halt, the president half expected Marsop to be waiting for him. But Marsop was not to be seen. Instead, a limousine and two Fords were on standby, the limousine for himself, and the other cars for the six Secret Service agents to precede and follow him. Also, Underwood noticed, two cars of army guards, Noy's personal security force, were on hand to flank him for the drive into the city.

Since, at Underwood's request, there was no motorcade and no sirens were used, the journey from the airport into Visaka was slowed, and the party did not arrive at the Oriental Hotel for three quarters of an hour.

Four of the Secret Service men rushed ahead to go upstairs

and check out the president's suite. The other two Secret Service agents accompanied Underwood into the hotel.

As Underwood entered the hotel, there were guests lined up on either side, held back by Noy's security guards, to see what kind of celebrity was arriving. From one group of onlookers, a man burst free in an effort to approach the president. He was immediately grabbed by a security guard and blocked by one of the remaining Secret Service men.

When Underwood saw who it was who'd tried to intercept him, there was an immediate expression of dismay on his face. Nevertheless, he ordered the agent to stand aside and allowed Hy Hasken to come forward.

"What in the devil are you doing here?" the president said angrily. "You're supposed to be on the press plane on your way back to Washington."

Without flinching at the president's tone, Hasken stood his ground. "Morrison said I could have an interview with you or him about the China trip," Hasken said. "Since Morrison is giving the interview to the other correspondents on the press plane, I thought I'd stay behind and try for an exclusive interview with you."

"No way," said Underwood with rising fury. "I'm much too busy for that."

"Mr. President, Lampang wasn't on your agenda—"

"It wasn't because I hadn't intended to be here. An emergency came up."

"Business or pleasure?"

"Certainly not pleasure," said the president heatedly. "This is a matter of state."

"I'd be curious to know . . ."

The president had been moving through the lobby, with

Hasken beside him. Now the president suddenly stopped and turned on the journalist.

"Hasken, when have you had enough? The last time you pulled something like this, you invaded my privacy; tried to prevent me from having a day's vacation. You succeeded in showing President Noy in a close-up in the worst way, dressed in a sarong, which made both of us appear frivolous and was entirely misleading. Now you're trying to invade my privacy again, and I won't let you."

"Mr. President, my job is to cover you, wherever you go. I'm merely fulfilling an assignment, as I'm sure you are. I hope you'll be more understanding."

"I just don't want you near me," the president flared. "I have more things on my mind than a ridiculous press interview. Just stay out of the way, and keep out of sight while I'm here. Thank you. Good-bye to you—and, I might add, good riddance!"

In his suite at the Oriental Hotel, Underwood began to unpack his traveling bags, and then stopped doing so. He had no idea how long he would be here—an hour, several hours, a day or more. The thing to do as swiftly as possible was to find out why he had been summoned and what was going on.

He telephoned Chamadin Palace, asked for President Noy's office, and got Marsop.

"I'm so glad you're here," said Marsop. "We need you."

"What's going on?" Underwood wanted to know.

"Can you come right over," Marsop asked, "or would you prefer I come to you?"

"I'll be right over," said Underwood.

A half hour later he was in Chamadin Palace and was escorted to Noy's office. Shown inside, he was surprised to see that Marsop was not alone. Noy's son, Den, was with him.

Underwood shook hands with the boy.

"How good to see you, Den."

"Good to see you, Mr. President."

Marsop came forward and took Underwood's hand. "I'm glad you're here, Mr. President."

"I came as quickly as I could," Underwood responded.

"I can't tell you how much we appreciate that," said Marsop. "Please sit down."

Underwood took a seat and surveyed the office. He saw that he was alone with Marsop and Den. The swivel chair at the executive desk was empty.

"Where's Noy?" Underwood asked.

With difficulty, Marsop found his voice. "She's been kidnapped."

Underwood was plainly shocked. He had not known what to expect, but this least of all.

"Kidnapped?" he repeated incredulously. "Noy's been kidnapped? Why? By whom?"

Marsop held up his hands to indicate he had no satisfactory answer. "We don't know by whom. We can take an educated guess, but it is not a certainty. As to why, that is easier. Noy's captors allowed her to speak to me on the telephone. She instructed me to tell the nation she will not run for election."

"That's outrageous!" Underwood exploded. "I expected her opposition to be unhappy. I did not expect them to go this far!"

"They are serious," said Marsop.

"What happened? Tell me from the beginning."

Marsop pointed to Den on the sofa. "It started with Den early yesterday afternoon."

Underwood came about in his chair. "What happened, Den? Can you tell me?"

The young man's reply was negative. "I get mixed up, maybe because I'm scared. It is better Marsop tell you."

Underwood directed his attention to Marsop. "All right, you tell me."

Marsop nodded. "Very well. Noy takes her son to school when she can. Yesterday morning she decided to do so. She took him in the Mercedes with Chalie driving."

"Who is Chalie?"

"The chauffeur. He was the family's driver before Den was born, when Prem was still alive."

"He is reliable?"

"Thoroughly. He had no part in this, as you will see. Anyway, they left Den off at the school, and then they drove back to the palace. Chalie was assigned to pick up Den at the school, as he did every day at two o'clock. Chalie returned Noy to the palace, and then went to park in the underground garage. Someone was hiding there, and struck him a blow on the head and knocked him unconscious. We found him later. He's alive, but with a fractured skull."

"Then another driver replaced him in the Mercedes."

"Yes and no. Another driver, but in a Mercedes that was a replica of the one in the garage. This car was waiting for Den when he got out of school. With his three best school friends he came across the school yard and jumped into the car, as he did every day. Only after he had been driven away from the school did he realize he was with another driver and something was wrong."

Underwood looked at the boy. "So you were abducted first. Any idea where they took you, where you were going?"

Den made a face. "No, except the driver turned a different way."

"A different way?"

"We always turned left to go to the palace. This driver turned right."

"Then what did you see?"

Marsop interrupted. "Den could not see a thing, Mr. President. Apparently a man was hidden on the floor in the rear. He jumped up, climbed the front seat, and blindfolded Den."

"So he couldn't see where he was headed?" said Underwood.

"Only that it took maybe twenty minutes. It's hard to know exactly."

"So maybe twenty minutes," Underwood said to the boy.

"I could not know," said Den. "It felt like longer."

Underwood understood. "It would if your eyes were covered."

Marsop went on to explain that the boy's blindfold was removed after they had him inside what Den guessed was a second-story room. The room resembled a living room, sparsely furnished, and there were four men in army uniforms in it.

Underwood listened, seeking some clue. There were none. The abductors had not been amateurs.

"Then they called Mother," said Den. "They told me I could see my mother again if she did as she was told."

"Could you hear what they told her?"

"She was not there. They talked to Marsop. I heard a little. About coming to some place alone to be traded for me."

Underwood gnawed his lower lip. "Did Marsop think they were lying about having you?"

"I guess so, because one of them with a deep voice said Marsop wanted to hear me, hear me speak. They took me to the phone. They said I could say, 'Marsop, I am here.' They told me if I said anything else, they would kill me. I was scared. I did what they told me."

"And Marsop knew that it was you they had?"

"Oh, yes."

Underwood confronted Marsop again. "Tell me how the exchange took place."

Marsop described how Noy managed to leave Chamadin Palace in her kitchen maid's clothes, undetected and alone. Then he explained how she arrived at the designated corner and was baited with the release of Den, and added that before she could follow him, two men grabbed her and took her away. "Then she was forced to call me."

"What she had to say was very clear?"

"It was exact. Obviously she had been rehearsed in advance."

"Did she sound frightened?"

Marsop offered a ghost of a smile. "You know her. She does not frighten easily. Noy sounded quite calm."

"Repeat for me the terms of her release once more."

"She will not run for election against Nakorn. I am to announce it on national television tomorrow evening. I am to say she is very ill, too ill to run. I am to say that the election, at her request, is to be held in one week."

"And after that?"

"After Nakorn is elected, Noy will be released."

Agitated, Underwood rose and began to pace. "Do you believe that, Marsop?"

"Why not?"

"You may be naive." Underwood gave Den a quick glance and returned to Marsop and said in an undertone, "They may see fit not to release her."

Marsop had not even considered such a possibility. "Not release her?"

Underwood dipped his head in assent. "That's right. She could be an embarrassment to her captors. Speak out. Tell how she was coerced."

"Would anyone consider this kidnapping to have been possible?"

"Enough to put Nakorn in trouble, give him real opposition."

Marsop was helpless. "But what would they do with her?"

Underwood glanced at Den, who had begun to whimper, and said, "You know."

"They would do such a thing? Even if we met their terms?"

"The stakes are high, Marsop. Tell me, when Noy spoke to you, how did you know she wanted me here?"

"She did not mention you by name, of course."

"Of course not. She couldn't."

"She suggested that I get someone from the outside to visit the palace and confirm that she was ill."

"You're sure she meant me?" asked Underwood.

"Who else from the outside could she mean—especially since you were relatively nearby, in China?"

Underwood stood still, briefly puzzled. "What did she think I could possibly do?"

Marsop threw up his hands. "I have not the faintest idea. Perhaps your importance and arrival here would give her captors pause about what they were up to."

Underwood was doubtful. "No one knows I am here."

"Tomorrow your press will have it in print. Not why you are here, but that you are here. Also, spies—our army has endless spies—will know of your arrival in Lampang and checking into the hotel. It will be known everywhere."

"Do you think my presence in Visaka could influence Noy's captors?"

"Personally, I do not think so," admitted Marsop. "However, you do have a relationship with Noy. She regards you as clever. She might guess you will start looking for people who could have some idea who's holding her captive and how she might be rescued."

"Looking for people," Underwood mused. Suddenly he sat up and snapped his fingers. "There might be someone."

"Someone?"

"Percy Siebert."

"The head of your CIA station in the United States Embassy?"

"Yes, Siebert. He knows Noy. He was with me when I brought him to Noy to speak of her husband's death."

"Of course."

"Furthermore, he has countless other contacts in Visaka. He might be the direction to head for. He might give me a clue about where to start."

"You will see Siebert?"

"As soon as possible." Underwood crossed to Noy's swivel chair behind her desk and moved a black telephone closer. He dialed the United States Embassy in Visaka.

An operator answered.

"Percy Siebert, please," said Underwood.

"Who is this, may I ask?"

"The president of the United States."

The operator's voice was uncertain. "The president?"

"You heard me," Underwood snapped. "I must speak to Siebert at once."

"He's out of the city, sir. I do not know his movements. I do

259

not know where he can be reached. He will be back in the embassy in the morning. I can give him a message, sir."

"You give him this message," said Underwood. "Tell Siebert the president of the United States called and wants to see him at the Oriental Hotel bright and early tomorrow morning." Then with emphasis Underwood added, "Tell him it is top priority. I must see him as soon as possible."

It was early in the morning as Matt Underwood gulped a quick breakfast and awaited the arrival of Percy Siebert.

A knock on the door brought in Secret Service Director Frank Lucas and two of his agents instead.

"Your visitor is outside," said Lucas.

"Send him in," said Underwood.

Lucas said, "Well and good, but I'd like to leave two of my agents in the adjoining room."

The president's response was emphatic. "I'm about to have a private talk with my CIA station head in Visaka. I prefer to have no one within listening distance, certainly not closer than the corridor outside."

"Well, I'd prefer—" Lucas began.

"I'd prefer nobody around." Underwood cut him off. "This is the CIA, and I don't want a word overheard. All that I want to know is that you've swept this room clean and the other rooms as well."

"They're clean, Mr. President. No bugs. You can speak freely."

"Good," said Underwood. "You and your agents post yourselves outside. When you've done so, send Percy Siebert right in."

While Lucas and the agents backed out, Underwood tried to

organize what he would say to Siebert when the CIA man arrived.

In a minute Siebert was in the sitting room.

The president pushed his breakfast tray aside, rose, and extended a hand to the CIA man.

"Good to see you here again, Mr. President," said Siebert. "This took me by surprise. Your message indicated there is some urgency about meeting."

"There is," said Underwood. "Take that chair."

Siebert sat down, alert and wondering, and Underwood pulled up another chair opposite him.

"This concerns President Noy, once more," said Underwood. "The last time I brought her up with you, it was a personal matter, a defense of myself. This time it is more serious."

"What is it?"

"Do you know that President Noy is missing?"

"Missing? I'm afraid I don't understand you."

Underwood studied Siebert's countenance to try to detect any contradiction in what he heard and what he already knew. He decided that Siebert was genuinely bewildered.

"Noy has been kidnapped," said Underwood flatly.

Siebert's eyes bulged. "I can't believe that."

"You'd better believe it because it's true." He continued to study the CIA man. "I was sure you'd know something about what happened."

Siebert was still astonished. "This is the first I've heard of it."

"I thought the CIA had its finger on everything."

"I wish that were true. It isn't. It's a fallacy of fiction. We try to know a good deal, and we do know a good deal, but we're only as good as our sources. No one even hinted at a kidnapping. What happened to Madame Noy?"

Crisply Underwood began to outline what he knew. He started with the call to Beijing from Marsop. "She wanted me here, so I came at once." Underwood then recounted what he'd learned from both Marsop and Den Sang. He backtracked briefly to explain how the kidnapping had come about. He spoke of the abduction of Den, of the trade for Noy, and of Noy's phone call to Marsop, ordering him to withdraw her from the election to assure her safe release.

Siebert absorbed it all and uttered one word: "Incredible."

"It is incredible, kidnapping the president of a country in broad daylight," agreed Underwood. "Now that you've heard it all, I'm hoping you can shed some light on it."

Siebert made a gesture of surrender. "I'm as much in the dark as you are."

"Think back. Not even a hint from anyone at any time that this could have happened?"

"I swear to you, Mr. President, I don't have a clue."

Underwood considered what Siebert was saying. "Then, you may have a clue to something else. Who could have done it and with what motive?"

Siebert spoke instantly. "I think that's rather obvious."

"I think it is, too, but I'd like to hear it from you."

"All right. Noy reverses herself and announces to the nation she will run for election against General Nakorn, and immediately—"

"According to your information, would she win such an election? You were present when she showed her confidence in winning."

"Polls have her a shoo-in. So do my best contacts. People

like her. Of course, Nakorn has a following, but not equal to Noy's."

Underwood was satisfied. "Very well. Let's go back to what you started to say. Noy announces for election and immediately —immediately what?"

"She's kidnapped. The ransom is a stiff one. She must withdraw from the election."

"And who benefits?"

"General Samak Nakorn. He would have the field to himself. It would be a Ya vote—a Da vote—he'd be the new president. Most people in Lampang, the majority, would be displeased. But those in your own government—yourself excepted—I mean Ramage and Morrison, would be mightily pleased. They could have an ally to massacre the Communists and be true-blue to the United States."

Underwood blinked at the last. "You're not suggesting that Director Ramage or Secretary of State Morrison engineered this kidnapping?"

"Good God, no. Ramage and Morrison are capable of many things, but not an act like this, especially when they know how you'd feel about it."

"So what you're saying is that the real winner in this, the one person to instigate the kidnapping and demand Noy's withdrawal from the election, is the Lampang Army chief of staff."

"General Nakorn. He'd come out the winner in this."

"Are you accusing Nakorn of doing this?"

"I'm not accusing anyone, Mr. President. I'm merely suggesting who stands to gain by it. Maybe Nakorn didn't do it. Maybe one of his overzealous aides decided to do him a favor. That's a possibility. But a greater likelihood is Nakorn himself. He's a ruthless son of a bitch, capable of any act of violence."

"So if I want to get to the bottom of this and save Noy, all roads lead to Nakorn."

"You have nowhere else to go. All other roads lead to a dead end. It's Nakorn or nothing."

Underwood weighed the possibility. He did not like it.

"You think a meeting with Nakorn provides any hope?"

"As president of the United States, give him the go-ahead to wipe out the Communists for your sake, and give him the added weapons to do so, and he may be cooperative enough to investigate this kidnapping. But not a certainty. He still wants to be president."

"And I want to retain the president who's been kidnapped."

"Difficult."

"I guess there's nowhere else to go but meet with General Nakorn."

"You may get lucky," said Siebert dryly. "Don't count on it."

President Underwood was in Noy's office in Chamadin Palace, seated behind Noy's desk, seated rigidly in Noy's leather swivel chair, awaiting his visitor.

Earlier, Underwood made his next move. He had telephoned Marsop in Chamadin Palace and spoken to him.

"I want to see General Nakorn," Underwood had said. "In Noy's office in the palace in an hour. Do you think you can arrange that?"

"I can try, Mr. President."

"I think Nakorn will come around. I'll be waiting for him."

"Uh, Mr. President—"

"Yes?"

"If Noy should call again to find out what progress is being made, what should I tell her?"

"Try to tell her I'm here from China and doing my best. Better, for the sake of the others holding her, let her know you are going to comply with the ransom demand. Assure her you will address the nation tomorrow evening and withdraw her name from the election—on one condition. That in no more than a half hour after your address, her captors will release her unharmed on the very corner where she was kidnapped."

Marsop had been quiet. "They can promise anything."

"Worth trying."

"Mr. President, do you still mean for me to give that television address to the nation?"

"Prepare for it, plan on it. Between us, I'm no closer to finding out who kidnapped her. But I'll keep trying."

"Please."

"Then the next step is General Nakorn. Get him for me."

"I'll get him," Marsop had promised.

Now President Underwood was seated in Noy's place, awaiting his visitor.

More than an hour had passed since Underwood had instigated the meeting, and he was becoming apprehensive.

That instant the inner phone on the desk buzzed, and Underwood snatched up the receiver.

"Yes?"

"Your visitor is here, sir," Noy's secretary announced.

Relieved, Underwood said, "Show him in."

He rose just as the side door from the reception room opened, and General of the Army Samak Nakorn entered in full uniform.

The president had forgotten that, while Nakorn was much shorter than he, Nakorn was much broader. He was a barrel of a man in an immaculate uniform, his chest filled with ribbons, and he was holding his braided cap.

Nakorn crossed over quickly, grasped Underwood's out-stretched hand and, following Underwood's gesture, sat down alongside the desk.

Underwood returned to Noy's chair, disconcerted that Nakorn revealed no significance in where the president had chosen to sit.

"Aren't you surprised to find me here?" Underwood asked.

"No," said Nakorn calmly. A smile flicked his face. "We have very good intelligence in Lampang. Even if it were not so good, Air Force One is impossible to overlook."

"Aren't you curious as to why I am here?" Underwood wanted to know.

"I am most curious," said Nakorn. "I haven't the slightest idea." His gaze wandered around the office. "I half expected President Noy Sang to be with you."

"If your intelligence is so good, you must know that she is missing."

Nakorn had been phlegmatic, but momentarily he seemed taken aback. "Missing? What do you mean by that?"

"Kidnapped," said Underwood evenly. "She's been abducted."

"I can't believe that. Who would dare—"

"That is why I wanted to see you. To find out if you can tell me who would dare to do this."

"Me?" said Nakorn. "I know nothing about any kidnapping. Why should I?"

Underwood was stony. "Because you stand the most to gain by it."

"In what way?"

"You've announced you are running for election. After that, she announced she was running against you. If she can't run against you, then you are elected."

For the first time Nakorn showed some animation. "Are you implying I had her kidnapped?"

"I am saying you could profit by it."

Nakorn was grim. "Much as I respect your high office, Mr. President, I feel that I deserve an apology. You do me a grave injustice. You insult me."

"I will apologize when I am convinced you are not involved. At the moment, I am less than certain. The kidnappers have relayed word that they will hold President Noy until she publicly withdraws from the race against you."

"This is news to me. I am looking forward to the election campaign against her. I do not want her to withdraw."

Underwood's irritation had mounted. He came out of the swivel chair. "Then find her," he said harshly to Nakorn.

Nakorn remained unmoved. "Do you have any clues to her whereabouts?"

Underwood considered informing Nakorn how it had all come about, but then he thought better of it. If Nakorn had any involvement, it would be unwise to let him hear what was already known.

"I have no clues," said Underwood. "Surely, with your vast military resources, you could find a means of tracing her."

Nakorn came to his feet. "In kidnappings there are limited means of searching. One goes to the victim's enemies, to begin with. In this case, through our computers I can find a list of persons who have threatened her in letters and speeches. I can also interrogate members of the opposition parties who stand the most to gain by her withdrawal. There is only so much I can do until I find a useful lead. But I'll certainly try."

"You might try one more thing," said Underwood.

"What would that be?"

"Interrogate closely your own aides and confederates, those who would like to see you elected above anyone else."

"I could not do that. Each and every one is loyal to me—and to their president, Noy."

"General Nakorn, I speak to you as commander in chief of the United States, and as an ally of Lampang. Unless I know that you are doing everything in your power to rescue Madame Noy, I am afraid our future relationship will be gravely impaired. Do you understand me?"

"I understand you. I can only do what is possible. I am not sure rescuing President Noy is at all possible before she withdraws."

"You will do what you can," said Underwood icily. "And I will do the same, you can be sure." He paused. "You know where to reach me if you should suddenly find the impossible, possible. Good day."

On the way back to the Oriental Hotel, Matt Underwood felt stymied. He'd seen Siebert with no luck. He'd met with General Nakorn with no give. He wondered to whom he could turn next. He considered returning to Chamadin Palace after a brief rest and questioning Marsop thoroughly. They could draw up a list together—the very list General Nakorn had spoken about—of Noy's enemies and her opposition. He'd discuss the names and possibly try to see several of them.

At the Oriental Hotel, once more accompanied by the Secret Service, Underwood took the elevator up to his penthouse suite.

Going along the corridor toward his suite, he could see Director Frank Lucas posted at the stairwell that led to his door, and someone, back turned, talking to him or questioning him.

As he neared them, Underwood could make out the second man. He was Hy Hasken, the television correspondent.

Lucas had gone ahead and unlocked the president's door and opened it, and as the president started inside, Hasken tried to follow him. Lucas blocked the way.

"I thought we might have a talk," Hasken said across the Secret Service director.

"I don't think so," Underwood replied. "I'm too busy to discuss China."

"Not about China," Hasken said.

"No? Then what about?"

"Lampang," said Hasken evenly.

"What about Lampang?"

"Something I've found out." Hasken glanced at Lucas and the other Secret Service men. "Do you want me to discuss it out here in the corridor—or would you rather discuss it with me in privacy?"

Underwood considered the television reporter briefly, with undisguised distaste.

He directed himself to Lucas. "Let him in for a minute, Frank. I want to find out what's on his mind."

Lucas unbarred Hasken's entry and let him through the metal detector. Hasken tracked after the president, shutting the door behind them.

The two stood in the middle of the living room. "What is it?" Underwood asked.

"This may take a little time," said Hasken. "May I sit down?"

"Sit down," said Underwood brusquely.

Hasken settled in a corner of the sofa, and Underwood came down edgily in the armchair beside it.

"I'll tell you why I wanted to speak to you," said Hasken.

"I can't wait," said Underwood.

"You're not here on state business," said Hasken. "I have a good hunch it is something personal."

"Is this what you're taking up my time to tell me?" said Underwood with considerable annoyance.

"There's more," said Hasken.

"There is? Fill me in on it."

Hasken drew in his breath. "What I have to say to you concerns Madame Noy Sang."

"Yes?"

"Madame Noy is unavailable or missing. My bet is on the latter. I say she's missing."

"That's a wild shot," said Underwood. "Where'd you pick up that nonsense?"

Hasken's gaze was fixed on Underwood. "It's not nonsense, Mr. President. I believe it's a fact. I can't prove it, not yet, but I'm sure it's a fact. Noy is missing, and my guess is that you're here to find out what is going on."

Underwood met the reporter's gaze. "I repeat, where'd you pick that one up?"

"By hanging around Chamadin Palace. By listening. By asking questions and hearing the answers. By checking out Madame Noy's usual routine for two days. By learning that such a visible person is suddenly not visible. I think you'd be wise to confirm it and let me in on it."

Underwood shifted restlessly in his chair. "There's not a thing to let you in on. You're taking a wild shot, and it's wide of the mark."

"You won't help me?"

"Even if I could, I wouldn't." He paused. "Not you."

"You're making a mistake, Mr. President."

"I'm not, but if I were, it wouldn't be my first. You're really fishing, Hasken, and there's nothing to catch."

"One more chance, Mr. President."

"Good-bye, Mr. Hasken," Underwood said firmly.

With an elaborate shrug, Hasken came to his feet. He stood over Underwood. "Let me say this, Mr. President. I'm going to find out why you're here. I'm going to find out why you're in Lampang when you're supposed to be on your way to Washington. When I do find out, I won't have you to thank for it. I'm going out on my own to run down Madame Noy. I'm just going to remind you of one thing, Mr. President. I'm the best investigative reporter in the business. Of the three thousand journalists covering Washington, there's no one better, no one who can do what I can do. I'm going to learn the truth about Noy with or without you."

Hasken's certainty shook Underwood. He watched the reporter head for the door, and one sentence that Hasken had spoken stuck in his brain. *I'm the best investigative reporter in the business.*

Underwood had been trying to play investigative reporter himself, but without success. He did not have that kind of imagination or devious turn of mind. He didn't and he was at his rope's end. Desperation time.

He knew he had to hold on to Hasken. It was time to put aside differences, get himself an ally who possessed the armament to give him hope.

Hasken, hand on the doorknob, was about to depart when Underwood called out. "Mr. Hasken!"

Hasken's hand left the doorknob and he turned. "Yes, Mr. President?"

"Come back here. I want to talk to you after all."

Without another word, Hasken made his way back to the sofa and gingerly sat on it.

"I'll make no bones about our relationship," the president began. "I've never particularly liked you. I've always found you too snoopy. But it is this very quality in you that appeals to me now. I'm willing to let bygones be bygones and settle into some sort of working relationship, presuming I can trust you."

Hasken nodded solemnly. "If you have to trust me to go on with me, if that's what stands between us, I assure you that you can trust me totally."

"I take your word," said Underwood. "What caught my attention and turned me around, made me call you back, was the remark you made that you are the best investigative reporter in the business. You have no doubts about that, do you?"

"None whatsoever. I have the skill and the patience. If something must be found out, there is every likelihood that I can get to the bottom of it. If not always, then ninety percent of the time. So you can have faith."

"I'm going to depend on you for something extremely important."

"You can do so."

The president nodded. "I'm not an investigative reporter, and you are. I'll discuss the outline of the problem with you, thoroughly, fully, if I have your pledge once more that you will not use what I tell you in your work. You will be tempted, but I must have your pledge not to make it public until the problem is resolved. Will you promise strict confidentiality?"

"I promise it," Hasken said sincerely.

"I had best pose the problem as a hypothetical case, and learn if you can suggest any way to approach it."

"Go ahead, Mr. President."

Underwood found it difficult to know how to begin, then at

last he began. "There's a local woman who has a son. She drops the boy off to school. She does not pick him up. She sends her car and driver to do so. Before he can make the pickup, the driver is knocked out, another driver substituted for him, and a similar car used for the pickup. The boy is abducted, held hostage in the city, and his mother is ordered to come alone to a certain street corner to get him. She does so and is kidnapped. She is held for ransom. I would hate to see the ransom paid."

Hasken shook his head. "You're not leveling with me, Mr. President."

"How so?"

"I don't want a hypothetical case. I want the real case. I want to hear the facts. It's obvious to me that the mother is Madame Noy Sang and her son is Den Sang."

Underwood sighed. "I found it difficult to bring their names into this—even with you."

"You must be completely frank," said Hasken. "Otherwise, I cannot help you."

Underwood surrendered. "All right. Noy and Den. As you seem to know, Noy is missing. She's been kidnapped. The ransom demand is that she withdraw as candidate for election."

Hasken gasped. "Do you have any leads, Mr. President?"

"No leads. Suspicions, but not a solid lead."

"Suspicions can become clues."

"How can we find Noy?"

"Well, now that I know it's Noy, and that her son was involved—"

"And Minister Marsop, too. He was drawn in when he took the call from Noy's son."

Hasken appeared reassured. "Okay, we may be getting

someplace. Maybe I can help you. But I'll have to hear the whole story, every detail of it, down to the most minor, seemingly unimportant fact. I'll have to question the boy. Then Marsop. But first you. Start talking . . . sir."

TWELVE

F ROM his suite in the Oriental Hotel, President Underwood put through a call to Minister Marsop at Chamadin Palace.

"Marsop? This is President Underwood at the hotel. I'm with someone who thinks he can help us."

"To find Madame Noy?"

"Yes, to find Noy."

"Is he a detective?"

"No, not really. His name is Hy Hasken, and he's a White House television correspondent from Washington, D.C."

"He will not let this matter be public?" asked Marsop anxiously.

"Mr. Hasken is sworn to secrecy. He is what we call an investigative reporter."

"I am familiar with the expression."

"Even though he's not really a detective, he works like one,

maybe even better," said Underwood. "He wants to interview both you and Den about everything that happened. Is Den there?"

"Yes, I thought it better to keep him out of school until everything is resolved. Den is in his bedroom, watching television."

"We'll need him and we'll need you. Mr. Hasken wants to review the whole matter with both of you personally. He'll probably have questions I did not think to ask."

"We will do the best we can."

"Good. Hasken and I are on our way over."

In thirty-five minutes the four of them were gathered together in Noy's office in Chamadin Palace.

Den and Marsop were seated erect and alert on the sofa, facing Hasken, who had taken a small notebook and pen from his jacket pocket. Underwood sat nearby behind the reporter. He wanted to be unobtrusive and allow Hasken to have center stage.

Hasken addressed himself to the boy. "I'm going to ask you a lot of questions, Den. No matter how silly or unimportant they may seem to you, I want you to answer each and every one in the best way you can. Will you do that?"

"I will try," said Den.

"Let's start with where you began and go right up to the moment you were released by the kidnappers. Shall we?"

"Yes."

"Now you left school. Who left and what happened?"

Listening to Den, Underwood heard it all again, and he couldn't imagine how Hasken would find any more clues in what he heard than in what Underwood had heard.

But suddenly Hasken was asking Den something that Underwood had failed to ask because he had seen no purpose in it.

"Your three school friends," Hasken said. "Do you want to tell me about them?"

"Tell you what?"

"Their names, let's begin there."

"Toru is my best friend. Then there are Sorik and Sassi."

"What are their backgrounds?"

Den was puzzled. "What does 'backgrounds' mean?"

Hasken, at once aware that young boys of that age would have little awareness of background, revised his question.

"Den, do you know what work their fathers do?"

The boy thought about it. "Toru's father has a factory."

"What kind?"

"Uh, I don't know. Yes, I do. He makes ceramic plates. Sorik's father makes—publishes a magazine about Visaka. Sassi's father is a lawyer."

"Do your friends ever talk about what their fathers are interested in?"

"Interested in?"

"Like hobbies that your friends know about."

"Toru's father collects foreign cars. Sorik's father writes stories, and lets Sorik help him. Sassi's father saves lots of money."

Hasken laughed. "A good hobby. Let's go back a bit. You're in the Mercedes and your eyes are covered."

Den went on from there, relating everything he had told before.

"You're sure it was two flights up to the apartment where they held you."

"Two flights up."

"How many people in the apartment?"

"Four men."

"Can you describe them, tell me what they looked like? Tall, short, heavy, skinny, moustaches, scars, anything?"

Den fumbled trying to describe the men. To him they were just four soldiers who looked alike.

"The room where you stayed," Hasken persisted. "Was it empty?"

"There were places to sit."

"Describe them if you can."

Den couldn't very well. He remembered wooden chairs, a table, and a couch.

"Were there windows?"

"Two."

"Could you see outside?"

"No, they would not let me near the windows. But I could see from across the room. There was another apartment across the street."

"Across the street. Not next door."

"It was further away. So it must have been across the street."

Den went on to the telephone call to his mother. He had not heard it all, except that he knew his mother was not near her emergency phone. Marsop had answered instead.

"Did you speak to Marsop?"

"Yes, they pulled me to the phone and said to me, 'Tell him you are here. Just so he can know it's you. Not another word.' So I said that, and when I wanted to say more, the man took the phone away from me and pushed me back to my chair."

As he concentrated on the questions and answers, Underwood could not see where this was leading, or that Hasken's so-called investigative reporting was turning up anything at all.

Hasken had finished with Den and was concentrating on Marsop.

"They told you to tell Noy to come alone to the southwest corner of Khan Koen Road and Bot Road?"

"To go beyond it three blocks and go back to the corner and wait for Den."

"Marsop, can you find me a map of Visaka?"

"I'm sure Noy has several in her desk." He was going through her drawers as he spoke, and at last he found a map and unfolded it. He scanned it quickly, then rose and took the map to Hasken and pointed.

"There it is, Mr. Hasken. The southwest corner of Khan Koen Road and Bot Road."

Hasken studied the area on the map. "It seems to border on a park. I can see the wooded area, beyond the corner."

As Marsop sat down, Hasken resumed questioning him.

When Hasken had finished his interrogation, he said, "Thank you, Minister Marsop. Thank you, Den. I'm sure you've told me everything you can remember. I appreciate that."

Hasken swung around in his chair and directed himself to Underwood.

"I think I have everything I need to know. It isn't much, but it may give us a start."

"Is it helpful?" asked Underwood impatiently.

"It might be. Now we're going to find out."

"How?"

Hasken was thoughtful for a half minute. Then he spoke again. "By starting where the whole thing began, and reenacting it every step of the way, as far as we can go. I'd like to start with the school, with the moment the school day ended and Den came outside with his three friends. Let's take two cars. You and I, Mr. President, can take the little Volvo I rented. Den and a driver—is Chalie well enough? . . . He is? . . .

Chalie can drive Den in the Mercedes, and we'll follow them
to the school." He jumped up. "Let's get going."

There were four cars in all heading for St. Mary's School.
With the chauffeur, Chalie, his head bandaged and Den
beside him, leading the way driving Noy's Mercedes 450 sedan,
the others followed. There was Secret Service Director Frank
Lucas and an armed agent in the front seat of the next car.
After that came Hy Hasken and President Underwood in the
Volvo. Another Secret Service car and agents brought up the
rear of the small caravan.

Arriving at the chain fence that surrounded the school, they
all left their cars and gathered before the open gate.

"You wait here," said Hasken. "I want to speak to the principal briefly. Den, take me to the office."

Underwood, surrounded by his Secret Service men, wondered what this would accomplish, but he crossed his fingers
and kept his silence. He watched as Hasken and Den hurried
across the yard.

Inside the school, Den led the way. Hasken followed him
across a stretch of tiled floor, around a corner, and then into a
reception room.

"The principal's office," Den announced.

A drab-looking gray-haired woman, obviously the principal's secretary, looked up.

"Den Sang," she called out, "we didn't expect to see you
today. Minister Marsop called and told us what happened."

"It was scary," Den said.

"Did someone really kidnap you?"

Den confirmed this. "They kept me just a little while, and
then they let me go."

The secretary studied Hasken. "Den, who is this gentleman?"

"He's an American reporter. He's trying to find out who kidnapped me. He wants to see Miss Asripon."

The secretary stood up. "I will tell her you are here." The secretary disappeared into the inner office, and quickly reappeared. "You may go in now."

Before they could start for the principal's office, Hasken put a hand on Den's shoulder. "Den, you wait here. I want to see Miss Asripon alone."

Hasken went into the office by himself.

Miss Asripon, a thin, small, worried middle-aged woman, was on her feet expectantly.

Hasken shook her hand and introduced himself.

Miss Asripon said, "This is in relation to the awful kidnapping attempt of Den yesterday?"

"Yes. I'm with the president of the United States, Matthew Underwood, who is outside with his Secret Service. As a friend, I'm trying to give him a hand. Actually, I thought I'd start my investigation here."

"I'm afraid I can't be of much assistance," said Miss Asripon stiffly. "I did not witness it. I only know what Minister Marsop told me earlier."

Hasken made it clear he understood that. "It's not you I'm after," said Hasken. "I really want permission from you to talk to three of Den's friends who did witness the kidnapping."

The principal said, "They're in their history class just now."

"I wonder if I could borrow them from the class for a short time?" asked Hasken.

"You have their names?"

"Toru, Sorik, Sassi."

Miss Asripon softened. "Fine young men. They're on the

third floor. It will be less disruptive if I fetch them myself. You wait in the courtyard with Den. I'll deliver them shortly."

Watching from amid his Secret Service guard, President Underwood observed Hasken and Den before the building, and then saw a woman hurry three small boys out the front entrance of the school.

Underwood could see that Den was having a joyful reunion with them.

The president broke free of his Secret Service detail. "Frank," he said to Director Lucas, "I think I should be over there with Hasken and the boys. Stay here. You can keep an eye on me. You have a faint idea what this is all about. So for now, stand tight. I don't want those kids intimidated by the bunch of you."

Starting across the gravel school yard, Underwood met Hasken and Den and Den's three companions halfway.

Politely, Den introduced Underwood to Toru, Sorik, and Sassi.

"Are you showing Mr. Hasken how you went to Den's car yesterday?" inquired Underwood.

"I'm showing him," said Den, waving to his companions to keep pace with him.

Den began to run across to the gate, as the three boys scrambled after him.

As quickly as they could, Hasken and Underwood stayed at the youngsters' heels.

At the gate, the boys came to a halt. "There was the Mercedes, just like it is now," Den said, indicating the car he had been driven to school in yesterday and the car he had just been driven in to show Hasken and Underwood to the gate.

"But that's not the Mercedes you jumped into," said Hasken.

"I thought it was," said Den. "That's why I got right into it."

"What about you boys?" asked Hasken, addressing Toru, Sorik, and Sassi. "Did you think it was the same Mercedes that always picked Den up?"

"Yes," Sorik and Sassi each answered.

"No, it wasn't," Toru piped up. He added, "When it started to drive off, I could see that it was different. I called out to Den, but it was too late. He was gone."

Hasken took a hard look at Toru. "You know about cars. You can tell one from another."

"My father collects them," Toru said.

"All right, Toru," Hasken went on. "What did you see that was different?"

"The wheels," said Toru promptly. "The Mercedes that took Den away had special custom-made wire spokes. Fancy ones."

Hasken was impressed. "Very observant of you, Toru. The regular Mercedes doesn't have those spokes on the wheels?"

"Never. Spokes like that have to be customed specially. Only one car dealer in Visaka does that."

"Who's that?"

"Muchizuki. Not far from here. He makes fancy things for cars that are different. He makes wheels with wire spokes."

"Muchizuki? Do I have the name right?"

"That is correct. I have gone with my father to see him many times."

"Does your father have spokes on his wheels?"

"No. It is too expensive."

"And Den's mother doesn't either."

"No, as you can see."

"But the Mercedes that picked Den up did have these spokes?"

"Yes. Beautiful ones."

"So Mr. Muchizuki must have made them?"

"He is the only one in Visaka to do this."

Hasken spun from Toru to Underwood. "Maybe we're getting somewhere, Mr. President."

"I hope so."

Hasken took the president's arm. "I think the time has come to see Mr. Muchizuki."

Toru joined Den in Noy's Mercedes, which Chalie was driving.

Hasken, after sending Sorik and Sassi back inside the school, followed Chalie, Den, and Toru, with President Underwood in the front seat beside him. Frank Lucas and the Secret Service detail drove in front of and behind Hasken's Volvo.

They had driven a mile when Underwood could see up ahead that Toru's arm had darted out of the car window and was pointing toward their destination a block ahead.

As they drew near, Underwood could see that Toru was pointing toward an automobile repair shop. There was a display window in front, with a yellow BMW filling the window and a spacious work area toward the rear. Alongside the shop was an alley that led to a parking area in the rear. Marsop drove around a Secret Service car, beckoned the others to come after him, and he turned into the alley with the other three cars right behind.

Once they were parked, they all jumped from their cars and followed Toru and Den into the shop. A small, begrimed man in coveralls was spraying the chassis of a Honda. Quickly Toru went to him and interrupted him to say, "I am Toru, and I have been here with my father many times."

"Ah, yes, yes," said Muchizuki. He peered past the boy at the others, and was troubled by the number of men who were filling his shop. "There is something I can do for you?"

Toru edged closer to the repairman and began to whisper to Muchizuki, bringing his friend Den in closer to explain about him, and then turning to identify Hasken and Underwood.

The repairman was instantly awed by the fact that he was receiving the president of the United States as well as a famous television personality from America.

After further explanations by Toru, the elderly repairman set down his can, wiped his hands, and accompanied Toru and Den. He did not shake hands, but bowed to Hasken and Underwood instead.

"You want to know if I make wire spokes for the wheels of the Mercedes," said Muchizuki.

"We're told you are the only one who customs these wheels," said Hasken.

"It is true," the repairman answered. "I have tried to import spokes from the United States and from Germany, but it is impossible. I have to make them myself by hand."

"Are you sure that you are the only one in Lampang who does this?" Hasken asked.

"The only one. It is difficult and costs high sums."

"Have you made many such wheels?" Hasken inquired.

"Four in ten years," said Muchizuki. "I have a sample wheel in my office. The other three I have made on order for customers."

"Only three?" interjected Underwood.

"Three. I remember exactly, since there are so few."

"These were ordered by men?" Hasken asked.

"Men who are interested in dressing their cars the best possible."

Hasken stepped forward. "Mr. Muchizuki, do you have the names and addresses of these three people?"

"I do, of course."

"Were they all sedans?"

"They were. You would like to know of these three gentlemen?"

"Their names and addresses."

"I have those. If you will excuse me, I will go through the work ledgers in my office."

"We will be glad to wait," said Hasken.

Muchizuki left them, walked to a corner glass enclosure that served as his office, and could be seen taking ledgers off a shelf and placing them on his desk.

Underwood watched briefly and looked at Hasken.

"What do you think, Hy?"

"If he actually has those three names, it could be the lead we need."

"That was a smart idea, interviewing Den's friends."

Hasken grinned. "In years of investigative reporting, I've learned that kids often observe more than grown-ups. They have been some of my best sources."

They continued watching Muchizuki in his glass enclosure, and they could see him making a few notes.

It was ten minutes longer before he emerged carrying a piece of notepaper.

He handed the slip of paper to Hasken. To Underwood he said, "Those are the names. Mr. Suraphong, who is employed by the Tourism Authority of Lampang, on Khong Road. Then, Mr. Prayoon, who owns a store called Imported Thai Jewelry, which is in the Loei Mall. Finally, Mr. Ratanadilak. I have no business for him, but his address is the Mai Sai Apartments. That's on Tassman Road. They all bought and used wire-spoked wheels on their Mercedes sedans. I hope this is useful for you."

Leaving for the rear parking lot, Underwood asked Hasken for the map of Visaka he had used in Noy's office. Hasken took the map out of his jacket pocket, and turned it over to Marsop.

Opening the map, finding a pen, Marsop marked the spot where they were. Then he found and marked the areas where Suraphong, Prayoon, and Ratanadilak might be found.

Underwood took the map. "Marsop," he said, "drop Toru back at the school, then you and Den go back to Chamadin Palace in case Noy is heard from again. Hy Hasken and I will check out our leads."

"Very well," said Marsop, leading the boys back to the Mercedes.

Underwood turned to Hasken. "Now let's start on these three names. Let's begin with Suraphong, the tourist fellow."

Hasken opened the door of the Volvo. "Off we go," he said, "and let the gods be with us."

The gods were not with them on their first two calls.

It took an hour to make the calls. Mr. Suraphong, a clerical type, left the Tourism Authority offices to proudly show them the spokes on the wheels of his cream-colored Mercedes. He had papers to prove it had always been cream-colored, never black, and intensive questioning made it clear he knew not a thing about politics, least of all about Noy.

Mr. Prayoon left the jewelry import shop in his wife's hands as he brought Hasken and Underwood out to his parking area to reveal to them his crimson Mercedes with its spoked wheels. He was even less knowledgeable about politics than Mr.

Suraphong, and while he'd heard Noy's name, he had no idea if she would run for election, and didn't very much care.

"Discouraging," Underwood told Hasken as they remained outside. "There's just the one with the crazy name."

"Ratanadilak," murmured Hasken, staring at the name of the one on the note-pad piece of paper the repairman had written on. "I don't know why it sounds familiar to me."

"It does?"

"Yes. You know, I'd like to get to a phone and ring Chamadin Palace. I'd like Marsop to check it out. Let's use the telephone in the jewelry store."

Presently Hasken was on the phone and speaking to Marsop. There was a wait while Marsop, on the other end, apparently checked out the name. When Marsop came back to the phone, Hasken listened, and broke into a broad smile.

Hasken gripped the president by the arm and led him outside. "I think I may have it, Mr. President," he said with an air of excitement.

"Ratanadilak?"

"Yes. I thought I'd seen it before on a press roster. He's a major in the Lampang army. He's an aide to Colonel Chavalit, and Chavalit is an assistant to General Nakorn." Hasken's excitement mounted. "I think we've nailed our kidnapper. The Mai Sai Apartments on Tassman Road. I'll bet that's where they've got Noy. And I'll bet there's a black Mercedes sedan there with wire-spoked wheels. Let's go."

Underwood did not move. There was a troubled expression on his face. "Hold it," he said. "I'm not sure I want to move in on them with this whole crowd of Secret Service. It could scare them off, and if there's lots of gunfire, Noy could get herself killed."

"Well, what do you want to do?"

"Have a word with the director of the Secret Service, with Frank Lucas."

President Underwood beckoned Lucas and drew him aside.

"Frank," said the president, "I want you to do me a favor."

"Name it."

"You know there's been some trouble over Noy. . . ."

"The woman you were with in Washington."

"The one. She's president of Lampang."

"I know that, of course."

"She's been abducted."

"I gathered that, also," Lucas interrupted. "I've had my ears open."

"Hasken and I have an idea where she is," Underwood went on. "We want to get her out of there as nonviolently as possible. The people who are holding her may give her up when they learn who I am, and that I've come to get her."

"They may not, Mr. President."

"In any event, I can't have you at my heels. The crowd of you may scare her captors and they may do her harm, or worse. Hasken and I have to do this alone."

"I can't allow you to take such a risk."

"You must. Make believe I'm Harry Truman. That's my command. He used to go it alone, and I must—this once. Frank, I'm dealing with a personal matter, not a presidential one. You need not be far behind, but you must remain out of sight. I think you can take a position four or five blocks behind Hasken and me. That would at least be a precaution."

Lucas's reluctance remained. "Forgive me, Mr. President, but the secretary of the treasury will have my ass if he ever learns about this."

Underwood dismissed the fear. "Never mind. I'd fire him before he could fire you. I'm still the president."

Lucas considered what the president had been saying. "Well, if you say so."

"I say so."

Lucas nodded. "You'll need a means of electronic communication, same as the agents on the detail have, so you can really call us if things get rough. Hold on."

The director of the Secret Service strode over to one of his agents. When he returned to Underwood he had a tiny radio transmitter in his hand. "This is a wire top," he explained. "A tiny radio transmitter powered by a miniature battery. You can hook it onto your belt. If you need help, press the button here. It will send an RF signal to this receiver in my ear. It'll give off a vibration. If I should hear it, I'll be on the run with all of us."

"Thanks, Frank," the president said, attaching the wire top to his belt.

Lucas had bent down, lifted a trouser leg, and unstrapped something. He held it up. It was a holster packed with a gun. "A Smith and Wesson .66," Lucas explained. "Each of us is equipped with two weapons. An Israeli-made Uzi submachine gun under our jackets, and small arms, usually this Smith and Wesson or a Sig Sauer P-226 strapped somewhere else, often to our legs." He handed the gun to Underwood. "If you're doing something so foolish, you ought to do something else that is just as foolish. Put this gun in your pocket. God, I never dreamt I'd see the day when I was arming the president of the United States. You're sure you'd fire the secretary of the treasury before he bounced me?"

Underwood held the Smith and Wesson. "Never mind. You'll never be fired. Show me how to use this gun."

Lucas showed him.

President Underwood pocketed the gun.

"I guess I'm set."

"One bit of advice," Lucas said. "In a situation like this, don't use the gun to threaten anyone else." He paused. "If there's real danger, use the wire top on your belt. Only if you must—shoot right back."

They were a block away on Tassman Road when Hasken squinted through the windshield of his Volvo and said quietly to President Underwood, "I see it."

Underwood leaned forward and followed his gaze, and then nodded. "I see it, too."

On the far corner was the five-story white stucco building bearing a black and red sign that read MAI SAI APARTMENTS.

"Let me park here," Hasken said. "We can walk the rest of the way and scout it out."

Parking alongside the curb, they both left the car, and side by side started walking toward the apartment building.

"What do we do next?" said Underwood.

"I want to go to the entrance and check the mailboxes," Hasken said. "I want to be sure that Ratanadilak's apartment is the corner one on the second floor."

"What if he used another name?"

"Why should he? It's his own apartment, I'm sure."

They were nearing the Mai Sai building.

"I'm afraid of one thing," said Underwood. "That they may spot us and make a run for it to another hideout with Noy. Do you think they'll see us?"

"You can be sure they will. They'll be on the lookout for anyone strange. Someone will be watching from the apartment window or down in the street. They'll know who we are, too. Mr. President, you haven't exactly an unrecognizable face, even in Lampang."

"That's what I'm counting on," said Underwood. "That knowing who I am, they won't risk harming us. I expect them to be impressed enough to let Noy go."

"Forget it," Hasken said curtly. "You're not going to get a chance to talk to them. That's a foolish idea, if I must say so. These are desperate thugs acting under orders. They don't give a damn who you are. They want Noy and her concession on television. Once they spot us, they may fire at us—but more likely, instead of creating all that commotion and attention, I'm positive they'll make a run for it. They must have a fallback plan." He glanced at the president. "Maybe we should use our own first fallback plan right now and summon the Secret Service."

Underwood was adamantly opposed to it. "That's sure to mean a gun battle. Noy could be hurt or even killed. I won't risk that."

They had covered the block and slowed down.

Hasken looked over his shoulder, down the intersecting street, and Underwood did so, too. They saw a shabby street-vendor selling ripe fruit. There was a woman lounging behind the wheel of a parked Ford. There was a teenager lolling against a lamppost, smoking a cigarette and reading a newspaper.

"One of them's a lookout," Hasken whispered. "We'll have to move fast. You'd better take over the entrance and examine the mailboxes for the apartment number. I'll go around the building to see if there's a back staircase, or a fire escape. Stand by for me at the entrance. Let's move normally, but fast."

Together, trying to be casual but going swiftly, they crossed the street. Underwood went up the front steps toward the mail-boxes as Hasken kept going past the building and around it.

Underwood had reached the mailboxes. He scanned them,

and there was the one he wanted on the second floor: RATANADILAK—204.

He concentrated on it, really stalling for time, wondering what to do, and at the same time wondering how Hasken had fared in the rear. As he stood transfixed, he heard footsteps. He whirled around to see Hasken coming fast toward him.

"There's a fire escape in the back, and I'm sure a corridor that leads to it from their apartment," said Hasken breathlessly. "One of them just poked his head out to see if the coast was clear. That means others are still in the apartment, and they're going to make a run for it."

Before Underwood could respond, he saw an older woman with a bundle of laundry coming out of the front door. "Let's keep the door open," he said to Hasken. "We can't use the buzzer. We can just go in as the woman leaves."

The woman had pushed the door wide, and Underwood held it open for her to leave, and then Hasken rushed inside with Underwood right behind him. As they dashed to the staircase, Hasken called out, "We'll break down the front door and maybe catch some of them inside. This is the time to contact the Secret Service for help. This is the moment, or it may be too late."

Underwood reached down to the wire top attached to his belt, then pressed the button, giving Frank Lucas the emergency signal, and with his free hand he yanked the Smith and Wesson from his pocket.

Together they raced from the ground floor to the first floor two steps at a time, and then swung up to the second floor. A corridor sign pointed to apartment 204.

Hasken was on the run with the president a step behind him.

At 204, Hasken gasped, "Let's hit the door together and bust the lock. Do you have a gun?"

Underwood displayed it.

"Good!" exclaimed Hasken. "You'd better be prepared to use it!"

As one they stepped back, each with a shoulder in front of him.

"Go!" shouted Hasken.

They smashed against the front door simultaneously. There was a metallic explosion as the lock snapped open and broke, and they flung the door free to enter the living room of the apartment.

They saw two of the soldiers hurrying through a second door into the corridor. A third soldier crowded behind them, and the fourth one, a hefty character who Underwood guessed would be Major Ratanadilak, had a gun out and was holding it against the side of Noy's head.

The crashing of the door and the bursting into the room by Underwood and Hasken froze the major and then diverted him. He whipped his gun away from Noy's temple and aimed it at Underwood, just as the president dropped down to one knee.

Ratanadilak's bullet grazed the president, and in that split second Underwood remembered the Secret Service director's advice. *Only if you must—shoot right back.*

Taking aim, the president was ready to shoot right back.

He saw that Noy was momentarily free, cringing against the wall, and he saw that the major was preparing to fire a second time.

Praying that he would not miss the officer and hit Noy instead, Underwood held his arm stiff, curled his finger against the trigger of the Smith and Wesson, and pulled it hard.

The report was a handclap in his ear, and then he saw Ratanadilak drop his gun, clutch his chest, and slowly crumple to his knees. Hasken crawled and then dove to retrieve the officer's gun, and Underwood leaped forward with his own weapon and pressed it against the major's forehead.

"You bastard!" Underwood yelled. "You tell me who made you kidnap her or I'll blow your brains out!"

Choking, still clutching at the wound in his chest, Ratanadilak was able to gargle one word.

"N-N-Nakorn," he gasped.

There was a second outburst of shooting, and then the other captors came backing into the living room with their hands up.

Pushing in after them, guns held high, was Director Frank Lucas and half his Secret Service team.

Underwood knew that they were safe at last, and then and only then did he reach out for the trembling Noy, and bring her into his arms, and hold her tightly, kissing her and kissing her again.

THIRTEEN

PRESIDENT Underwood and Hy Hasken drove Noy Sang back to Chamadin Palace in the newscaster's rented car.

At the door, Noy took Underwood's hand. "Matt, come and have dinner with us tonight. You can move your things over from the hotel, sleep in a guest room, and be up as early as you wish to catch Air Force One to Washington in the morning."

"Accepted," said Underwood.

"Around eight," said Noy, and then she left them.

Underwood and Hasken drove in silence back to the Oriental Hotel.

Arriving there, the president shook Hasken's hand. "You were brilliant, and I want to thank you."

"My pleasure," said Hasken. "See you in Washington."

"You'll see me a good deal before then. Meet me at Muang Airport tomorrow morning at ten when I'll be taking off. I want you to come along with me. We can hash over a few things."

"Thank you, Mr. President."

As Hasken drove off to return his rented car, Underwood went into the hotel and up to his suite. There his valet helped him repack his effects.

When they were ready, a limousine that Marsop had provided was waiting for them.

It was seven forty-five when the valet carried Underwood's bags up to the guest bedroom before leaving to find himself a place to sleep in the staff's quarters.

Underwood was in Noy's office when she appeared, brightly dressed for dinner. She went to Underwood, and hugged and kissed him. "The doctor gave me a clean bill of health," she said. "Matt, would you mind waiting a bit? I have two items on my agenda that I must dispose of before dinner."

Wondering what they were, President Underwood took a seat on the sofa.

Noy swung toward her desk chair, slipped into it, and buzzed her secretary. "You can tell Marsop to come in."

Marsop appeared, and he was smiling. "I've taken care of the television stations. I've cancelled my scheduled appearance on your behalf. You are not conceding the election. You are still very much a candidate."

"I'd say I am," said Noy. "Did you bring our old friend here?"

"General Samak Nakorn is in the outer office under heavy guard."

"Good. Be sure he has been disarmed, then send him in. Leave the guards outside."

After Marsop had left, Noy remained at her desk, winked at Underwood, and said, "Now the general's sentence."

Moments later the side door opened and General Nakorn came in alone. He was in full uniform, his chest glistening with medals. He gave Underwood a glance, then walked woodenly to a spot before Noy's desk.

Nakorn saluted her, and seemed to indicate he wanted to sit.

Noy did not permit him to sit. She had him remain on his feet, militarily stiff and erect.

Noy spoke. "This is your trial, General," she said, "and I am judge and jury. It will not last a minute, so you can remain standing."

"I was not responsible," said Nakorn.

"This is on your word?"

"My word is good enough."

"I have others' words against you, and better, witnesses to prove you were responsible," said Noy. "I have your major, who is now in the hospital and will survive to speak against you if he has to again. I now have a confession from Colonel Chavalit. I have the other three persons who held me in the apartment. You have no case. I am personally going to sentence you."

Nakorn's lips were tight. "What is my sentence?"

"I could have you executed. I won't. Too easy. I could send you to prison for life. Again, too easy, and I don't want you in Lampang. I am sending you into exile in Thailand. You will be behind bars tonight. In the morning you will be flown to Bangkok and left there. You will stay in Thailand for as long as you like, but you will never come here again. I have left instructions at every point of entry into Lampang that if you are seen here, you are to be shot on sight." She paused. "Do you understand, Nakorn?"

"I do."

Noy stood up. "You may leave now. I have guests for dinner."

Nakorn pivoted. As he walked through the doors, a guard grabbed him and snapped handcuffs on his wrists.

Noy took Underwood by the arm. "Business is done, Matt," she said. "Now it is time to celebrate with Den and Marsop for dinner."

An hour after dinner, Den was sent to bed and Marsop departed. Noy suggested that Underwood had better get some sleep, since he would be awakened early and would be flying all day tomorrow.

"Let me show you to your bedroom," Noy said. "Follow me."

Dutifully, Underwood trailed after her up the stairs to the floor above.

Passing one oak door, Noy tapped it. "My master bedroom," she said. She tapped the door not far from it, and then turned the knob. "The guest bedroom, your very own. Good night, Matt."

Without kissing him or touching him again, she turned her back to him and walked to her bedroom.

Underwood watched her leave, then entered his own bedroom and saw that the silken cover to his canopied bed had been thrown back and a downy pillow waited for his head. His two bags were locked, and only his wardrobe bag was unzippered. It had been left open for him to put away the clothes he was wearing. His travel suit, fresh shirt, underwear, and necktie had been laid out for him with soft travel shoes and silk socks.

Turning down the lights one by one, he left on only a dim lamp beside the bed. Underwood slowly undressed.

He found his navy blue robe and was about to toss it on the bed when he heard the creak of a door.

He whirled around, and to his surprise—no, not to his surprise, because he had dreamt it and fantasized it so long—the door between Noy's bedroom and his own was opening slowly, and soon Noy was standing in the doorway.

She was wearing only a sheer pink negligee. Even in the dimness of the room, he could make out the dance of her full breasts and see the dark triangle beneath the filmy robe.

Noy slowly approached him, her eyes on his face, on his penis, on his face again.

She went into his outstretched arms as he hugged her tightly.

His hard penis pressed against her.

She tried to release herself from him to throw off her robe, but he reached up and pulled it down her body and flung it aside.

She stood naked before him.

He was having trouble with his breath. "Noy, are you doing this because you are grateful to me?"

Noy reached for his head. "Matt, I'm doing this because I'm deeply in love with you."

"God, darling, how I love you." His heart was thumping as he brought her to him, against him, the touch of her skin inflaming his body. He crushed his mouth against hers, and she went limp in his arms.

Her breasts were what he felt, larger, softer, yet firmer than he had imagined. He had them in his hands; bent; had the nipples, one, then the other, in his mouth. The sweetness of them made his erection grow larger.

He was on his knees, kissing her belly, her hips, her thighs, going downward between her legs, and entering her with his tongue.

He heard her moan, felt her sway, felt she was going to faint, and quickly rose, catching her, his mouth all over her pliant flesh.

"Matt—Matt—Matt—don't wait—"

With that, he lifted her off her feet—she was as light as a feather—and he carried her to the bed and lowered her on to it.

She eased to one side on her back, and opened her legs and thighs to him, her arms outstretched, imploring.

He was on his knees, kissing her full breasts, her pointed nipples, and then kissing her lips above, and her navel and inside her thighs, and kissing her wet lips below.

He was almost out of control, his penis high and firm.

Then, as he was about to enter her, she sought him and pulled him down upon her, and he felt himself sinking inside her almost endlessly.

She screamed, and he clutched her and went deeper.

The excitement of the coupling was almost unbearable.

But it went on and on.

He made love to her once, and once again an hour later, and then a third, lingering time.

After that, they fell asleep in each other's arms, sated, exhausted, and happy beyond human desire.

In the early morning Noy brought in her tray of breakfast and shared it with him. Underwood remained under the cover, the tray on his lap, as Noy perched on the side of the bed and ate with him.

Later, she removed her robe and showered and came in to dry herself before him.

Watching her, he found his voice and spoke what had been on his mind this past hour and these recent minutes. "Noy—"

"Yes, Matt?"

"Noy, I want to divorce my wife and marry you."

She started to look over her shoulder and then fixed her gaze on the boudoir mirror beyond him. "I thank you, Matt, but that's impossible."

"It's not impossible. We deserve to be together."

"No, Matt, that would spoil everything. You're the president of the United States. Alice is your first lady. You cannot leave. The scandal would hang over you—us—forever."

"It doesn't matter."

"You must go back to your wife. And, like me, you must run for office again. You cannot abandon the people who believe in you. You must run for reelection again to preserve what you believe in. And I am determined to preserve what I believe in."

"That's all you have to say?"

"There is more." She turned to face him. "Matt, if you didn't run, I could never see you again. I'd be a president and you'd be a plain citizen. But if you do run and are elected, and I run and I'm elected, we will both be presidents once more, and we will be able to see each other like this from time to time without any problem. Think about it, darling. It's the only way for us to continue to be together."

"In love," he said quietly.

"Always in love," she whispered.

President Underwood stood outside the Muang Airport, staring across the field as he watched Air Force One receive its final checkup before departure.

He turned to Hasken, who stood beside him. "Hy," the president said, "you deserve an exclusive newsbeat for all you've done for me. I'm going to give you that beat here and now."

"Yes," said Hasken eagerly.

"I'm running for a second term. I'm running for reelection. The news is all your own."

Hasken kept his eyes fixed on the president. Hasken said, "So Noy wouldn't let you leave your wife."

The president blinked. After a long pause, he shook his head. "No, she wouldn't."

"That's the big story, Matt."

"I know it is. But we're swearing that's strictly between us. It's a story you alone know. The story for the world has nothing to do with my wife or Noy. The story for the world is that I'm going to run again."

"And keep your first lady. And maybe—just maybe—see Noy from time to time in the future?"

The president gave a twinkle of a smile. "To discuss matters of state, like giving the United States a bigger air base in Lampang. She can meet with me and arrange that, once she's elected."

Hasken grinned. "You're quite a guy, Matt."

President Underwood smiled. "Only because I know quite a woman, Hy."